I0646349

HELEN ROW TOEWS

THE
SECRET

By Helen Row Toews

Runestaff Chronicles

This book is dedicated to Charles Leslie Row.

You will always be my hero.

Vinci Books

vinci-books.com

Published by Vinci Books Ltd in 2025

1

Copyright © Helen Row Toews 2022

The author has asserted their moral right to be identified as the author of
this work in accordance with the Copyright, Designs and Patents Act 1988.
This work is a work of fiction. Names, characters, places and incidents are
the product of the author's imagination or are used fictitiously. Any
resemblance to actual persons, living or dead, places and incidents is
entirely coincidental.
All rights reserved. No part of this publication may be copied, reproduced,
distributed, stored in any retrieval system, or transmitted in any form or by
any means, including photocopying, recording, or other electronic or
mechanical methods, nor used as a source for any form of machine
learning including AI datasets, without the prior written permission of the
publisher.
The publisher and the author have made every effort to obtain permissions
for any third party material used in this book and to comply with copyright
law. Any queries in this respect should be brought to the attention of the
publisher and any omissions will be corrected in future editions.
A CIP catalogue record for this book is available from the British Library.
Paperback ISBN: 9781036701604

The EU GPSR authorised representative is Logos Europe, 9 rue Nicolas
Poussion, 17000 La Rochelle, France
contact@logoseurope.eu

Chapter One

The air outside of Larkender castle was filled with the beating of leathery wings and voices raised in anger. A shadow fell across the two arched windows of Kayden's library, blotting out the afternoon light. He laid down his pen and raised a hand from the heavy sheaf of papers on the worn desk before him. Rubbing the tiredness from his eyes, he pushed back his chair to peer at the narrow opening cut into the thick stone walls.

The space was small and sparsely furnished. Only his desk, pushed against the outside wall, several cozy chairs, an end table set between them and a heavy tapestry hanging over the fireplace, adorned the room. He assumed the momentary lack of light had been caused by the passing of his dragon, Alandrial. Although it was unusual for him to set flight before sundown. The blue sky had deepened with shades of late afternoon. All light would soon be gone.

The hollering continued. *What was all the commotion about?*

He didn't need to worry. His friend and warrior, Talbot,

was there—and of course Alandrial. If there was trouble, which there hadn't been for two years, ever since Malahd had been defeated, his friends would deal with it.

Gathering his papers together, Kayden slid open a drawer, dropped the pen he'd been using inside, and stood. The wad of paper in his hands and several pens were the only two luxuries he'd brought into the land of Erinbourne after having visited his family in Canada a short time ago. Although most Erinbournians knew of the four great portals—one of which led into the alternate place called Canada, where Kayden had grown up—it would be difficult to explain the differences between the two lands, and so he kept his paper and pens hidden.

Kayden stretched his hand to ease the cramps he'd gained since beginning this self-appointed task. The manuscript was complete and now all that was left was to read it through and ensure everything was written correctly. He tucked the papers beneath his arm before moving across the room to pull a heavy old chair, belonging to his predecessor, King Ludwig Larkender, closer to the hearth.

A fire crackled its invitation and a thick candle lay ready to be lit on the small table nearby. Settling himself within the soft depths of the armchair, Kayden laid the manuscript on his lap and smoothed his hands over the top page.

Telling the story from his grandfather's point of view had been more emotional than he'd expected, but he couldn't think of any other way to do it. It was easy enough to put himself into his grandfather's shoes and imagine how bewildered and disbelieving he must have been, because Kayden had felt that way too. He'd also entered Erinbourne under strange circumstances, roughly five years ago.

Yet, Kayden was only twelve when his grandfather, Charles, had passed away, and writing about him—actually *being* him, as he wrote his grandfather's story—had been difficult. Thankfully, Gran had given him the journal his grandfather had written of his adventures in Erinbourne. Kayden had never felt closer to his grandfather as he did when lost in the yellowed pages of Grandpa Charles' old notebook.

A few faded pictures accompanied the diary. Kayden treasured them and picked one up off the table now. It was a photo depicting his grandparents on their wedding day and he gazed into their happy faces.

Charles had looked particularly handsome in his dark suit on that occasion. He had longish, sandy-coloured hair, as was the style back then, and laughing blue eyes that had crinkled at the corners even when he'd been young. A tall, broad-shouldered man, he stood proudly beside Gran with a protective arm around her waist. A livid red scar on his left cheek was quite prominent in the picture and now, after all these years, Kayden knew how his grandfather had gotten it.

Grandad had always been evasive when it came to that scar.

Gran's hair was a rich auburn and was piled high atop her head with flowers threaded through the coils. She was fair skinned with a scattering of freckles across her nose and had the light-coloured, amber eyes that were a sign of Garde heritage. A tiny woman, but Kayden knew she'd been a force to reckon with back then.

He set the picture back on the table. There were other photos as well, always showing the two together: one of Grandad wearing his customary cowboy hat while posing at the Calgary Stampede, and another of them beaming at the camera with their first and only child, Chris. Kayden turned his attention back to the manuscript.

After translating his grandfather's spidery writing, Kayden had learned a few details he didn't think his grandmother had ever been told. His grandfather wrote that he'd protected her from information he felt would cause her more grief. Gran hadn't read the memoir, not wanting the pain of loss it would evoke.

Kayden was the only one to whom the secret was revealed and felt he would have to share it with Gran, next time he was home. For now, it raised some interesting questions in his mind. Of course, Gran's detailed account had also helped when piecing events together. He'd faithfully copied down her every word. He was sure everything was accurate.

The story would have been quicker to write if he'd been able to use a computer, but such technology did not belong in this world. Instead, he'd penned the tale of his grandparents' adventures in longhand.

A sigh escaped his lips. He laid the title page aside and bent his head to begin reading. It was important for each detail to be exact as far as Gran had told him. Thankfully, she had an excellent memory.

A roar of rage penetrated the thick stone walls of Erinbourne Castle, but Kayden was oblivious to the possible reason for Alandrial's fury. The sights and sounds of the ranch he knew and loved in the foothills of the Canadian Rocky Mountains drifted over him as he read the opening page, and Kayden became lost in the story of how twenty-year-old Charles Bramley found himself in the alternate universe of Erinbourne...

Charles gathered the reins and drew his saddlehorse, Champ, to a halt as he crested the ridge. Beneath him, where the Bramley land butted up against the tallest mountain of this particular range, stood his father's missing herd of cattle.

"Finally!" he said aloud, taking off his cowboy hat and dragging a sleeve across his dripping brow. It had taken all morning to find this bunch, and not a moment too soon. He glanced at thunderheads rolling over the mountains.

The group of thirty-five cows, calves, and the young bull that accompanied them nestled in a lush green gully just before a sheer rock face reared into the air. They were protected against the prevailing winds, and lay together lazily chewing their cuds.

Charles smiled as he returned the damp hat to his head. Couple the imminent storm with the scorching heat of a mid-July afternoon and he was glad to be heading home. Right after he assured himself the calves were all healthy and accounted for, of course. Responding to the pressure of Charles' legs, Champ moved forward. They wound their way down the rise on a parallel path to the resting animals, lest the cattle be spooked and run.

Charles reined up again as a cow lumbered to her feet. She watched him warily, swishing her tail against the flies, her mouth continuing to grind. He counted each body and leaned back in the saddle, satisfied they were all there. He and Champ could turn their attention toward home, which was at least another three hour ride.

A sound like a crack of thunder, so powerful it rattled his teeth, split the heavens.

Charles ducked. His horse bolted and Charles scrambled to hold on. Only he was unseated and flopped back across Champ's hindquarters. They topped the hill again in a headlong rush for home before he could pull himself forward enough to grasp the saddle horn and haul the runaway horse to a stop.

The animal pranced uneasily as Charles twisted around to look back. The storm was still a good way off. What had made that fearsome sound?

A movement caught Charles' attention. Holding a hand to shade his eyes, he squinted toward the tallest peak. Something black was hurtling through the sky. It was huge.

Was it a plane, crashing after hitting one of the mountain tops?

No. As it grew closer, it looked like an eagle tumbling end over end as though shot from a cannon. But this thing was far larger than any bird Charles had ever seen. It rolled toward him through space at a remarkable speed, soon reaching a spot almost directly overhead.

Charles was mesmerized. Although his horse strained to sprint away, he held Champ still.

As he watched, the bird's wings shot out at right angles to its body and, with difficulty, it righted itself and checked its headlong flight. The enormous bird flapped unbelievably long wings and began circling as though looking for something. A snake-like neck protruded from the body at one end and an equally lengthy tail unfurled from the other. The tail slashed at the air.

Charles' attention turned back to his horse and he slackened the reins. Champ was right. They needed to get out of here.

The horse lunged forward, needing no encouragement to run. Charles flattened himself across Champ's neck as they streaked down the knoll and across a meadow on the other side.

They were nearing a forest of pines when, without

warning, a sack dropped into Charles' line of vision and thudded to the ground in front of them. Champ shied violently to avoid it, lunging to the right. However, Charles didn't. With a heavy thump, he hit the ground. He lay on his back, winded and listening to the sound of Champ's receding hoof beats as he thundered for home.

Great.

Charles opened his eyes to look for the winged creature above him, but it was nowhere to be seen. At least that was one thing to be glad of.

What in the heck had fallen, and where had it gone?

Rolling onto his knees he stood, reconciling himself to a tiresome trudge back to the ranch, with a massive storm at his heels. He didn't even have a coat, because it was tied to the saddle. Walking over to pick up his hat, Charles rammed it on his head with disgust.

He might as well take a few moments to find the thing that had caused the problem. His eyes scanned the area.

There it was. He walked through the grass to the brown cloth bag, as long and narrow as his arm, tied at the top with bindings that ran from one end to the other. He picked it up and was shocked at the weight.

Deftly, he loosened the ties and slid the bag away, revealing an intricately designed pole about the length of his arm and the thickness of his wrist. Awed, he turned it over in his hands to examine it. It was heavy as though made from real gold, with indentations and various markings engraved along its length.

On one end, three gemstones, each the size of a hen's egg, were inlaid into an elaborate setting of gold. A ruby, a sapphire, and an emerald all flashed with rich, brilliant colour. They were hypnotic, and he gazed at them for some time, feeling unworthy to touch such beauty.

Yet, one gemstone was missing. The claws that should have held it in place had been pulled back and the stone was gone.

Charles scanned the earth, thinking it might have dislodged and been lost when it fell, but he couldn't find it.

He turned his attention back to the kingly item and reached out a hand to trace the glimmering stones. They were cold as ice. When his fingers passed over the gems they lost their sparkle, turning as lifeless and dull as the chipped stones along his driveway at home.

Where in the world had this thing come from?

He slipped the pole back into its protective covering, fastened the top together, and drew the cords over his head and shoulder to lie across his back. He couldn't just leave it lying there. It must belong to someone.

He set off walking and was just nearing the first scraggly pines when a gust of wind almost blew him off his feet. He staggered and grabbed for his hat. Tall grasses swirled and flattened with the force of the gale, and a few of the smaller trees snapped off and whirled into the forest.

Had the storm gained on him so quickly?

He twisted his head around to see that the white thunderheads, their dark underbellies filled with the promise of rain, were still hanging threateningly over the mountains. So what was causing the extreme wind? He hurried for the sanctuary of the sturdy pines, bent almost double in an effort to stay standing.

A dark shadow surrounded Charles, growing blacker by the second. Something was bearing down on him from above. He looked up, one arm shielding his face from the blast of wind and the other holding his hat.

Huge talons, each one as sharp and deadly as a spear, sprang from the end of a claw opening directly over him.

Above that, all Charles could see was a bank of armoured plates, appearing to have been carved from stone.

He ran, but was seized as easily as a hawk snatches a mouse from the prairie grass and lifts it writhing into the air to be consumed.

Chapter Two

Charles had been taken by a dragon. He wasn't sure how he knew, or how it could possibly be so, but he knew the thing that had flown above him in the sky was a dragon.

He dangled from the beast's claw with his arms and legs pinned, unable to move beyond a little useless squirming. He knew about dragons, of course. They were mythical beasts from fairy tales and fantasy books he read in his spare time, but how could one be real?

"What are you doing? Let me go!" Charles screamed, but his words were torn away by the wind. The only response was the slow, steady beat of the dragon's wings as the creature bore him toward the mountain.

Charles' mind reeled and his head drooped as he watched the landscape disappear behind him. With every thrust forward, Charles travelled further from the safety of his home.

What was happening? What did this creature want with him? Would it land on the mountaintop to eat him? Would he be picked apart like some flapping fish on the bank of a river, or swallowed whole and his bones ejected later as owls did with their prey?

He lifted his eyes. Their speed was increasing. Charles could feel the beast tense with the strain of moving its wings faster and faster, pulling at the air until they were hurtling toward the highest peak of the mountain range. He looked back. Behind him, like tiny ants, the cattle he'd struggled to find lay placid and content, oblivious to the turmoil over their silly heads.

It was unbelievable. Not thirty minutes ago, life had been normal…Almost boring. Now, here he was, held in the talons of a dragon and careening to certain death against the side of a rock. Closer and closer they came to the mountain, their speed increasing exponentially.

"Don't you see you're gonna hit it!" Charles yelled.

His words had no effect upon the beast, and Charles closed his eyes, stiffening himself, involuntarily preparing for impact—and a painful death.

The world exploded around him. A searing pain flew up his body from one end to the other. Where the golden rod lay across the middle of his back, the pain was worse. It scorched Charles' flesh like a white-hot flame. His mouth opened in a scream of agony, but the sound of his cry was swallowed into the explosive din of their impact with the mountain.

The world went white.

Nothing existed apart from the collision. It was like the report of a cannon shot beside his head. When finally he became aware of his body, it felt thin, stretched like a rubber band, and wracked with throbbing pain, as though he had been wrung out by huge, unseen hands and tossed aside to die. He floated in a sea of sightless pain until he could neither feel nor hear anything.

Charles awoke still dangling from the claw of his captor.

Am I in Heaven? No. If I was in Heaven, I'd be free of this monster carrying me. But how did we escape death?

His body hung limp. He ached from the punishment he'd been put through, and from the talons that still bit into his flesh. His mind could not accept what had happened and struggled to make some sense of his fate.

Opening his eyes just a crack, he looked down. They were flying high above snow-capped mountains. He shivered. Once, when he and his mother had flown to see her parents on Vancouver Island, he'd looked down at the tops of the mountains in just this same way—with a few distinct differences. Peering at the lofty peaks out the window of an Air Canada jet was clearly not the same as soaring over the mountains in the clutches of a fire-breathing dragon.

Fear gripped him. His stomach churned and he was sick.

Don't look down again. You have to figure out what's happening to you and how to get away.

But Charles knew there was nothing he could do at this point, and likely nothing he could do when he was released either. What *did* one do when captured by a dragon? Did dragons eat people? The whole situation was too farfetched to even contemplate. Maybe it was nothing more than a bad dream.

Charles squeezed his eyes shut and then opened them halfway again, hoping somehow it would all be gone. Nope. He lifted his face, his hair slick against his head in the great wind created by their flight, and tried to focus on where they were going. At this altitude and speed, he was freezing cold, but somehow the temperature helped to bring him back to his senses.

Another huge creature leaped from atop a peak to the left of them. A second dragon! Swiftly it rose to meet them in the sky.

A person rode astride its back, raising their sword into the air. The shiny edge glinted before it was lowered to indicate they continue on the same course.

To his right, far into the distance where the mountains gave way to flat countryside, there appeared to be farmland. Tiny checkerboard patches of varying colours glowed in the afternoon light. Charles considered how long they must have been flying. That was odd. There shouldn't be that much open area yet. Not when you flew straight west of Calgary toward the coast.

Ahead of them, the mountain range curved to the right in its never-ending sweep across the land, and lowland followed the bend.

The dragon dropped lower as he tilted his wingtip toward the earth. His long scaly neck stretched in front of him. The beast was staying closer to the peaks now, skimming over their tops.

Charles tried to calculate the time of day or how far they'd flown, but it was hopeless. He had no idea how long he'd been unconscious. The sun was to his left, although lower than it had been. So, he might say it was about six o'clock, but he couldn't be sure. And as for how far—who knew how fast a dragon could fly?

Then he had a horrible thought. What would his parents think when Champ returned to the ranch without him? They would be filled with fear. Charles imagined his mother crying and wringing her hands with worry. They'd likely organize the neighbours to search for him and tirelessly scour the foothills near their home. But he was far beyond their reach. *He* didn't even know where he was.

He snapped out of this inner turmoil as he caught sight of a waterfall tumbling down the side of a steep outcropping of jagged pinnacles ahead. When they were closer, he determined the pinnacles of rock were actually the points of some sort of castle or fortress built into the side of a mountain. Openings along the face of the rock looked like windows and a wide ledge ran horizontally several hundred metres below.

The dragon sailed past the face of the mountain fortress and began a slow spiraling descent toward the ancient-looking structure. Charles caught his breath. They were landing on a circular area hewn from the top of the mountain home. Soon, he would learn the purpose of his abduction.

The dragon extended his wings and flapped against the air to slow their arrival. Dragons must land here all the time. He watched as the one they'd met in mid-air settled onto the rock, folded its wings, and crouched to allow its rider to dismount before taking again to the air. The rider joined three other people who had clearly been watching for them.

Rock rushed to meet Charles. The stern faces of the waiting group disappeared in a blur of tears as his eyes adjusted to the lack of wind. Wincing, Charles averted his face and prepared himself to be crushed, but the dragon released his steely talons and dropped Charles from a height above the onlooker's heads. It made his landing painful, but not life-threatening. His body bounced and his head rocketed off the stone.

He was so cold that he felt brittle, as though his limbs would shatter when they hit the rock. Only they didn't. He came to rest on his back, eyes closed, and struggled to catch his breath. Stars danced behind his closed lids, and he was close to blacking out.

The sound of footsteps strode toward him, followed by a man's voice, low and furious.

"Who is this? What happened today? I take it you failed?"

Someone jumped onto the stone near Charles' head and he realized there'd been a rider on the dragon that had carried him. Feeling nothing could be gained by sitting up and demanding answers, Charles lay still, listening to his fate and struggling to concentrate after the blow to his head. Besides, he didn't think he could move at this point.

"We found Ludwig, as you thought we would, and there was a battle," a woman said. "Thankfully there were two of us and we were able to ambush him before he could use the sceptre. He was easily defeated. He and his dragon are dead at the foot of the Ildune Mountain range."

"And the sceptre?" the man asked.

"That is why I brought *him*," the woman answered, prodding Charles with the toe of her boot. "During the battle, Nagilla and I were driven through the periphery of our world and into the next. I was unaware such a thing was possible, but it seems under the right circumstances, and with enough velocity—"

"What!" the man interrupted. "You crossed over to the other side—and returned? Without using the portal?"

"Yes. However, the trauma of violating that border and considerable pain of entry caused Nagilla to drop the sceptre. Before we could retrieve it, this...person picked it up and strapped it to himself. I had no option, but to bring them both. I feared the tear in the border between us would close and we would be trapped on the other side."

"Yes, yes, spare me the details. Where is the sceptre now?" The man's voice grew impatient and thick with greed.

The toe of a boot edged into Charles, and he was flipped onto his stomach. He felt a knife slice through the leather thong across his shoulder and the bag was lifted away.

"Excellent work, Laveza." The man's voice was no less sinister, but became buoyant with glee. "Give it to me! You and Nagilla shall be rewarded."

"And the young man?"

"Kill him. I have no use for such a hindrance. Nothing else matters now that I have the sceptre."

Footsteps marched away.

Hands grasped Charles under his arms and dragged him across the stone. As banged up, cold, and disoriented as he was, Charles could do nothing to prevent it. Yet before they reached the edge of the cliff, Laveza strode past him and spoke to his captor in a low voice.

"Take him to the dungeon, Armon. He has no idea where he is and would have no place to go if he escaped. I have a few questions for him before he is flung to the ravens."

"Yes, ma'am."

As strong hands dragged him away, Charles sank into oblivion.

Charles awoke in semi-darkness. Experimentally, he moved each leg and then his arms. Nothing appeared broken, but his hands were shackled and chained to the cold stone wall at his back.

A meager flame spluttered from a torch fixed along the wall where he slumped, and he wondered where he'd been taken. He was even colder than before, if such a thing was possible. His teeth chattered, and his bones felt as though they'd turned to ice. The jeans and thin cotton shirt he'd worn for the heat of a July day were no match for the frigid temperatures he'd experienced since his abduction. And now to be flung into a dungeon! What was this, the Middle Ages?

There was a noise somewhere to his left, and Charles snapped his head up. At the far end of the enclosure, a door was illuminated by light and two figures passed through.

He stiffened. The light revealed how huge and empty the space was, and the small round grate at the center of the room where a thin stream of steam arose.

The two made their way toward him. The smaller of them was a young girl carrying a tray set with dishes and a candle. Beside her strode a tall woman dressed in light-coloured pants and a long tunic belted at the waist. Boots reached her knees and a sword was slung over her back so that the hilt was just visible over her left shoulder. Her face was severe and pinched, and her dark hair cropped into short untidy tufts. She exuded authority and menace. When she spoke, Charles recognized her voice. She was the rider who had brought him to this awful place.

"Put the food beside him. And unlatch his hands." Laveza crouched in front of Charles, and narrowed her eyes as she searched his face. "You will tell me what I wish to know, but not tonight. Tonight, you shall be left to…settle into your new lodgings."

With a mocking smile, she stood.

"You are fortunate. My master does not often take prisoners and you would have been executed by now if not for me. However, I feel you may be useful. Information of the world beyond our borders would be most enlightening." She wheeled about and addressed the person at her side. "Stay with him until he has eaten and shackle him again. If he gives you any trouble, use your knife and kill him. He is not *that* important to our cause."

Laveza turned on her heel and strode away.

The girl knelt to place the tray and a blanket onto the floor, keeping her eyes lowered. She then reached behind Charles and fumbled with the metal bindings. They clattered to the floor and Charles moved his hands to his lap, hoping to chafe some life back into his aching wrists.

He tried to speak, but his throat was raw and he only croaked. Painfully, he swallowed. "Thanks," he said. He had plenty of questions, but didn't know where to begin and kept his head bowed.

"What is your name?" the girl asked softly.

Charles looked up as she pushed the tray closer and nodded, urging him to eat. She was a slight young woman, of perhaps his age of twenty, with long straight hair pulled tightly away from her face. Other than that, all he could make out was that she wore a skirt made up of a mixture of holes and patches. It was held up with a belt from which hung a pouch. He had no doubt that within the pouch there was a lethal knife. He had no wish to see her use it.

He smiled at her in the flickering light of the candle, hoping to reach out to her for help in some way. Still, she did not meet his eyes. "I appreciate the food. But more than anything I'd like to know where I am, who these people are, and what's going on. Am I going to be killed?"

Elegantly, she shrugged. "It would cost my life to tell you who they are and what their plans entail."

He sighed, yet felt a glimmer of hope. She seemed

different than the others he'd met so far. He grabbed a lump off the tray that turned out to be a bread of some sort, tore a piece off with his teeth, and chewed.

"My name is Charles," he said around the mouthful of bread. "Not sure what point there is in telling you that since apparently I'll be dead tomorrow."

He tossed the bread back onto the tray with a clang. "And I don't even know what this place is or why I'm here! I have parents at home that'll be out looking for me. They'll be worried."

"Please, try to eat something..." the girl said. She hesitated. "I can tell you that you are in Erinbourne, and my name is Alainea. I have heard their recent conversations, since they believe me to be of no threat to them or their plans. It seems the dragon and its rider breached barriers that were set in place since the beginning of time. These barriers have remained to prevent any knowledge of, or travel between, our worlds. However, somehow they passed through and brought you back with them."

She stole a glance back to the doorway where she and Laveza had entered. Lowering her voice to barely a whisper, she leaned closer. "And I shall tell you that my father is Respiele Larkender. He is the master of this castle and will kill anyone who angers or opposes him—and that includes me."

"He would harm his own daughter?" Charles said in alarm.

She did not respond.

"Do you oppose your father? And can you please explain more about this place I seem to be in? Or how I can get home?"

Alainea scrambled to her feet and laid a warning hand

on the pouch tied to her belt. He gathered what that meant and fell silent.

Alainea said nothing more. Charles sensed she was worried she'd already said too much. Feeling as though a dry biscuit and a cup of water was a poor meal to offer a man facing his execution, he ate reluctantly and in silence. The second he placed the cup back onto the tray, she clamped his wrists back into the chains and whisked up the tray. Her skirt swished as she bustled away without a backward glance.

"You can't just let me die," he called after her. "I haven't done anything to deserve death. Please help."

The door to the cavern swung shut with a thud and she was gone.

Charles slumped against the stone wall. None of this made sense. He went back and forth over the bizarre events since he'd found the herd of cattle, but his mind churned endlessly in circles without coming to any conclusions. He'd never heard of Erinbourne. And these people looked like they'd stepped out of the 1400s.

Plus, dragons? He shook his head as if to clear the dreamlike situation he found himself in.

At least, when the girl re-fastened the metal bracelets around his wrists, she'd left his hands in front of him. Awkwardly, he dragged the blanket over himself and shivered. It wasn't much against the chilling cold, but it was something. His head drooped as he dozed, his sleep filled with dreams of swords, dragons, and beheadings.

A tiny scratching noise awakened him. He remained still, but listened attentively. The fitful flame in the bracket nearby had all but gone out, leaving a sour smelling smoke to flood his nostrils.

The scratching came closer, accompanied by a snuffling

noise. Something small bumped into his foot. It was too big to be a mouse.

Charles lifted his lids and found himself looking into the sparkling black eyes of a rat.

"Hey there," Charles said. "You're stuck in this dungeon too? I bet there are some crumbs up here if you want to look."

His response surprised him. Rats were dealt with harshly back home, not welcomed. Yet, as he awaited his doom, it seemed only right he should be glad of some company, whatever it was.

The rat sat up on his hind legs and regarded Charles. Small round ears wiggled and his long, hairless tail curled around his feet. The animal wasn't afraid, which Charles found strange. It cocked its head to one side and stroked long, translucent whiskers with a paw. It was twice the size of any rat Charles had ever seen. Yet he felt no concern, despite being unable to defend himself.

The rat dropped to all four feet and moved alongside Charles, his nose snuffling out the few crumbs that had fallen. The rodent nibbled them, not ravenously, as Charles would have expected, but thoughtfully as though it was accustomed to much better offerings elsewhere.

"Well, suit yourself," Charles said. "I know it wasn't a gourmet meal."

The torch sizzled and its light grew dimmer.

"We'll be in darkness soon. Sure wish you could chew through these chains. I bet you know how to get out of this place too."

He looked at the rat and it sat up on its haunches again, twitching its ears. Although the rat faced away from him, Charles got the feeling it was listening intently to his voice.

"The name is Charles," he said. Under other circumstances he would not have considered talking to a rat in a gloomy cell while his hands were bound to a wall, but the little fellow felt like the only friend he had. "My parents and I have a ranch in the foothills near Calgary. Ever been there?"

The rat shook his head.

Charles stopped dead and stared at him.

Okay, that had to be a fluke.

"Anyway, today I was out checking cattle and this stupid *thing* fell out of the sky. Why did I have to go pick it up? I should have just minded my own business, but oh no, I had to go grab it. It was the dumbest move I've ever made too, because look where it's brought me."

Charles raised both hands with a clatter of chains and brushed the hair from his eyes. "I'd just like to go home. Somehow, I have to get there."

His voice sounded bleak, even to his own ears. He was fast losing faith that he'd ever see home again.

The last vestige of light wavered and was gone, leaving him and the little animal in complete darkness.

Charles sighed. Tiny pattering sounds told him the rat was making his way to the grate at the center of the room and disappearing. Alone with his thoughts once more, Charles wondered how he could possibly escape this prison and the unbelievable world he appeared to have been dropped into. It seemed hopeless.

Chapter Three

Charles dozed fitfully throughout what he supposed was the night. Unable to sleep any longer, he sat staring sightlessly into the darkness.

Silence surrounded him, enhancing his fear of what the day would bring. Despite that, when footsteps echoed in the hall outside the room, and the flickering light of a candle appeared, he allowed himself to hope all of this had been a terrible mistake. He leaned forward, willing it to be the girl, Alainea, and when she alone walked through the door, he exhaled with relief.

She placed a tray on the rough stone floor and reached up with the candle to light the torch closest to where Charles lay. Then she stuck the candle back in its dish, picked up the food, and walked toward him balancing everything carefully. Their eyes met, and even in the dim light, Charles fancied he saw pity in her glance. Perhaps he could convince her to set him free, although he had no clue how to get home.

"Thank you," he said with a heartfelt smile as she

approached. As before, she placed the platter beside him and crouched down to remove the shackles. Released, he rubbed life back into his hands before attempting to eat.

"You are welcome. I brought you food and drink. Something more nourishing this time." She plucked a cloth away from a bowl of hot cereal, a wedge of pale cheese, and two slices of bread. After the trek through frigid corridors, the porridge was only mildly warm, but it looked wonderful. He tore into the meal.

"It's great," he mumbled.

She regarded him a moment, and then spoke. "Obviously, we cannot keep cattle for milk or cheese on a mountaintop, but there are farmers in the valley below who have been—convinced to sell us a few things."

She seemed to be volunteering information, and Charles looked at her over the bowl as he spooned food into his mouth. He nodded encouragingly. The porridge warmed him a little and at least served to fill the gnawing ache in his stomach.

"Are you a prisoner here too?" he asked it with hesitation, as he reached for the cheese, but it was a question he'd started to consider during the night. Alainea seemed unhappy, burdened with a heaviness he could certainly understand if she lived in a place like this against her will.

"In a way, yes." She stood and moved to settle herself more comfortably some distance away. "There are prisons of many sorts."

He glanced at her, trying to read her expression, but her face was hidden in shadow.

She added, "I have spoken to Maurice."

The statement sounded momentous. Maurice, whoever he was, must be a person whose opinion and worth bordered on divinity. She did not look at Charles, but directed her speech to the wall beside him as though unwilling to meet his eyes again.

"Is that a good thing?" Crumbs dribbled from his mouth as he spoke, but he was too hungry to care.

"Maurice is an astute judge of character," she said as though he hadn't spoken. "He and his family, along with my mother and I, are the only Garde left in this fortress. The others were either killed or driven off before I was born. No one else is trustworthy. However, Maurice seems to think you could be. And that you need our help."

"Help?" Charles mumbled around his bread and cheese, which, to his surprise, was quite delicious. He reached for a battered tin mug of water to wash it down before trying to speak again. "I have no idea who Maurice is or how he could know anything about me. No one has been in here or spoken to me since you and that other woman, last night. But yeah, I need help and lots of it."

Again, Alainea continued without paying the slightest attention to him.

"Maurice also believes I need as much help as you do. He says I should confide in you." She looked up and searched his face. "Indeed, you will not last long here, and time grows short. May I trust you?"

Charles met her unwavering gaze. Despite his lack of understanding, he felt a kinship with this girl. Whatever it was she needed, he would help.

Besides, he wasn't getting out of here without assistance.

He sat up straight. "Yes."

She held his eyes, as though looking through to his very soul.

"I believe you." She twisted her hands together in her lap. "We must move quickly."

Charles swallowed the last morsel of bread and grabbed the cup to drain its contents.

"I'm going to need to know a few details," he said. "Life has been pretty strange since I was picked up yesterday."

"Of course! I do apologize." Alainea glanced back at the open door to the dungeon with a frown. "It must be a short version, though, as Laveza will wish to speak with you as soon as you have eaten."

"Great," Charles said, following her gaze. "I can hardly wait for that."

Alainea leaned forward and tapped his boot with her fingertips. "Listen carefully. The reason you were brought here was because you were somehow in possession of, the Golden Sceptre of Power. There was a great battle yesterday. I do not know all the details, but the king was killed and this artifact was taken from him. The sceptre bestows immense power upon whoever possesses it. Now that my father, Respiele, has it, he will increase in strength and might, affording him the ability to take over our world. That must not be allowed to happen."

Whirling around, she put up a warning hand, squinted back out the doorway from where she had come, and listened. Satisfied no one was coming, she continued in a throaty whisper.

"The power comes from the gemstones, but you may have noticed that one is missing. My father himself removed the Amethyst, many years ago, before fleeing from King Larkender and secluding himself here. If the Amethyst were to be joined with its brothers on the sceptre, they would form an absolute power. There would be no stopping Respiele."

She took a long breath and plucked at a tear in her garment. "Fortunately for us, the Amethyst was taken away several days ago. Each gem carries a power independent of the others and this person wished to have it in his possession as a powerful ally. He went to gather forces in the north. At present, the Amethyst is in the clutches of one more dreadful than my father—the sorcerer, Malahd."

"So, you want help with what exactly?"

"I am not sure you are capable of helping. But before Malahd returns tonight with the Amethyst and the additional troops, I must secure the sceptre and escape this fortress. I shall take you with me."

"You're kidding." Getting themselves out of here seemed tricky enough, but she wanted to take that strange sceptre too? The whole scheme sounded like a pretty tall order. From what he'd seen already, these people didn't mess around. He and Alainea could both be killed for the smallest misdemeanor—she had said so herself—let alone if they were caught trying to steal the most prized possession in the land.

"If we succeed in getting the sceptre," Charles said, also watching the doorway for the dreaded arrival of Laveza, "how in heck would we escape? There must be a lot of people here, an army maybe, and we're halfway up a mountain."

"That is of no consequence." Alainea brushed his concerns aside with a wave of her hand. "I have—"

She leaped to her feet and reached for her knife, swivelling her head to the doorway where a light was bobbing along the corridor.

"Pretend you are still groggy from yesterday," she hissed. "Tell her you have a headache or concussion. Say as little as possible."

At the other end of the dungeon, Laveza entered, holding a crude-looking lamp.

"Is he shackled?" she barked at Alainea. When the girl shook her head, Laveza waved a hand. "Do it then. Immediately!"

Alainea scrambled across the floor to Charles, her back to the advancing woman, and met Charles' eyes as she bent to fix his hands behind him once more.

"I will send Maurice for you. Follow him," she whispered in his ear. She picked up the tray without another word, straightened, and dipped her head to Laveza. "Is there anything more you wish of me?"

"No. Leave us."

"The boy remains dazed," Alainea said, hovering nearby. "It might be best to let him rest longer."

"I do not recall asking for your opinion. Get out." Laveza's gravelly voice sliced into the chilly air.

Alainea turned and hurried away.

Charles felt as though the one hope he had was fast disappearing down the hallway, but he didn't allow his glance to betray her. He determined to do as Alainea had told him—to appear ill and unable to answer Laveza's imperious questions. With a heart as chilled and despairing as the rest of him, he subsided against his chained wrists and allowed his head to drop to his chest as though holding it up was too much of an effort.

"Look at me," Laveza demanded.

A metallic, sliding sound told Charles she had unsheathed the sword strapped to her side. Before the razor-sharp tip of it was pressed beneath his chin, his head lifted.

"I want to ask you a few questions," she said. "Whether you choose to answer will determine the outcome of this little chat."

Charles lifted his lids a crack, pretending it was hard to open them for long. He moaned.

"What is this land you come from? Who is in charge of it?" Applying pressure to her blade, Laveza pushed his head higher. "Is it defended, and if so, how well? Do they possess gold or other riches?"

The edge of the blade sliced into his soft flesh. It stung.

"Answer me."

His body strained to follow the angle of her sword and save him from a more serious injury. He was fearful she would end his life here and now if he didn't volunteer some sort of information, but if he moved his jaw he might cause her sword to pierce him further.

"I can't talk," he said between compressed lips, staying as still as possible.

As she removed the sword, she drew the razor-sharp edge along his cheekbone. Pain seared along the mark, and warm blood trickled down his face. He shook his head. Droplets flew away and splattered the stone floor. Laveza smiled.

"The land…" Charles started and then stopped to clear his throat of the lump of fear lodged there. His head sank to his chest. "The land is called Canada."

Throughout the night he had pondered why this person wanted knowledge of his homeland. There were no *good* reasons for it. She sought information with the hope of invasion, and he had to deter her somehow.

"It's a land of warriors," he said. His voice sounded weak. Good. "There are armies placed along the mountain borders and we have advanced methods of warfare…"

Purposely, he made his voice trail off at the end and he slumped lower, his head lolling.

Laveza kicked him in the side with enough force to throw him sideways, the chains following with a loud jangle. He cracked his head on the stone. The air was expelled from his body in one loud groan of pain. He thought he might pass out. Struggling to catch his breath, he took a deep gulp of air. His lungs felt like they were in a vice.

"You are lying. Think very hard about what to say when I return." Laveza snarled above him. "If you will not talk, it is not worth the effort to keep you alive...I suggest you find the answers to my questions."

Wheeling about, she strode from the dungeon.

Charles lay sideways on the cold stone, his arms stretched taut by the shackles that bound him. He concentrated on taking a shallow breath in and another out to minimize the pain. He must have cracked or broken a couple of ribs. How could this be happening? One minute he was riding the range and the next, he was beaten and held as prisoner in some mountain fortress by crazy people.

He stayed in the same position, his body shivering from shock. Once that subsided, he found himself hesitant to move for fear of finding he wouldn't be able to. Slowly, using his arms as much as possible, rather than the muscles of his torso, he pulled himself upright.

Take it easy. Breathe and try to relax.

As he did so, he found he wasn't as injured as he had thought. He lifted each arm in turn and flexed any and all muscles. Apart from soreness and bruising, he seemed okay. Certainly no bones had been broken, and for that he felt grateful.

However, he knew when Laveza visited him again there would be no more chances. Even if he told her all she wanted to know, there was no reason to keep him alive. Once she gathered any information she could, she would dispose of him exactly as she'd threatened. He had to trust that Alainea would send the man, Maurice, to help him escape.

Taking a deep breath, he shuffled along the floor to sit up straighter. There had been no sounds from the hall outside, and the torch was spluttering again, its dying sending a thin shaft of foul-smelling smoke into the air. He watched the door, wondering what Alainea was doing.

Where was this Maurice guy?

A slight sound caught his attention. He swivelled about to trace its origin. In the dim, flickering light, something small poked its head through the grate at the center of the room. It was indistinguishable at this distance, but he had a feeling it was once again the rat, coming to look for crumbs.

The little animal pulled the rest of its body through, stretched high on his hind legs, lifting his nose, and taking great sniffs of the air. Appearing satisfied, the animal dropped to all fours, scurried over to Charles, and sat beside him.

"If you want crumbs you'd better hurry," Charles said. "One way or another, I'll be leaving soon, so there won't be any more."

Unsure why he was again making conversation with a rodent, Charles almost smiled to himself. He guessed when a person faced the bleakest moments of their life, they could find companionship in the most unlikely of creatures.

The rat did not snuffle around for crumbs. Instead, he reached behind his body, his tiny paws tugging at something attached to his back. As he wiggled it free, Charles saw what appeared to be a tiny bag with straps crossing over the animal's chest. From it, the rat produced a key.

Charles' mouth dropped open in an amazement as the rat pattered behind Charles and began, one after the other, to unlock the restraints. They fell to the floor with a muffled *clang*.

Charles pulled his hands free and looked at the creature

in shock. Words failed him. The rat slid the key back into the bag, looked him in the eye, and then scampered off to the doorway. Almost there, he looked over his shoulder to where Charles remained sitting on the floor. The rat sat up on its hind legs and with both front legs, he very clearly beckoned that Charles should follow.

Charles rose stiffly, stretched his cramped, cold limbs, and tiptoed after the rat. He wasn't sure whether he should put his faith in a rodent or not, but it seemed unwise to ignore the rat's help thus far.

He could make sense of all this later.

Once they reached the entrance, the rat ran to the far side and leaned around the thick stone wall to peer down the hallway. Apparently, the coast was clear, because he motioned that Charles should follow him again and they set off to the left at a swift pace.

The hallway was not that wide. It would only allow two people to walk abreast, and the roof was low. He was forced to duck a few times where the obstinate rock dipped further. Sconces were placed along the walls at intervals, which helped. Unlike the ones by his prison cell, they burned bright.

Coming to a sharp corner, the rat put up a warning paw. Charles stopped, waiting for the animal to give the signal to continue. They then made several turns, descended a short flight of stairs, and finally came to a low door set into the stone. The rat slipped beneath it at one corner where a small space had been carved, and disappeared.

Charles looked both ways down the corridor and pressed himself flat to the door. It was recessed only a smidgeon into the rock, hardly enough to conceal him from whoever might walk these halls. He had no wish to be chased, especially when he had no idea where he was, or where to go next.

Why had he followed this creature?

Without warning, the solid door opened behind him. Charles took a few unsteady steps backward, lost his footing, and toppled inside, flinging his arms wide with a yell. There were a few frightened squeaks. Just before he hit the floor, someone's arms slid beneath his own to catch him.

"Shhh," Alainea hissed. "You'll alert the guards."

She pushed Charles upright and he spun around to see her dressed in dark grey pants and a tunic, with a heavy woolen vest fastened overtop and a belt at her waist from which hung the cloth bag she'd had before. Her appearance was much different than it had been in the dungeon. There, Alainea appeared helpless, dressed in little more than rags, with a demure, almost frightened aura.

Now, she was a warrior. He admired her for it, and for her beauty. Long auburn hair was twisted into one thick braid that hung over her shoulder. But her eyes! They were an unusual shade of yellow and thickly fringed with dark lashes.

And she was strong, he realized with surprise. He was over six feet tall and muscly, yet she had caught him as though he were a feather.

"Are you going to stand there gaping at me all day, or shall we prepare ourselves to escape this place?"

"Sorry," Charles muttered.

"I see Laveza left her mark on you." Alainea eyed the gash on his cheek. "It should be cleaned once we reach the kitchen."

"Okay, thanks." He shifted his gaze.

The room was small, barely big enough to fit the three of them. A free-standing closet stood at the far end, and what looked like a pile of rags heaped in the corner next to it. There was no window, just two sconces recessed into the walls on either side. It was poor light, but enough to see by.

On the floor sat the rat, peering at him with interest.

"You have met Maurice," Alainea said, following his gaze. "My trusted friend and the only reason my mother and I have stayed sane all these years. Now, I must outfit you for this venture and then we shall seize the sceptre. It is nearly noon, and Respiele will be looking for his lunch."

She bustled away to the tall wooden chest, flung open the doors, and began rummaging inside.

"Maurice?" Charles shook his head as if to clear a fog that had descended on it. "Maurice is a rat? How did *he* tell you anything about me? Rats can't talk!"

The rat drew himself up to his full height, folded his front paws across his chest, and turned his head away with a squeak. Charles clapped his mouth shut. Without a doubt, the rat—Maurice—had understood every word and was angry about it.

"Wonderful." Alainea poked her head out of the wardrobe to look at Charles in irritation. "Now you have offended him."

She turned, holding a sword and scabbard which she thrust at Charles as she marched past him to peer out the door.

He accepted the weapon awkwardly and shrugged. "I'm sorry. I didn't know."

She closed the door behind her and turned to face him, leaning against it. Her face softened. "It is my fault. I forget you are from the other side. I am descended from an ancient people called the Garde. We communicate easily with all creatures in this land."

She nodded meaningfully toward Maurice, who stood like a statue, stiff and unforgiving.

"Maurice," Charles found himself saying, "I'm deeply sorry for doubting your intelligence. Where I come from, animals can't talk...and they certainly don't have the abilities you have. I apologize."

Maurice swivelled toward Charles and nodded in acknowledgment, but remained rigidly at attention. It was going to take more than a glib apology to win the animal over.

Charles looked at the weapon in his hands. "What do I do with this?"

"Are you telling me you are not able to wield a sword?" Alainea sounded incredulous.

"That's what I'm telling you."

Alainea raised her eyebrows. "Well, there is no time to learn now, but you cannot leave this room without some way to defend yourself. In most cases, the first person to deliver a cutting blow will win. Use it to block your attacker if nothing more. Otherwise, the best advice would be either to get it to me, or run." A flicker of a smile crossed her face. She took the belt and scabbard out of his hands. "Are you left or right-handed?"

"Right."

"Good, for the time being it will ride on your left hip, but first you must change out of that strange garb you are wearing. I have other clothes for you over there, on the floor by my bed mat."

"Strange garb?" he repeated, looking down at his faded blue jeans and orange plaid button-up. "What's wrong with what I have on?"

The rat squeaked something up to her.

"Maurice says you look foreign and will attract imme-

diate attention. Please change, and be quick. I must don my
dress and go to the kitchens. Respiele takes his meals alone,
making this my best chance to get the sceptre. We will go
together."

She motioned to the pile of clothes on the floor, then
grabbed the voluminous old dress she had worn when
Charles had seen her before. She pulled it over her head,
concealing the clothes she'd put on for their getaway, and
moved back to the door to give him space.

With one hasty glance to make sure her head was
turned, Charles looked at two pairs of strangely made
pants, a long, cream-coloured shirt, a swath of material he
supposed was a coat, some boots, and a small bag with
straps to carry across his body.

"The lighter breeches go underneath for warmth and to
keep the woollen ones from scratching." Alainea, although
turned away from him, seemed to have eyes in the back of
her head as she answered the questions that ran through his
mind.

"Thanks, but I'll just keep my own underneath."
Hopping on one foot to keep his balance, Charles pulled on
the coarse pants, glad he was able to keep his jeans. He
drew the long tunic-style shirt overtop his own and tucked it
in. Then he threw the strap of the bag over his head and
adjusted it so the pouch was under his right arm. Lastly he
held up the heavy, chocolate-coloured material and turned
it in an effort to find the armholes.

"It is called a cloak," Alainea said in a sarcastic drawl.
She had turned to eye him. "Just drape it around your
shoulders and pull the hood over your head to hide your
face."

"Thanks."

Long, leather boots completed the ensemble. Charles

balked at this. Already he mourned the loss of his cowboy hat, and now his boots. The boots had been expensive and he'd just gotten them worn in. He didn't want to change into ones that had belonged to some nameless man before him. Probably some dead guy, considering the way things seemed to go around here.

"Are you ready?" Alainea asked. Her voice was strained.

Charles realized how petty he was being, worrying about material possessions when their lives were at stake. If not for this girl, he would soon have been dead anyway.

"Almost," he said.

He pulled off his boots and pushed them under the rags she had called her bed, before pulling on the others. They were a much lighter construction with a thick sole to protect his feet and had laces running the full length. He tightened them and stood, flexing his feet. A little too big, perhaps, but he wasn't going to complain now.

"Ready," he said.

Both Alainea and Maurice turned to survey the results. The rat squeaked again and almost looked as if it was smirking.

"He says you almost look respectable now." She smiled and Charles' face grew hot.

What's wrong with you? Embarrassed at the praise of a rat.

Alainea showed him how to strap the sword and scabbard to his side, and secure the weapon so it didn't swing too much as he walked.

She straightened, and Charles looked into her amber eyes. With a nod, she turned, tugged the door open, and leaned outside to listen, then slid through with Maurice and Charles close behind.

Single file, with Maurice scampering between them, they hugged one side as they hurried along the hallway back in the direction Charles and the rat had come. It was an uphill climb, and Charles found it cumbersome to move with the sword. The last thing he wanted was for it to clang into the stone wall and attract attention, so he held the scabbard with one hand as they progressed.

There were a great many doors built into the rock as Alainea's was, and he wondered how many people lived here. He was amazed at the labyrinth of rooms and hallways, hewn from the solid rock. The corridors echoed into the distance, and he marvelled at the time it must have taken to create such a place.

The path way flattened and broadened, where time and the passage of many feet had worn the stone smooth. As they rounded a corner, a broad door came into view at the end of the corridor. Although it was still some distance ahead, the muffled babbling of many mouths, and the clatter of dishes was audible.

The bolts rattled as the door was pushed partially open and voices floated toward them, echoing along the rock. Alainea yanked Charles behind her as she ducked into a narrow passage and down a flight of steps leading to a stout wooden door. He held his breath as two men passed above, deep in conversation. One grimaced, picking food from his teeth with a dirty-looking finger, and then they were gone. When their footsteps faded, Alainea led Charles and Maurice from their hiding place. They passed the wooden door at a run.

"It is the dining hall. Everyone will be eating at this hour. Hurry," Alainea whispered. She doubled her pace.

Steadily they descended. Alainea halted before a massive, double door made from thick timbers. She put her hand on Charles' arm. He leaned closer to listen as her voice was barely discernable.

"Stay here until I am assured that only my mother is inside. The other servants should be away, serving the meal, but if anyone comes, turn your face away and do not speak. I will be back in a moment."

She hauled the door open and disappeared within. Maurice stood on his hind legs, his whiskers twitching as he kept watch.

When Alainea poked her head back around the door and beckoned, Charles followed Maurice as they entered a rectangular chamber filled with the banging of pans and the smell of food cooking. Fires roared in two massive fireplaces along the center of the outer wall, and next to each one was a tall, but narrow window only a few centimetres across. Between the shelving, sconces burned bright, and a broad beam hung low from the ceiling over a wide table where a woman worked. From the beam hung bunches of dried herbs, onions, and garlic, along with pots and pans. Shelves filled with jars and dishes and other containers of what must have been food lined the walls, while barrels were grouped in a corner.

"This is my mother, Elspeth," Alainea said, moving to the woman's side.

Charles focused his attention on the tiny lady. She barely reached her daughter's shoulder.

Alainea waved a hand toward him. "Mother, meet Charles."

He nodded as Alainea stooped to plant a kiss on the woman's lined cheek.

"Is Respiele's dinner ready?"

The lady looked up and pushed stray hair from her face with the back of her hand. Flour dusted her arms and her fingers dripped with dough from kneading bread. She looked tired and sad, but she managed a brief smile for Charles.

"I am so sorry that you are here, Charles. It was an unfortunate mistake," she said, shaking her head. "I wish you both safe travels, but I confess I am worried."

Facing them, she answered her daughter. "It is by the fire, my dear."

Elspeth's voice cracked. Charles couldn't tell if it was from emotion or hard work. He remained silent. It seemed to him that the mere sound of his voice might trigger an alarm somewhere in this place and their attempt to escape would be thwarted.

Maurice hopped onto a stool. He watched Elspeth, his whiskers twitching.

Alainea picked up a shallow bowl from a stack on her mother's workbench. Then, snatching up a cloth, she used it to grasp a kettle of water hanging over the fire and pour a measure of it into the dish. Turning, she hurried to Charles and dipped the end of the cloth into the steaming water.

"Bend, please, and hold still," she said.

Obediently, Charles leaned toward her, and she swabbed the wound across his cheek with a light touch.

"It will leave a scar, I am afraid."

Charles shrugged. "If that's the worst that will happen to me here, I can handle it."

Alainea allowed him a brief grin before she set the things down and marched back to the fireplace. Retrieving a tray covered with a cloth, she placed it on the bench beside her mother. From the pocket of her ragged dress she withdrew a small pouch and untied the lace holding it together. She flipped the cloth off one end of the tray and sprinkled what looked like dust onto a bowl of thick stew. She stirred it with a knife she'd snatched from the table and then flipped the covering back.

"He should sleep well and soundly after that," she said. Satisfaction gave strength to her words.

Charles took a sharp breath. She was drugging the man she called Respiele—her father. Charles had been wondering how she hoped to wrestle the sceptre from the man's grasp.

Maurice squeaked to the girl.

"Yes," Alainea said in answer. Pulling up the hem of her outer clothing, she stuffed the empty pouch into the bag strapped to her waist underneath. "We shall need a little food to be getting on with, Mother. Do you have something for us?"

She stepped back expectantly as the woman bustled past her.

"Yes, take these." Elspeth reached for two packets she had secreted on a shelf behind a curtain and thrust one out to Alainea. "There is enough bread and cheese to see you both a good distance."

A tear rolled down her weathered cheek. She reached for Alainea and clasped her close. Then, letting the girl go, she stemmed a sob with her apron.

"I will return for you. You shall not be forced to endure this misery much longer." Alainea wrapped her arms about her mother again and held her tight. "I love you."

Blinking furiously, Elspeth nodded before walking across the room to hand Charles the other parcel.

"Put it in your bag," she said in a low, quavering voice. The tiny woman reached out to touch his arm. "Please, take care of my Alainea."

Her eyes glistened. She moved back to the workbench and, forcing another smile, waved them both away.

"Hurry," she said. "You must go now or it will be too late."

Alainea picked up the tray and spoke to the rat. "Will you lead the way as far as the top, and stay with Charles while I go in to Respiele?"

Maurice inclined his head, jumped to the floor, and scampered to the door.

"Charles, I want you to follow Maurice and do exactly as he does. I will go ahead with the tray. By the time you arrive, I should have the sceptre and we may be off."

She grabbed another long bag from a hook by the door and flung it back to Charles.

"Water," she said.

She hauled one half of the double doors open and, with a final glance at her mother, slipped through.

Charles slid the strap over his head and adjusted the sloshing bag on his back, under the cloak. He looked to Maurice for instruction. The little rodent sat on his haunches and held up a warning paw. Elspeth chopped vegetables behind them and sniffed. Then, waving, Maurice signalled that Charles should follow, and scurried into the hallway.

With a soft thud, Charles pulled the door closed behind him and drew the hood further over his face before tiptoeing after the rat. He now realized what a benefit it was to have the soft boots. His footsteps were almost soundless.

There was no sign of Alainea. Maurice scurried along the edge of the wall, getting them past the still boisterous dining hall door. Charles didn't look up, but kept Maurice in his line of vision and stepped as lightly as possible.

Footsteps hurried toward them.

Maurice stopped dead in his tracks, stood on his hind legs, and swivelled to look at Charles with alarm. Charles was surprised to learn how expressive the face of a rodent could be. The rat chattered his teeth together and motioned that Charles turn and run the way they'd just come. There had been no other hallways for quite some time, but there was a door about twenty paces back. Charles made for it now.

The footsteps were getting closer. They were loud, as though the shoes were fitted with metal, for they rang against the stone floor.

Panic washed over Charles. What if the door he had in mind was locked? Or what if someone was inside the room he intended to enter? Not that he had any other choice. From the look of fear in Maurice's dark eyes, he knew he couldn't just slip past whoever was coming.

He sped up.

The handle of the recessed door appeared around a slight bend. Charles lunged forward, grasped it with both hands, and twisted. Despite cobwebs, and the fact that it looked as though it hadn't been touched in decades, it turned easily and he gave the door a push. It resisted. Something prevented the door from opening and he braced himself and shoved harder. It sounded like he was heaving against piles of gravel lying on the other side. Somehow, he managed to squeeze himself through the opening. His feet crunched over whatever it was. Afraid to move again, he held his breath as he leaned into the massive door and closed it behind him.

The heavy footsteps grew louder and marched past outside.

Charles sagged with relief and turned to see where he was. A narrow opening was cut into the solid rock at the far end where a thin stream of light filtered through. It was some sort of storage room.

Dusty bottles and jars of all shapes and sizes lined shelving from floor to ceiling, consuming every inch of space. A few of them still contained what looked like pebbles that shone through the filth. Many of the jars were smashed, and he peered at the floor where he stood to see piles of broken glass, realizing that was why it crunched. But there was something else there too. Piles of the round rocks lay in heaps as though the jars they'd been in were smashed on purpose.

Even in this poor light, and covered in dirt, they were multi-coloured and pretty. They glowed through the grime. It was the only colour he'd seen in this horrible place, and they called to him. Not understanding why he did it, he stooped and grabbed a fistful of the pebbles and shoved them into his breeches pocket. Then, knowing he must find Maurice again, he eased the door open and listened.

He could hear nothing. With one hand holding the sword, he yanked the wooden door shut and trotted back along the corridor, looking for the rat.

Maurice was curled up in a ball along a crevice, as though napping. He blended in so well with the rock, Charles nearly missed him. Maurice shot from his hiding place and with only a short, backward glance to ensure Charles followed, continued on.

Maurice went faster, and Charles realized they'd lost precious minutes. He was forced to jog in order to keep up with the speedy rodent. They flew around corners, winding along a steep path that led up rather than down to where Alainea's room had been. The way became narrower and uneven. Finally it became steps, cut into the rock, and Charles knew they were entering one of the tall turrets he'd seen while dangling from the claws of the dragon.

As they neared the top step, Maurice slowed and

stopped, looking back to ensure Charles was doing the same. Ahead of them was a half-moon landing with another large oaken door fitted into the rock against the wall ahead. The door wasn't closed all the way, and muffled voices argued from within. He recognized the deep angry tones of the voice from yesterday. The same person who had ordered his death—Respiele.

"I don't want it!" Respiele shouted.

There was a loud clatter and a bang. Charles envisioned what must be happening. The tray had been flung across the room, splattering the contents of the meal and the medicated soup against a wall. The soothing voice of Alainea followed, but Charles wondered what she could do now to wrest the sceptre away from a man that was filled with such rage.

There came another sound, although this one was dull and more of a *thump*.

"Maurice! Charles! Are you there?" Alainea cried. She sounded frightened. "Come here!"

The rat was around the corner and through the door in a second. Charles leapt across the space behind Maurice and pushed the door wider to enter. With a sharp breath, he took in the scene that greeted him. A man lay sprawled across the floor. The table and chair he'd vacated as he fell was upturned and soup dripped down a tapestry that hung in the small spherical room. The sceptre, wrapped in its protective covering, still rested in Respiele's hand.

Alainea dragged the table and chair out of the way. "Help me to get him into bed."

She grasped Respiele under his arms, and gasping, she hauled his torso off the floor. His head lolled and the sceptre fell with a clunk.

"Is he dead?" Charles rushed to grab Respiele's feet. He

lifted with Alainea and they shuffled toward a narrow bed piled high with thick, woven blankets. Leaping in front of them, Maurice used his teeth and paws to pull the covers back, allowing them to lay the man down.

"No." Alainea busied herself with tucking her father's tall frame beneath the blankets.

Charles stood back to study his face. In sleep, the man didn't look as cruel as he had sounded yesterday. His mouth was thin and cheekbones prominent, giving him a hungry, dissatisfied appearance. Still he reminded Charles of his grandfather with dark hair curled off his forehead, his eyes wide-spaced, and bushy eyebrows.

Alainea moved Respiele's head into a more comfortable position on the pillow, leaving behind a smear of blood.

"You hit him on the head?" Charles asked unnecessarily.

"Of course. Hold him up, will you, please?" Alainea answered with an irritated snort.

Charles took Respiele's shoulders and pulled him forward while she flipped the pillow around to hide the blood. Charles lowered the man onto the clean side.

"Thank you." Turning on her heel, she addressed Maurice who had jumped to the floor and stood, poised for flight. "Tell Mother to spread word that Respiele didn't want to eat since he was up all night and wants only to sleep in preparation for the battle ahead. He does not wish to be disturbed. Go quickly, my friend, and we shall hope it gives us enough time to get away before they come to check."

Maurice said something to her, drew himself up, and bowed before disappearing through the door. Alainea gathered the dishes that had been thrown from the tray and slid them out of sight under the bed. Charles righted the table and chair as she tore the ragged dress from her body and used it to scrape as much of the soup from the wall as she could with one swipe. She looked around, satisfied that the room appeared as normal as possible.

Lastly, she reached for the sceptre. After looking at it as though deep in thought, she thrust it out to Charles.

"Take this and give me the sword."

Without hesitation, Charles did as she said, and the familiar weight of the golden sceptre fell across his back. The strap had been repaired.

"If you are not accustomed with how to use a weapon, there is no point in you carrying it further. Come."

She was already halfway out the door as she slung the sword around her waist and secured the scabbard. Charles pulled the door closed behind them and followed the girl who had become his only hope. Leaving the mighty ruler of this fortress of doom tucked in bed, they sprinted down the steps to attempt their daring escape.

Chapter Four

Before they'd reached the bottom of the narrow hallway, Alainea took another route. Charles hadn't noticed the slab of stone jutting into their path on the way up, because the opening behind was only visible from this direction. Alainea slipped behind the stone, and into the gloom beyond.

He followed. There were no torches here, and he felt his way along the contracted passage with a hand on either side. Not only was it barely wide enough to pass through, but he was forced to stoop to keep from rapping his head on the ceiling. It had been made for people much smaller than him. The food bag and flask of water bumped his hip, and the golden sceptre weighed on him. Underfoot, the stone was rough and wound steadily lower. Charles stumbled occasionally. He mourned his normal life of only yesterday.

Oof! He ran right into Alainea before noticing a pale flickering light leaching into the passageway from around another of the stone slabs. Alainea stood still, listening for any movement from the other side. Then, she inched around the block with Charles right behind her.

He stepped into a huge room filled with weaponry. Shields hung in clusters along one wall and suits of armour down another. Everything appeared primitive and deadly. Different sizes and types of swords hung opposite them, alongside an area for bows and arrows plus other evil-looking items Charles could not identify.

Alainea crept into the room in a crouched stance, wary and watchful. Stopping before a low table filled with knives, she selected a small dagger, sheathed in a pouch, and handed it to Charles, motioning that he secret it in the bag that housed the food. He did so, all the while mirroring her movements as she tiptoed silently toward an enormous door at the other end of the room.

Snatching a bow, and quiver of arrows, Alainea shoved them over her head and drew her sword. Balancing it in her hand, she looked back at him to nod encouragingly.

This was it. He took a deep breath. Alainea snaked out her hand to reach for the handle of the door. She pulled it back and plunged through.

They were in yet another corridor. Alainea broke into a run and flew down it to their right. Charles sprinted behind her, amazed at how quiet she could be, or perhaps the beating of his heart was so loud it covered all other sound.

Here, the way was broad and the footing smooth, allowing for the passing of many people at one time. Charles only hoped they hadn't taken too long upstairs with Respiele. After negotiating a curve, a door appeared. It was chiseled out of solid rock and rounded at the top like an archway, but fitted with enormous hinges. At the top, a glimmer of natural light shone through and he knew they were at the entrance.

Running footsteps echoed down the passage, reaching Charles and filling him with dread. People were coming.

Fast. Had his absence been noted? There was a shout behind him, and even as he and Alainea stretched their strides to reach the door, Charles knew they weren't going to make it. Slowing to a stop, he and Alainea turned to face whoever was coming.

Laveza and two burly men came to a halt several paces away. The woman drew her sword.

"Go," she said to one of the men. "Check on Respiele. It seems as though we have thieves and a traitor in our midst."

One man rushed to do her bidding. The other remained at Laveza's side, unsheathing his sword with a metallic clang.

Charles knew he was no match for the sword, so he positioned himself to best evade the pair when they attacked. He would not be taken prisoner again. Beside him, Alainea raised her weapon.

"We shall quit this place, Laveza, whether or not I must fight you to the death," she said.

Laveza laughed, the venom of it reaching out to twist around Charles' mind like a vice.

"I always thought you were trouble," she spat. "He should have had you killed long ago. In any case, you cannot leave now. The party has only just begun."

She lunged forward, thrusting her sword in a move calculated to pierce Alainea through. Alainea jumped to one side and parried with a strike of her own. The women delivered blow after blow to one another, breathing heavily as they fought back and forth, their swords ringing as they battled. Finally, Alainea forced Laveza back along the passage.

Her companion, the heavy-set man, stepped forward with a smile curling his lips. His eyes fixed upon Charles who backed up hastily. The warrior paced after him, appearing in no particular hurry.

Charles felt the solid rock wall beneath his seeking fingers and knew there was nowhere left to go. His eyes darted side to side, assessing whether he had a chance to successfully dodge this man's attack.

The man slashed his sword through the air. Charles dove toward him, somersaulting across the rocky floor with the sceptre grinding into his back. He came up on his feet the other side of his aggressor. With a howl of anger, the man whirled, attacking again. Panting, Charles sprang. The tip of the man's sword dragged down one arm. Charles heard the thin cloth of his shirt rending and felt the sting of his wounded flesh.

Then, without warning, something flew from the shadows above them. It smacked into Charles' assailant. The man reeled sideways. The thing clattered to the floor.

It was a rock. Another stone was hurled from the shadows, finding its mark, this time between the man's shoulder blades.

Enraged, the man turned his attention to the shadowy ledge where the rocks had appeared from. But, as he squinted to see his assailant, the soldier was pounded in the back of his head from across the hallway. Then a volley of rocks were launched from both sides. He dropped to his knees and fell to the floor, flinging up his arms to protect his head. Not being able to cover every vulnerable spot at once, he was at the mercy of the invisible aggressors. A final blow to his forehead, from an immense round rock, felled the man. He toppled like a tree amid another shower of stones and lay still.

Not waiting to learn who was responsible for this welcome assault against his foe, Charles took in what was happening further down the passage. Alainea and Laveza continued to wage war. It seemed the two were evenly matched. Something had to be done to help Alainea since reinforcements from within the fortress were most surely on their way.

Charles reached for the knife. Yet, no matter how nasty Laveza was, he couldn't bring himself to harm her. The only other weapon he had was himself. Throughout school and even since graduating, Charles had enjoyed participating in two distinct sports—football was one. While he wasn't keen on being stabbed by a stray sword, he couldn't see any other way but to tackle the woman. Hunkering low, he threw his shoulders back and squatted at a forty-five degree angle. From this stance, he watched for an opening in the battle.

The sound of metal crashing against metal filled the chamber as the two women lunged at one another, parried, and shifted their weight to seek advantage. Tirelessly they fought, their breath loud and ragged.

Then, Alainea stumbled. She yelped and crashed to the floor. Laveza pounced on the girl's arm, pinning it to the stone. With her own sword, she spun Alainea's away from her grasp.

Laveza had won. With her back turned to Charles, she lifted her weapon to strike a final blow.

Head back, eyes up, and focused on the goal, just like his coach had taught him, Charles threw everything he had into the few running steps before impact. Then, planting his left foot, he propelled every ounce of his bodyweight toward Laveza. He brought both of his arms up and under her, picking the woman off her feet. He carried her several steps before slamming her to the granite floor.

Groggily, Laveza pushed onto one elbow and brought her feet under her to rise.

What should he do now? Charles looked around for something to use as a weapon. His eyes caught a movement and he ducked as a stone, lobbed from somewhere near the ceiling, knocked her back down. Laveza was unconscious before she hit the floor.

Alainea was on her feet and running toward him. Charles swivelled from side to side, squinting into the shadows along the passageway to see who or what had been their silent ally. There was a narrow shelf running the length of the stone walls, just under the roof. There he met the sparkling black eyes of twenty or thirty rats. In a twinkling, they backed away and were gone.

Unbelievable.

"Hurry!" Alainea tugged at his cloak.

Charles tore his eyes from the sight. The pounding of countless feet advanced along the corridor. He sprinted beside Alainea to the huge door. She wasted no time in drawing back the bolt and dashing out into the bright afternoon. Sunlight blinded Charles and he flung up an arm to shield his eyes as he rushed through to freedom.

But was it to freedom?

He piled into Alainea as she skidded to a halt outside. They were back on the same broad platform where he'd arrived in the claws of the dragon. From an enclosed lookout tower, built on the far side, two guards spotted them. One raised a horn to his lips and blew three short blasts. The other ran toward them, plucking an arrow from a quiver on their back and fitting it into a bow.

"Stop!" the man yelled.

Alainea grabbed Charles' arm and dragged him toward the edge of the landing area. Charles braced himself. Any moment, he expected to feel the shaft of an arrow pierce his back, but he ran with Alainea knowing he faced death if he were captured again. He gulped in the thin mountain air and ran faster as other voices were added to the din behind them. More warriors had arrived from within the fortress.

Following Alainea, he dashed to the edge of the platform. He teetered there, his toes gripping the brink. Stones skittered away from their headlong rush and rattled into the yawning space beneath their feet, bouncing from rock to rock. It was a sheer drop. He sucked in a terrified breath. There was no escape to be found here. He swiveled around to look at her standing behind him. Footsteps and bodies pounded toward them, and voices shouted.

"Jump!" Alainea growled. She drew her sword and threw a glance over her shoulder to the people advancing on them.

"Are you crazy?" Charles yelled at her as he faced the mob, feeling trapped and furious. "We'll be killed!"

He looked beyond at the warriors pouring out of the door. They bristled with weapons and could have killed them easily, but they didn't. These people knew there was no escape for him and Alainea. They were trapped...and after all they'd struggled through.

"Do *not* kill them!" someone hollered. Charles knew why. It was only because he teetered at the brink of a precipice with the prized sceptre at his back. No one wanted to be responsible for losing that.

Alainea's eyes flashed fire at him. She kept her back to the advancing mob.

"I said jump." She shoved him hard. He felt himself tumbling backward, arms and legs clawing at the air, scrambling to reach for a foothold on the rocks. He flew over the cliff and into the abyss.

Charles screamed. The world revolved about him. Mindlessly, he pedaled at the air, reaching for something to hang onto.

In thrashing, he smashed into another body. Alainea must have jumped with him! Why? Then he felt her take hold of first one and then the other of his hands and grip them tightly. They plummeted through space together.

The blue of the sky and the lumpy grey wall of rock flashed before his eyes and became a blur in which nothing at all was visible. Time slowed. He lost all hope. Tensing every muscle in his body, he prayed he would die upon impact and not be left broken and suffering at the bottom.

Then another sound took over from the roaring of the wind in his ears. It was deafening, as though a freight train was passing only an arm's length away.

Alainea tugged him closer.

"Be ready to grab on and hold tight," she screamed into his ear.

Barely had the words left her mouth, than something rocketed up from under them. Charles slammed into the mass and bounced painfully across a hard exterior. Alainea's hands were torn away from his own, and he scrabbled for something to hang onto. He slid, gasping for breath, clawing at the rough surface with hands and feet in an effort to hang on. Spinning toward the brink, he found himself skidding over the edge, looking at rocks only a few metres below.

Alainea grabbed his ankle and held fast. His torso already dangled precariously, and he would have slipped over completely if not for her. Slowly, she hauled him to safety. Using fingers and toes, Charles held on, struggling to find breath, his mind whirling as his rescuer came into view. The great leathery wings of a dragon lifted high above him and dug into the air to propel them, swooping over the rocks at the base of the mountain.

He concentrated on breathing, laying his cheek against the rugged skin of the beast that had just saved his life.

"Are you alright?" Alainea hollered against the rush of wind that marked their passage. "If so, I need you to crawl over to me and hang on tightly. You must prepare for what comes next."

Charles raised his head and opened his eyes only wide enough to see her slight outline flat against the dragon. Was she actually smiling? He'd just been through the most terrifying ordeal of his life, and they weren't clear of it yet. What was wrong with her? It would take a miracle just to stay where he was, let alone start crawling about. Already the wind buffeted him so much that he felt himself slipping backward.

Cautiously, he rolled onto his stomach, gripped the knobby hide of the beast, moved his feet to find a toehold, and hung on. Lowering his head, he didn't attempt to answer her. Hollering was beyond him.

"There is no choice in this matter," she yelled. "You *must* get to where I am…now. Respiele's riders will not be long behind us and we cannot battle them. We must hide and bide our time."

Charles' hair was slicked flat to his head in the gale that rushed over him. It seemed difficult to open his eyes against the force of it. Also, with the regular undulations of the wings, the broad back of the beast rolled up and down causing him greater alarm. Yet, he knew Alainea had gotten him this far. He needed to follow her direction. What did he know about riding a dragon! He pushed one reluctant arm forward to drag himself along the beast's back.

Finally, he was lying level with her, but still some

distance away. She held out what looked like a crude rope harness that she herself was bound within.

"Take this end and pull yourself closer," she yelled, tossing him a length of flat, woven cord.

He grasped it and after some concentrated wriggling, he lay beside the girl. She fit the system of bands around him and across his back and chest. The other ends of the rope disappeared around the dragon's neck and body.

"Feel more secure now?" With one cheek resting on the dragon, Alainea smiled reassuringly at him before lifting her head to squint into the distance. She didn't have to holler quite so much now he was closer, but still raised her voice lest the wind whip her words away. "Now, listen carefully. I have made this dive several times, but it is rather alarming and you are a much broader person. I only hope we fit. Move the sceptre to your side as it will add to our width."

"Dive! You hope we fit!" Charles croaked. "We're diving somewhere? Where, underwater?"

"Of course not." Alainea frowned as though he'd asked a question too foolish to consider. "Dragons cannot swim. No, several years ago I found a tunnel that leads deep into the mountain. I do not believe anyone else knows of it, which makes it a perfect place to secret ourselves. However, the entrance to this place is narrow and must be entered at precisely the right angle and velocity."

She looked over the long neck in front of her. "We are close. Make yourself as flat as possible and grip the rope tightly."

With one last wide-eyed look at the girl, Charles concentrated on shifting the sceptre and pressing himself into the hide of the dragon. The beast changed course. The tops of mountains whistled past in a blur. The dragon had been increasing their height all this time, he thought with surprise, and now they were among the mountain peaks rather than at the base of them.

The dragon tensed beneath him and altered its direction, angling downward. Charles' body shifted forward alarmingly, but the harness caught him. He would have fallen off if not for the ropes, and he was glad of them, no matter how flimsy they felt.

Beneath a rocky overhang there was an opening in the mountain. It didn't look big enough for them to pass into, but that was where the dragon was aiming. Alainea shuffled backward, working against gravity to flatten herself as best she could. Charles did the same.

The dragon snaked its long neck out straight and long, and with a loud swishing sound, folded its wings beside its body. They hurtled through space. Charles held his breath and winced, waiting for impact or to be snagged on the rocky edges of the hole, and crushed.

Then, with a *whoosh* they entered the tunnel and everything went black. Rock grated painfully along Charles' back. He tried to force his body flatter lest he be scraped off and lost. The unexpected icy air, as they left the sunlight behind, sucked his breath away. He squeezed his eyes shut, willing himself to remain on the dragon, and with Alainea.

The cavern began to broaden and their speed slackened. Charles worried that with his added weight, they'd be slowed too much, and would become stuck in the passage, wedged in a prison of their own making. But they burst free into a large, open space and the dragon unfurled his wings to brake and bring them down to land.

Charles stayed where he was, thankful to be alive. He caught his breath as Alainea loosened the bands across Charles back and slid off the creature. Hesitating, he finally shrugged out from under the harness and sat up.

A torch flared to life on his right and Alainea's face flickered into view.

"Use the rope to lower yourself," she said. "We must move deeper into the cave."

Charles grasped the rope and pushed himself over what he supposed was the shoulder of the enormous reptile. He dangled in mid-air and then dropped to stand beside the girl. A dancing light played across the broad side of the scaly brown hide as the dragon moved away from him. It was huge, nearly the size of his house, and he shook his head, still having trouble to believe any of this was real.

With the merest of glances to see that he was following, Alainea marched away. Charles flexed his shoulders, feeling the soreness of his back from where their travels had taken him. However, the scratches were unimportant, and he jogged after her.

The space was so large, the light of the flame in Alainea's hand didn't reach the edges, but Charles caught a fleeting glimpse of skeletons along the way. They were animals of some sort, maybe cows, and he wondered who or what had brought them here to devour.

Hastily, he turned his thoughts to other things.

The rock underfoot inclined sharply and he slid, falling onto his butt with a rattle of loose stones.

"Be careful and be quiet," Alainea whispered. "Not far now."

Picking himself up, he followed the bobbing light. The dragon alternated between walking and hopping ahead of them, surprisingly silent for such a huge creature. Its long tail slashed back and forth which was the only part of it that Charles could see.

Alainea turned to face him and held up one hand. "We wait here until the darkest part of the night."

Gesturing with the torch, she indicated several boulders and seated herself upon one. The dragon made a complete circle and faced them, peering at Charles with glittering eyes.

"This is Dranich," Alainea said, waving at the dragon with an arm. "She is pleased to make your acquaintance."

"How do you know?"

"Pardon me?"

"How do you know your dragon is pleased to meet me? She doesn't look all that thrilled." He shuffled uncomfortably under the dragon's scrutiny. "You can talk to her without speaking?"

Alainea's tinkling laugh echoed off the walls. She clapped a hand over her mouth and her eyes darted back the way they'd come. "I communicate with all the creatures of this land through telepathy, but Dranich and I are different…almost an extension of one another."

She directed her gaze back to Dranich and her eyes softened.

Rising, she moved to a rock closer to Charles and leaned toward him. "Despite being a distance into this mountain, we must be quiet. Dranich has taken a risk in helping us. If we were detected by Respiele now…"

Charles nodded. "Please tell Dranich I'm very grateful to her for saving my life and am happy to meet her too."

He inclined his head respectfully toward the creature and was further startled when she winked one dark gleaming eye.

"She knows already. Dragons are very intelligent. She understands what you say." Alainea stood and placed her hands upon her hips. "Now, wrap yourself in the cloak and try to get some sleep. If we are able to rest, we will be better prepared for—"

"Sleep!" Charles erupted, then repeated in an undertone, "Sleep? I can't sleep after all this. Can you please explain a few things to me before you nod off?"

Alainea caught the sarcasm in his words, because she looked to Dranich before answering.

"Yes, of course. You deserve that." She settled herself again beside Charles and folded her hands on her lap. "What do you wish to know?"

"I'd like to know where I am and how I can get home. Or, if I can get home at all…?" His voice, low and hoarse, died away as the awful prospect hit him.

Would he ever see his family or the ranch again?

"I already told you, you are in the land of Erinbourne… and yes, there is a way for you to return to your home," she said. "One gatekeeper, in particular, will assist you in that matter. Hope is not lost."

She reached out and patted his hand.

"I shall make the history brief," she said.

Charles watched her closely, noting how sad she appeared in the light of the torch.

"Erinbourne is—was—ruled by a wise and judicious king, Ludwig Larkender. His rule was made absolute by the fact that he held the sceptre. My father, Respiele Larkender, is his brother. Sadly, when they were young, the two quarrelled and Respiele stormed out of the castle to seek his fortune elsewhere." Alainea sighed heavily.

"Before Respiele left, he seized the Amethyst. With it, he fled into the west, to the Araleesh Mountains, and carved a home for himself from its eastern face. In time, he gathered a following of like-minded people who wished to see King Larkender overthrown." She looked up to Dranich, her voice fading away before she gave a slight shudder.

"Each of the gems possesses a distinct power. The

Amethyst, when in the hands of someone with a heart that is corrupted, exerts a mind-bending influence. This is what I believe has happened to my father." She tugged at a loose thread on her cloak.

"Please, don't feel you have to go on if this is painful," he said.

Alainea flashed him a look, as though remembering he was there.

"No, it is important and you should know. Respiele is not a sane man. I like to think he once was, but I have not known him to be so. He has never treated me as a father should, nor my mother as a wife. He wrenched her from her people, forcing her to work for him, and in time to become his concubine. All against her will." Alainea stood and began to twist her hair.

"At the center of each mountain range that borders Erinbourne, there lives a race of people known as the Garde. As I told you, my mother and I, Maurice and his folk, the dragons and many others are of the ancient tribe of the Garde. They were the original inhabitants of this land, set in place by the Creator as guardians of the portals leading to your outside world. The Garde have many abilities beyond those of normal men and women like Respiele. When he grew in strength, Respiele waged war on those innocent folk and drove them from the mountain. All of them apart from my mother, whom he enslaved." Alainea flipped her braid behind her back and spread her arms wide.

"Respiele recently sought the services of a sorcerer to help him win the war. Malahd is his name. He moved into the fortress and somehow influenced Respiele to trust him with the Amethyst. This sorcerer took the Gemstone of Power with him two days ago when he journeyed east in an attempt to win over further followers. That is the reason the Amethyst is not already joined with the other gems on the sceptre. If Malahd had been in the fortress, and if the gems were together on the sceptre, I cannot begin to imagine the destruction the two of them would create. We would never have gotten it away as easily as we did. My world would be in utter ruin. That is why I must stop Respiele. Even at the cost of my own life, if necessary. I will return the sceptre to King Larkender or, if he is truly dead, to his descendants." She whirled to face him. "I am only sorry you happened to be caught in the middle."

Charles took a few moments to digest what she'd said. His brain felt sluggish—an alternate universe, a king, mountain portals, talking animals and mythical beings. It was a lot to take in.

"It's okay. I want to help you. I'm just not sure what good I can be, but I'll try." Bringing his hands together in front of him, he stared at the rock beneath his feet. "What should we do next?"

She straightened her shoulders and stopped before him. "We wait here until I can be sure that two of Respiele's dragon riders have returned for the night. They will want to keep them fresh to ride out in the morning in search of us. There are four, not counting Dranich. We have a better chance to make our escape if there are fewer of them when we set out to look for the king."

"Okay, but how do we get back down that passage?" Charles thought it was a reasonable question when he tried to envision Dranich forcing her bulk up that same narrow way. The dragon wouldn't have room to use her wings, but he couldn't help smiling in response when the torch lit up her grin.

"There is another avenue. It will be a little frightening

for you, but it is the only way. Now sleep." She blew out the torch and Charles could hear her settling down on the unforgiving rock to rest.

He wondered what "*a little frightening*" might mean to Alainea as he wrapped his cloak about himself and tried to relax his mind and body. He'd been in a constant state of fear since this whole episode had started.

Could it get worse?

Chapter Five

Charles woke to Alainea shaking him. A sharp pain, both in his ribs and across his back, reminded him of where he was.

He reared up in alarm.

"It is time," she whispered.

Charles got to his feet, feeling stiff and sore, to follow her. She lit the torch as she walked toward the dragon and waved it like she was standing on an airstrip directing planes.

The harness hung near Dranich's front leg. The dragon crouched low in order for him to get on. Swallowing hard, he grasped the ropes and hauled himself up her rough shoulder, hoping he wasn't hurting her. He drew the straps over his head, fastened them in the same way Alainea had done for him before, and tried to make himself comfortable.

The light was extinguished. The torch clattered to the ground, leaving them in darkness. Alainea leapt over him and hitched herself to the dragon with the other half of the bindings. Then, Dranich was off.

They ambled along in the darkness, swaying to and fro

as Dranich clawed her way along the rocky chamber. Charles was beginning to settle into the rhythm and loosen his grip on the rope when Alainea shuffled closer to him and whispered, "Hang on," into his ear.

He'd just opened his mouth to ask why when Dranich thrust herself forward. The world dropped away.

They were falling, dropping through space like a stone. Charles' stomach rose up to meet his throat. He lifted off the dragon, his body flying up behind him as they plummeted. He clutched at the ropes, pulling himself back down, thankful they were securely fastened. Dranich kept her wings tucked to her sides, gathering speed for whatever lay ahead.

Alainea had been right. It was terrifying.

The only thing that kept Charles from spinning off into the cavernous hole was the wonderful harness, and he wound it about his hands even as it slipped dangerously high on his shoulders. His cloak flapped behind him and his face flapped along with it as the force of their descent into nothingness tore at his body. The ropes burnt into his shoulders as he fought to stay with the dragon and the girl.

Then, they levelled off and Dranich unfurled her wings and soared. She must have night vision. How else could the dragon see to know where they were in such inky darkness?

"Stay down," Alainea said.

Charles flattened himself again, and Dranich folded her wings as they shot into another narrow tunnel. This one was not so tight. There was very little space between him and the surrounding rock, but at least it didn't scratch his back.

He discerned a slight lightening of the gloom. Although his cheek was pressed into the hide of the dragon, he kept his eyes open this time. Fresh air mixed with the dank smell of cold rock. And there was something else—the scent of pine! They were near a forest which had to mean they would be close to ground level when they exited the mountain.

Charles shifted his head, hoping for an end to the darkness. It started as only a pinprick of faint light, but with relief he saw they were close to the end of the tunnel. The light was from a starlit sky waiting for them beyond the cloistering silence of the mountain.

They burst through. Dranich spread her wings and caught the fresh night air, spinning them over treetops under the light of a waning moon. Charles gulped at a breeze that washed over him in a cleansing wave. He was still alive and he lifted his head to rejoice.

Silently they soared as close to the ground as possible. It made sense to Charles that Respiele would have lookouts perched at high points along the mountains, watching the skies. They would need to stay shrouded in shadow if they were to escape the notice of Respiele's dragon riders. Trusting in the knowledge and expertise of Alainea and Dranich, he lay still and thought of all she had told him as they glided soundlessly into the east.

While it was still hard to accept the bizarre events of the last two days, he couldn't deny that they had happened. Surely then, he would be able to return home one day since Alainea had said it. He imagined telling his parents what had happened and wondered if they would laugh him out of the house. He doubted they would believe it. Still, he was always honest with them and hadn't been a boy with a wild imagination. Maybe he could bring something back with him—to prove where he'd been and the things he'd done.

His reverie was broken with the crashing arrival of another dragon who burst upon them from a copse of trees to their right.

Charles wrapped the ropes around his hand and tried to hunker even lower, expecting they would attempt to outrun their pursuer. Only they did not.

Dranich turned back upon herself, rearing straight up into the sky with a powerful thrust of her wings. She made a complete circle overhead and came down on the long snake-like tail of the dragon who followed, throwing it off-balance. The rider collected himself, drew back on a huge bow that seemed fixed in place on the back of his dragon, and lifted it to take aim.

Alainea lunged to her knees, flipped her bow over her head, and shot an arrow straight and true. The rider crumpled, slid from the beast he rode, and dropped to the ground below. His dragon glided a little further and then, seeming to realize what had happened, left the rider behind and caught up to them.

Charles shrank back, thinking the beast was attacking them itself. Instead, the dragon drew up beside them and lowered its head in a sign of esteem before winging back the way it had come.

It all happened so quickly that Charles blinked, wondering if he'd really seen it. But he had, and he stared at Alainea with new respect. What a woman this was. He could tell it would not have been easy for her to kill someone, but clearly, she was determined to do whatever was necessary to save her world from the clutches of Respiele.

Charles couldn't see her face as she slung the bow across her shoulder and took her place once more. He laid his cheek against the rough hide and closed his eyes. It wasn't safe to voice his thoughts even if he had known what to say. Besides, he couldn't think of a thing. She had done what needed to be done and someone lay dead back there, because of *their* choices, not *hers*.

They flew on into the night. After considering what had happened, Charles wanted to ask her what the rider-less dragon had been doing. It almost seemed to be thanking them. Why though? And why wasn't the beast concerned about its rider? But this was only one of the myriad of questions he had for Alainea if they ever had a chance to talk.

A large bird swooped at them from the darkness, matching their speed and turning its head to stare at them. Charles prepared for another attack, but the bird was only the biggest snowy owl he had ever seen. He breathed a sigh of relief.

They flew throughout the rest of the night. Charles dozed periodically and wondered if Alainea did too, but he supposed not. She was a warrior. Whether Respiele had trained her to stand with him in battle or not, she was a formidable opponent. Did the man know she was not in agreement with his plans for world domination? He guessed if Respiele didn't know before, he knew it now.

Why was she treated so badly? Her only tasks at the fortress seemed to be as Respiele's servant. The woman, Laveza, had spoken to Alainea as though she were worthless, not the daughter of their leader. Charles felt pity for this girl and her mother, but suspected they would not want it.

The world was brightening. Off in the east, a thread of gold emerged against the horizon and shadows began to appear. A mountain range appeared on his right, taller than the one where Respiele's fortress was situated. The tallest peak pierced the sky and he stared at it. For some reason, it was familiar.

"It is the Ildune Mountain," Alainea said, as though reading his mind. She turned her head to speak to him in low tones. "Home of the Southern Portal and the Garde who live there. Durgot Flandish is Gatekeeper there. You will meet him."

"Why do I recognize it?" Charles stared at the mountain in wonder.

"It was from the south that you came," she said. "Above those peaks is where Laveza, and her dragon Nagilla, broke through the barrier and entered your world. You have seen that mountain before..."

She broke off and slid forward to peer down at the rolling landscape below. "And near here, somewhere, is where King Larkender fell in battle. We must now begin to watch for him."

Wisps of mist lay in pockets along the ground, making it difficult to scan the area with any certainty. Dranich swept across the ground disturbing the foggy areas, causing them to swirl in their wake.

"Respiele's riders will be upon us soon," Alainea said, keeping her gaze trained on the earth below. "When one of their numbers is missed, it will not take long for word to spread. They will soon know where we are headed."

She caught Charles' eye before continuing her search for the king. Her voice floated across to him easily now that their speed had diminished. "The dragons do not want any part of what Respiele does, yet they are enslaved, as is my mother. I shall free them all one day."

"I believe you," Charles said.

"Keep watch for anything unusual. Trees flattened, a dead dragon, burnt areas. All of these could point to the battle that took place and lead us to the king."

He lay on the side furthest away from the mountains and therefore had the best view of the fields and hollows that were directly to the north of it. The occasional farm appeared below them, surrounded by plots of land, each a different hue of green. They passed over a field of blue that tossed in the breeze of their passing like the waters of a large square lake. He wondered if it was flax, or if they grew the same crops here as they did where he was from. It was likely growing season meaning that some crops would be in flower.

Animals grazed below—horses, sheep, cattle—but there was nothing that resembled farm implements. Not that he'd expected it. This land seemed to be set back in a time long before such innovations.

Charles caught sight of something large and dark in a bluff of thick trees. Was it just a boulder, or something more?

"Can you ask Dranich to take us lower?"

"You already did," she said dryly, as Dranich circled and angled closer to earth.

The countryside was taking on rich hues of gold and orange from the rising sun and the mist was burning up in a hazy cloud of evaporation. Charles could see much better now and as they turned, he stabbed at the air to show Alainea where he had seen the mass.

"Over there. Do you see it?"

"Yes!"

Dranich was already banking and preparing to land in a clearing close by. Before she even touched down, both Charles and Alainea had shed harnesses and were sliding to the ground. Only Alainea was faster and by the time Charles arrived she was standing over the body of a great golden dragon.

"Her name is Oraneth," Alainea said softly. She brushed away a tear and went on in an unsteady voice. "She was from the Araleesh Mountains. They all are."

Oraneth lay with her tail crumpled behind her and

armoured neck thrust back to reveal several arrows protruding from her chest. Lacerations covered Oraneth's body, but were worst on her hindquarters where chunks of flesh had been ripped away. The grass around the dragon was matted and stained with dried blood. Her once proud head, with its long horns and thorny neck, were twisted unnaturally. The pain of seeing this beautiful creature in death tore at Charles' heart.

"I am so sorry, dear one." Alainea reached out and touched Oraneth's head. "Oraneth has not been dead for long. Perhaps an hour," Alainea muttered, glancing at Charles. Then, sniffing, she became stiff and businesslike. "Do not just stand there. Help me look for the king!"

Dragging a sleeve across her face she turned and darted about the area, searching. Trees had been shorn off at their roots with the force of the dragon's fall, and vast splinters of wood lay in the long grass, under shrubs, and in the surrounding trees.

Charles walked around to the other side of the dragon. He figured if the man had been riding the creature, he wouldn't have been thrown too far away.

He was right. Pinned under the dragon's tail was a young man, his face, what could be seen of it between smears of dirt and blood, was pinched and deathly white. Alainea could be forgiven for not noticing him, for only the man's head and shoulders were visible. Even then they were partially hidden in a hole the man must have dug in his effort to crawl out from under the heavy weight.

Charles gave a short, shrill whistle before resting his fingers on the man's neck. It was unbelievable. The pulse was weak, but he was alive. Alainea came running and flung herself down beside King Larkender's head.

"Is he…?" Her face was ashen, her eyes bright with unshed tears and hope intermingled.

"He's alive." Charles scrambled to his feet and assessed how they could move the dragon's tail away. "Dranich could pull the tail off of him—with the harness."

"Oh! That is wonderful!" Alainea clasped her hands together then looked to where Dranich was already moving toward them. "Yes, I believe she could."

Lunging to her feet, she ran to undo the length of rope she'd added in to accommodate Charles. Bundling it in her arms, she ran back. Together, he and Alainea wrapped a makeshift noose around the very end of Oraneth's tail, since it was the only part of it that Charles could partially lift for her to slide the rope around.

Dranich lumbered across the trampled grass to stand beside the fallen Oraneth. Bending low, she touched foreheads with her kin. A low wail of grief issued from her mouth, and two tendrils of smoke rose from her flaring nostrils.

Charles leaped back in alarm as Dranich rose on her hind legs and reared into the air. She threw her head back with a roar of flame issuing from her mouth that seared the nearby trees.

When she dropped back down to all fours, Alainea rushed to her side, speaking out loud to the dragon.

"My sweet Dranich. It is a sad day." She stroked a spot between her dragon's eyes with a loving hand. "But we do not have the luxury of time to mourn. We must save the king, and he is trapped. Please help us pull Oraneth's tail away and free him."

Dranich swivelled her huge lizard-like yellow eyes toward Alainea in silent answer.

The young woman sprinted back to where the king was

pinned and knelt beside him. Raising her arm, she motioned to Dranich. The dragon came close enough that Charles and Alainea were able to bind the ends of the rope around Oraneth's tail to the harness already about Dranich's neck. Then, Dranich extended her wings, lifting off the ground, and slowly, the dead dragon's long tail rose into the air, exposing the torso and legs of the crushed king.

He was in worse shape than Charles had expected. He saw now why Respiele's riders had confidently reported of the king's death. Several wounds marred the man's legs and forearms, but the most serious was to his stomach.

Charles sat back on his haunches. Dark red blood oozed from around an arrow that had pierced the king's abdomen clean through. Perhaps the dragon's tail had staunched it somewhat, because now blood flowed freely, trickling across the king's torn shirt to pool on the ground.

Nothing could be done for this man. Certainly nothing in *this* world. Even if they had been back home in Canada it would have been tough to save the king's life. It was obvious he had lost a lot of blood and his wounds were too extensive to heal on their own without major surgery. By the time they could get him to a doctor he would be...

"Give me the Golden Sceptre of Power," Alainea said beside him. She yanked the black arrow from the king's flesh and hurled it aside. Blood gushed out of the gaping wound all the faster. "Hurry!"

With fumbling fingers, Charles flipped his cloak aside. He tore the long case over his head, untied the thongs at the top, and pulled the covering away. The gleaming rod fell into his hands and he handed it to her, wondering what she could possibly use it for.

Alainea reached for the sceptre. It had been nothing more than a cold, beautiful ornament in Charles' grasp, but when she held it the thing seemed to come alive. The sceptre fairly vibrated. The gold became so luminous it was almost too bright to look at, and the jewels mounted at the top began to revolve in their ornate setting until they were a blur of flashing colour.

Charles fell back in astonishment.

Alainea bent to the king, holding the sceptre over his broken body, murmuring unintelligible words. Even from a few metres away, Charles could feel a strange warmth radiating from the sceptre and enveloping the king in a glowing light.

The king stirred. Where once he had lain barely breathing in a hollow created by the frantic scratching of his own two hands, he now sighed with a sound of deep contentment. His chest began to rise and fall in a regular rhythm.

More astonishing than that, however, were the king's wounds. Charles scrambled forward on his knees, his jaw dropping open in wonder. Before his eyes, the gashes were closing. Even the cavernous, bloody wound was drawing together to heal itself. It was like an excerpt from a film reel where the scene was played in reverse. And all the while, the multi-facetted gemstones whirled in a mesmerizing blur of sparkling colour.

Then, each cut and abrasion was gone. The king took a shuddering breath as the sceptre slowed. The light that had hypnotized Charles faded, and the spinning gems slowed until the sceptre was nothing more than a pretty ornament again.

No wonder Respiele wanted the sceptre. It was amazing!

"Will it work for Oraneth?" Charles asked, his eyes flicking toward the dragon.

Alainea took so long in answering that he cleared his

throat and opened his mouth to ask again, but she spoke before he could.

"No." Her voice sounded brittle and frail. "It cannot give life where none exists."

Inching forward, she cradled the king's head with her arm and nodded to Charles. "That flask of water you carry. Give some to him."

Charles removed it and handed it to her. Alainea held it to King Larkender's lips and gently wet them.

"My king," she said, "try to drink a little."

The man's eyes fluttered, and his tongue flicked at the offered water. Alainea tipped the flask and, while most of the water trickled down his chin, the king's throat worked as he swallowed a few drops.

"We must get him away from this place," Alainea said, looking at Charles over the king's head. "Riders will soon be combing the area, knowing I would search for him. They will be exceedingly angry and desperate to retrieve the sceptre. Laveza knows where the battle took place."

She looked down and a tear dropped to the king's ragged vest. It rolled a short distance before melting into the material.

Charles' mind felt foggy after the horrific events of the last few days. It was still like some awful nightmare.

"Right," he said, with effort. "Where?"

"King Larkender must be taken back to Larkender Castle along with the sceptre where he can recuperate." She whirled around to the dragon. "We will use the harness to bind him to Dranich and she will return him to the castle."

She thrust the sceptre back into Charles' hands. It was cold and lifeless once more.

"Wrap it up again, please. If he is to have any chance of

winning the war he must have the sceptre. It shall be sent with him."

"Okay. But is the king safe to move?" Charles asked, taking care to slide the rod into the case with reverence. "Shouldn't we go with him?"

"Dranich will see to his safety. Our path lies in a different direction."

Alainea nodded and laid the king's head down again. She and Charles went to untangle the ropes from Oraneth's tail. They readied the belts and ropes to receive the king. Then they hurried back to him. Between them, they managed to lift the weakened man and shuffle him across to Dranich who had lain down, allowing them to drag the king aboard.

Charles knelt with Alainea, as she worked with nimble fingers to piece together the straps and tighten them around the king's torso and legs. Lastly, she slung the sceptre around King Ludwig's neck and over his shoulder before fastening it securely.

To Charles' surprise, the king spoke.

"You have saved my life," he said in a quavering voice. "And recovered the sceptre. It was from my own foolishness that it was taken. I cannot thank you enough."

Charles leaned close to hear the last few words. It was a wonder the man could speak at all.

"King Larkender, please do not tire yourself needlessly," Alainea said. "It is important you leave at once, but heed me closely. When you have recovered, you must prepare for war. Respiele will be furious with what has just transpired. He was readying his troops to march upon you before this attack took place. If he had retained the sceptre he would have succeeded, but now…Well, we have a fighting chance."

The king drew a hoarse breath. "Oraneth?"

Alainea squeezed her eyes shut. "She is dead. I am so sorry."

"D—dead?" His voice cracked. "My dear friend is dead." The king's head fell back and tears rolled down his cheeks. "Has she been released?"

"No," Alainea answered. "May I?"

"Who are you child?" King Larkender asked in a halting voice.

"I am Alainea Ilstyne, daughter of Respiele. You are my uncle sir. My dragon and I stand with you."

King Larkender flinched. "His daughter?" Blue eyes focused on her from beneath partially closed lids. "I sense the truth in what you say. Yes, please release my dear friend."

In one fluid movement, Alainea slid to the ground and ran back to Oraneth. Kneeling, she placed both hands on the dragon's head and bowed her head. She mumbled a few words in a strange tongue, then stood, and stepped away.

A sudden, raging wind descended from above. It whirled about them, broken branches and grasses ripped from the earth rising into the sky along with the gale. Oraneth rose into it. Her body shimmered in the sun and became almost translucent. She hovered over their heads, appearing to have come back to life as her wings spread wide and her head lifted proudly on her neck. Oraneth's tail slashed through the sky, and her body shattered into a million tiny shards of light. They swirled like a twinkling mass of stars up into the sky and were borne across the heavens on the wind.

Alainea raised both arms over her head and lifted her face to the sunlight. Then, she jogged back to Dranich and scrambled up the dragon's side to speak urgently to the king.

"Oraneth is at peace, but you must leave, now." She patted his arm. "Dranich will carry you to Larkender Castle as fast as possible. Respiele thirsts for war. He believes you to be dead and your people vulnerable. He will march forth on the morrow with plans to attack you from the southwest. Remember there are many who will stand with you to drive this evil from our land. I will speak to all I can. Farewell."

The king's fingers lifted in acknowledgement.

"Thank you," he murmured.

Catching Charles' gaze, Alainea jerked her head to indicate they should move and allow Dranich to carry the king to safety.

Both of them dropped to the ground beside Dranich. The dragon rumbled from deep within her chest.

Leaning forward, Alainea rested her head against Dranich's nose and brought both hands up to hold the jutting angles of the dragon's face.

"Go," she said aloud. "Keep him safe my friend."

Releasing her, Alainea stepped back. The yellow, cat-like eyes of the dragon swivelled to look at Charles, who bowed his head in respect.

Dranich gathered herself to launch into the sky.

"You are too late," grated a voice from behind them. "Stay where you are."

Charles and Alainea whirled around. Two men picked their way around the tree stumps, only a few steps away. One of the warriors held a bow stretched taut with an arrow aimed at them, waiting to be let loose. Not far away, the warriors' dragons waited, and a third, with its rider, circled down to land.

"Fly!" Alainea screamed.

Drawing her sword, she launched herself toward the man who, as Dranich moved, turned his arrow toward the fleeing dragon. Dranich sprang into the air, her wings catching the wind in one smooth stroke after another, pulling her aloft. The arrow whistled after her. It clattered against her scales, followed by three more arrows. All fell uselessly to the ground.

"Kill them!" the man said with a snarl to his companion. He drew back to load another arrow.

Alainea leapt across the distance that separated them and drew her sword. She flung herself at the man, driving him to the ground with the force of her blade before he could arm his bow again.

Charles was not far behind.

The second man dropped his bow and reached for his sword as Charles swung a fist with everything he could muster. He caught the warrior across the jaw, sending him reeling backward. He staggered and caught himself before he fell. He reached once more for his sword. Charles leaped after him, planting himself in a solid stance to deliver a combination of punches he knew well. Before the man was stable, Charles jabbed him twice full in the face with his left, then quickly followed with a right cross. The man, his nose streaming blood, crumpled to the ground.

Charles stood over him, wondering what was to be done. They were not in a position to take prisoners, and these warriors would either report back to Respiele, or hunt him and Alainea down.

However, Charles was saved from the worry. The man had pounded his head on a rock as he went down and lay in a widening pool of blood. Charles bent to check the man's pulse.

Dead.

He raised his head to stare at Alainea. He had killed a man. He hadn't meant to, of course. He had never even seen a dead body before, let alone been the instrument responsible for it. He felt the colour drain from his face and his stomach clenched.

Alainea nodded. "You have a few hidden talents yourself."

"I belong to a boxing club back home," Charles said, his voice uneven.

Flexing his hand, he watched Alainea deftly unsling her bow and fit an arrow into the grooves. Holding the bow with her left hand, she angled herself, pulled back, and took careful aim.

Following the trajectory of her arrow with his gaze, Charles was amazed. Was she going to try to take down the dragon pursuing Dranich and the king? It was already so far away. Yet, with a *twang* of released tension, the arrow flew from her bow and she stepped back to watch its passage through the sky.

"There is but one chance," she muttered, only half to Charles.

He raised a hand to his eyes, shielding them from the morning sun, and looked at the figure mounted on the back of the pursuing dragon.

Of course, she wasn't shooting at the creature; she was aiming for its rider. The pair streaked through the sky in pursuit of Dranich, the king, and the Golden Sceptre of Power. If Alainea's arrow failed in its mission, both the king and her dragon would be killed and the sceptre returned to an insane man bent on ruling the world.

Chapter Six

Somehow, the arrow hit true.

With a release of held breath, Charles and Alainea relaxed as the dark rider toppled forward over the shoulder of the dragon and plunged through the air to disappear in a grove of trees.

"You did it," Charles whispered, amazed at such an ability.

Alainea shrugged and turned a tremulous smile on him. "Unfortunate to end the man's life, but there was no other way to stop him."

The rider-less dragon veered sharply, altering its course and streaking across the sky where the Araleesh Mountains lay. The two dragons who had waited for their riders now also took to the sky and careened off into the west.

Alainea looked down at first one and then the other warrior, both sprawled on the ground, dead.

"We need to go," she said, catching Charles' gaze. "It is plain to see this is all shocking to you."

She slung her bow over her shoulder and straightened

her tunic. "They would have done the same to us. Then they would have killed Dranich and the king. All would have been lost. I could not allow that to happen. Do you understand?"

Charles nodded.

"I'll follow wherever you lead," he said simply. His words were met with a thin smile before she whirled and jogged back toward the west, following, not in the direction Dranich had taken to the north, but behind the dragons who had flown without their riders.

"Why aren't we going to meet with Dranich and the king?" Charles caught up to her once they cleared the tree-line. "Where are we headed?"

"I can do nothing more for King Ludwig." She spared Charles a glance as he hurried across the grassy field beside her. "He will be well taken care of and knows now to prepare for battle."

"Then what are we doing next?" Charles eased into a steady rhythm beside her. Despite being unused to running long distances, he felt enlivened with the events of the morning.

It must be adrenalin.

He pushed images of the dead warrior out of his mind.

"My mission is to alert any who will fight for King Ludwig and to save the dragons. Dranich is one of only five dragons left alive in Erinbourne. Three lost their riders this morning and will return to take further orders from Respiele. They are forced to do so."

"They're forced?"

Alainea shook her head and frowned. "There is no time to explain, but I will when we stop." She repositioned the sword and held it with one hand to stop it from knocking into her leg. "War is upon this land whether it knows it or not. We can help spread the word so the people will not be taken unawares. I hope many will fight with the king. If they do not, I fear it will be too late."

Charles slowed. His thoughts raced as he tried to make sense of this new information.

"How long can you keep up this pace?" she called over one shoulder.

He hastened to catch up and stay abreast of the girl. "I usually ride whenever I'm out, but I think I'm pretty fit. It'll be easier now without the sceptre to carry."

"You ride what? A horse?"

"Of course." He steadied the flask of water riding on his hip and wondered if she was joking. "There aren't any dragons where I'm from, if that's what you mean."

A snort issued from her lips, followed by almost a laugh.

"I knew that much," she said, grinning at him. "Your expressions are quite revealing."

Charles smiled back at her. The morning sun made her auburn hair gleam in its bouncing braid, and her pale cheeks were flushed pink from the exercise.

They jogged in silence, moving from one bluff of trees to the next as long as the cover wasn't too far off the path Alainea chose. If it was, she quickened their pace across open areas until they reached some form of shelter again. She seemed to have a clear sense of which way to go and Charles didn't doubt her unerring ability to lead.

He saw nothing of civilization apart from the stone fences that seemed to border each field. They ran off into the distance over plots that had been cultivated and planted or left as grass to feed animals. Occasionally, they passed a few cattle, a horse or two, or some sheep, but he saw no farmhouses or buildings of any sort. Some of the crops, like wheat and oats, were familiar to him, but others were not, and he looked at them with interest as they hurried through.

The trees were different, too. Nothing like the poplar and pine he was used to back home. There were several varieties here, but all of them were taller and their branches were symmetrical which made them appear man-made. Strange, because they weren't. They were too random to have been planted.

Eventually, after waiting as long as possible, Charles put up a hand. They were in a dense part of a forest, and it had forced them to slow down as they wove around trees.

Alainea stopped.

"Just need a drink," Charles said, panting. He flopped onto the mossy ground and reached for the water at his side. "Don't worry. I won't drink much."

Lifting the container to his lips, he allowed several teaspoons to moisten his parched throat and then handed it to Alainea.

"Here, have some," he said.

Reluctantly, she accepted it and took a sip. Handing it back, she absently wiped her mouth with a sleeve and scanned the sky above them. Charles stared at her. He had so many questions waiting to be asked.

"Can you communicate with other dragons that might be nearby? Or with Dranich now that she's gone?"

Alainea took a long moment before she replied. "Dranich and I are connected. Her thoughts are my own. She is part of me and we may reach out to connect with one another, at a distance, mainly by way of our emotions. Not necessarily in words, which is the way you mean. Although I can send my thoughts to her if need be. We do not have conversations from a distance, but I shall surely know if anything happens to them, and when they reach Larkender Castle."

Sighing, Alainea dropped down to sit cross-legged in front of him, still keeping her eyes trained above.

"Other dragons are more difficult. While they will talk to me, at close range, and have never been willing accomplices in Respiele's plans to overthrow our world, they also are linked to only one person, which is to the Garde who was joined to them at the time of their birth. And it is *not* a Garde who rides them at present. They are bound by dark magic to these riders. When a dragon is released from one rider, through his death, they return to the mountain, to Respiele. He will then choose another of his warriors to take over. Again, it will be against their will and there will be no understanding between them. Common people cannot speak with animals. Only those of the Garde may enjoy that privilege."

"I see," Charles said, not really understanding at all. It was a complicated business, for sure. "So, that's how Dranich knew to be under the ledge when you pushed me off it?"

"Yes." Alainea looked at him finally and lifted one eyebrow. "Tell me about your life in this land you come from?"

"My life?" Charles repeated the words, trying to think of something interesting to say. He shrugged. "It's pretty quiet and uneventful, compared to this."

He lifted an arm and swung it around to emphasize his remark.

"I mean, where I'm from, things are different, and it's more modern too. We travel in cars and farmers use tractors to work the fields, not horses."

"A trac-tor?" Alainea stumbled over the word. "It sounds interesting."

"It's a machine." His mind struggled to define vehicles and machinery, then gave up trying. "Just a different way to travel or work. One isn't better than the other."

He picked up a twig from the ground and twisted it idly between his fingers. "I live with my parents on a ranch raising cattle. I'm an only child and was born to them late in their lives. They talk of retiring soon and moving to Vancouver Island. Then I'll be taking over."

"Retiring?" she asked with a puzzled frown. "You mean they would leave your home to live in this other place? The island?"

Charles nodded, and Alainea reached into her satchel to remove a chunk of the bread and cheese her mother had packed. Unwrapping them, she tore each one in half and handed the share to Charles.

"We might as well eat something while we're taking a break."

"So, what will you do once this is all over?" Charles asked. His mouth was full of the surprisingly tasty food. The cheese was creamy and melted like butter, while the bread, although it looked dark, hard, and nasty, was delicious.

Alainea's chewing paused and she looked into the sky where a lazy hawk wheeled overhead.

"I have no thought of tomorrow. My life thus far has focused on the preservation of myself and my mother. It consumes each day, leaving no time to dream of a future." She dropped her gaze to her hands. "Perhaps I do not have a future. As Respiele's daughter, I foresee only trouble ahead."

"Nonsense." Charles faced her. "You're smart, young,

strong, and brave. You will—I mean *we*—will make sure your mother is released from that prison and then you'll find a house in a village somewhere. There's lots of things you could do. I'll bet the king would give you a job after what you've just done for him."

"Perhaps," she said with a wistful smile. "Shall we go?"

In answer, Charles pushed himself upright and brushed leaves from his legs. He hadn't known this girl long, but his thoughts rested on her plight with concern. It was clear she had no worry for herself, or whether she made it out of this predicament alive. Her only fear was for her mother and the creatures she had taken under her care—the dragons.

She darted off again, winding through the trees like she was running an obstacle course. They emerged from this stand of timber. She ran several steps up a slope on the other side, then she turned, grabbed his arm, and pulled him back the way they'd come. Grim terror was etched on her face. He needed no words to know she had seen, or felt, something that threatened them.

She dove into the shelter of the brush at the edge of the bluff, dragging Charles behind her. Branches scratched and tore at his face and hands, but he was oblivious to the pain as he scrambled to conceal himself.

Peering through the lofty treetops, he could see another of Respiele's dragon rider spies wheeling high above them in lazy circles, scanning the ground for any sign of movement.

"Do you think we were seen?" Charles whispered.

"No. It would be upon us by now if that were the case."

They were silent, both watching the sky for the beast to move off, but it didn't.

A flock of sheep appeared over the knoll ahead of them.

The animals were unaware of their presence, and nibbled at the already short grass on the hillside.

"I have an idea," Alainea said in a low voice. "You said you come from a farm, correct?"

Charles nodded.

"Then you should have no qualms with what I am about to suggest."

The sheep grazed closer and closer to where they crouched in the bushes. There were only about twenty of them and they were large, round, and woolly. He'd never had much to do with sheep, and he watched them with curiosity.

"I propose we hide among them. I have asked the sheep to move toward the next patch of cover, taking us along with them."

"Hide in a herd of sheep?" Charles asked with incredulity. "Aren't they skittish creatures, afraid of everything?"

He sat back on his legs and stared first at her and then at the milling throng of animals.

"In truth, they are a flock, not a herd, and no, they will not run. You will be forced to crawl, of course, but the sheep are prepared to aid us. Ready?"

Without waiting for him to answer, let alone agree, she crept out from the cover of the bushes and disappeared into the group of sheep. They enveloped her. Charles knew he had no choice but to follow. With one final glance overhead, he crept from the battered bushes and pushed his way between the backs of the tight-knit animals.

If only his friends could see him now, crawling across a field on all fours, trying to blend in with a bunch of sheep. It was no easy task either, and somewhat painful too, he soon realized. The animals pressed in around him, jostling him, and driving their sharp little hooves into his hands and the backs of his legs. Plus, it was hard on the knees.

Each breath he took was filled with the scent of warm sheep, and the fine fibres of their coats found their way into his mouth and nose. The sun rose hot in a clear sky. Soon it felt like he was crawling across a desert under several layers of thick wool blankets. He could see nothing of where they were going as he didn't want to raise his head and stand out from the crowd. He'd lost sight of Alainea too, but believed she was ahead of him, somewhere. He trusted she was able to communicate with these fluffy creatures and could keep them on course.

Eventually, they stopped.

"Come up to me," Alainea called to him.

Keeping his head down like a battering ram, he shoved through the fluffy bodies until he reached her side. A tall stone fence blocked their path. The sheep moved uneasily, but they stayed close.

"Their owners live just beyond this fence, and the sheep assure me that the couple are faithful to the monarchy," Alainea said. "I believe they might help us if asked. In any case, we have little choice but to try. That dragon rider is not going anywhere."

Charles didn't chance a look. He simply nodded his willingness to follow her lead.

"When we leave the flock, move quickly. There is a bluff of trees on the other side of this wall, and beyond that, the farmyard. All we can do is hope the rider is looking the other way when we break cover."

She reached for rocky projections on the stone wall and Charles shuffled up to do the same.

Before they could leave the flock, however, something

whooshed over their heads very low. Charles couldn't help but look up in surprise. He caught sight of an expanse of white wings too broad to be any kind of bird he was familiar with back home.

"Wait!" Alainea drew her hands back from the wall and rested on her haunches among the sheep. Her eyes widened and she gulped. "I cannot believe it possible, but if I am not mistaken—that was a Silpeth."

Puzzled, he waited for her to explain.

"I have only read of them in legend. They appear as great white owls normally, but have the ability to change their form into that of a huge, winged horse. It is said they are valiant beyond measure, loyal to the king, and, I am sure, would not take kindly to Respiele's plans." A slow smile curved her lips. "It is too wonderful to think they are here, even if it is only one of them."

She looked across at Charles, her face lighting up with relief and joy.

"The Silpeth come from the Mareele Islands as far into the east as is possible to travel without entering your world." She raised both hands to her cheeks and lowered her head. "It spoke to me just now. It impressed upon me to remain still a few moments more. He was too late to assist the king, but is grateful for what we did to save his life."

Both of them eagerly turned to peer into the sky. The dragon seemed tiny at this distance, but it could clearly be seen suspended in space. It stretched its dark wings against the blue sky of mid-morning, a long tail coiled beneath its huge body.

Abruptly, it reared back and the tail slashed. Something flashed between it and their vision, and then a jet of pure fire seared the air. The dragon dove and gave chase.

"Now!" Alainea yelled.

Both of them grasped the rocky wall and heaved themselves over it, landing on the other side at a dead run. They made for the shelter of another copse of trees, but the cover was not good. They darted through and out the other side, heading for the sanctuary of a log building. It was a long structure surrounded by corrals, and probably used to house cattle in winter. If they had winter here.

The only entrance, a set of double doors facing a dilapidated farmhouse and several other, smaller outbuildings, were closed, but not locked. Alainea wrenched one open and leaped inside, only waiting for Charles to enter before she slammed it shut. They stood in the gloom panting.

Alainea walked to the one grimy window the barn possessed and rubbed her sleeve on it to squint outside.

"I see nothing of our hunter," she said, turning away, "but that does not mean it is safe to continue our journey as we have. I must think and hopefully speak to the owners of this place."

Charles bent to rub his sore knees and asked a question he'd been wondering about all morning. "If the dragons don't want to be part of what Respiele is doing, or carry the riders they do, why are they? They must know about the— what did you call it—a Silpeth?"

She nodded.

"Yeah, well, they must know that the Silpeth are good guys. Yet we just watched that dragon shoot flames at it. Surely dragons are powerful enough to fight Respiele and do as they please?"

Alainea walked over to a stack of fragrant hay and subsided into it before answering. "The dragon would never have tried to destroy a Silpeth. It would have been for show, a diversion allowing us time to escape."

She nestled into a more comfortable position.

"The dragons obey Respiele, because he has something very precious to them they cannot afford to lose." She sighed, drew up her knees, and hugged them to her chest. "He holds it over them as intimidation. They do not dare to defy him or he will destroy this precious thing and all of their futures in one fell swoop."

"What is it?" Charles said. He lowered himself into the hay beside her. He was impatient. How important could this thing be to force every dragon in this kingdom into subservience? He couldn't understand it.

"An egg," she said, her voice dipping down so low he barely caught the words. "The last of their kind. Dragons do not live forever. Certainly they outlive many other creatures in my world, but they are not immortal. And they are subject to the same ills and wounds that take every other life. That egg was—*is*—their final hope to continue their species."

"But surely they could…" Charles felt his face flush, but he stammered on. "I mean, they could mate and create other eggs, couldn't they?"

Alainea fixed him with her unusual amber eyes. Even in the semi-darkness of the space, they seemed to blaze with anger. "Five months ago, Respiele had every male dragon in this land executed, in order that he might hold the one remaining egg as leverage. He wanted to seize control, and used the dragon's fear of extinction to further his own ambition. He cares nothing if they live or die. His only desire is to use their abilities for his own evils."

Alainea clutched handfuls of hay in each hand and ground them into dust with the force of her emotion.

"Every dragon that lived through that killing spree is a female. The last remaining egg is a male. There *is* no other way. If it is destroyed, the dragons will be lost forever.

I must return to Respiele's fortress, find the egg, and save the dragons. Even if I die in the process."

Chapter Seven

Charles woke as a shaft of light intruded on his eyelids. He raised himself to an elbow, his stomach growling with hunger, and struggled to catch his brain up with all that had happened since his abduction.

Remembrance flooded back with a groan that was stifled once he squinted into the light. A man, dressed in a long, coarse-looking tunic and breeches, stood in the doorway holding an ancient-looking oil lamp high in the air. The heads of two curious cows were behind him while a lean-looking dog slunk into the space at the man's feet, his ears flat and his lip curling away from bared teeth.

"Who are ye?" the man demanded, crossing to where Alainea had leapt to her feet, one hand on the hilt of her sword. "And what be ye doing in my barn?"

The man lifted his lamp, shining it full into their faces. Charles clambered upright, feeling the tension build. The man's face wavered in the flickering light with shadows of suspicion.

Charles' gaze darted to the open doorway where the

evening's coolness seeped in. How long had they been asleep? He opened his mouth to formulate some sort of answer to the man's question. Though telling him they had been pursued by Respiele's warriors and needed somewhere to hide before beginning their quest to save the last of the dragons sounded crazy even to him. He closed his mouth and looked to Alainea.

"We are no threat to you, good sir," she began, with a tilt to her chin that brooked no argument. "My name is Alainea Ilstyne and this is Charles...."

She broke off, darting a look at him as she waited for him to supply the missing name.

"Bramley," Charles finished.

"Yes," she said. "We are commissioned by King Lark-ender to gather all those eager to end the menace brought upon us by Respiele. Be you for, or against?"

Charles noted, for good reason, that she did not include whose daughter she was.

The fellow eyed them both before responding, but his face had softened at her explanation. He was not a follower of Respiele. Alainea's body relaxed and her hand dropped away from her sword.

"There are farmers in this area as what provides food and milk for the likes of that tyrant," the man said. "I am not one of them."

He lowered his lamp and motioned that they step to the side. Turning, he walked back to the entrance, hung the lamp on a hook, and pushed the double doors wide to accommodate the cattle waiting outside. Two docile cows swung past and filed into stalls set against the far wall under the window, waiting for their feed.

Milk cows. Charles smiled with the familiarity of it all as the farmer leaned outside to retrieve a large silver pail from beyond the door. He looped it over his arm. The dog came forward, ears pricked to greet them personally, and Alainea bent to lay a hand on its head before the animal moved to sniff Charles. Apparently, he passed inspection, for the dog's tail began to wag and Charles stroked its ears.

"The name is Ben Hardy and my dog is Jay. He's right smart, Jay is. Ye can tell me more as I milk these old girls," the man said, patting the closest cow on the rump.

Using an old wooden bucket, he scooped a portion of grain from a bin near the stack of hay and poured a measure of it out for the two animals. Then, as they bent their heads to eat, he pulled a short stool close to one cow's hind end, sat down. and placed his pail on the straw, beneath her udder.

"And if I can be of benefit to yer cause, well, all ye have to do is ask."

Jay took up a place beside his master and lay down, his head against his paws.

Charles exchanged relieved glances with Alainea as they both moved closer. Ben rested his forehead on the flank of the cow as he began to squirt steady streams of milk into the pail.

"I am glad to know you, Mr. Hardy," she said. "We are making our way to the Araleesh Mountain range in hopes of raising an army of those unafraid to confront Respiele. He plans to overthrow the king within the week. I believe he will march into the north on the morrow. Could you gather those people you know who will fight for our king, and help us to pass undetected from this area so we may alert more people to the war that is coming?"

"I will," Ben said without hesitation. "Is that why ye are here, hiding in my barn? Is someone after ye then?"

He looked up at them, all the while continuing with his work.

"Yes," Charles said, anxious that Ben know he was not unable to speak for himself. "Respiele's dragon riders are searching for us. We were nearly captured today, but thanks to your barn we were able to escape."

Ben dropped his piercing gaze back down to his task. "Aye, I knew something was happening. Two days ago, there was a fearful clash this side of the Ildune Mountains. Dragons everywhere. And then one fell from the sky. Me and the missus, we went inside and bolted our doors. Was that part of this uprising?"

The milk continued to flow from his expert touch and the cows chewed their grain contentedly.

"It was King Larkender you saw fall," Alainea said.

Ben started, almost tipping the pail into the deep bed of straw at his feet, but she lifted a hand to reassure him.

"The king is alive. He is on his way to the castle now, and will gather troops to meet Respiele on the field of battle."

"Thank goodness for that!" Ben said. "I will give ye a horse to ride out tonight. It be nearly dark now and ye can travel far on the road. The town of Braklyn be within reach and there are supporters there, sure enough."

"Thank you," Alainea said. "How far is this town and how shall I know who to speak to?"

Ben rose slowly and pushed the stool out of his way. He walked to where a hook jutted from the wall. Hanging the pail on it, he picked up a burlap sack, wiped his hands, and turned to faced them.

"It be a three hour ride from my door, and I'll think on how best to reach true supporters. Have ye eaten lately?" he asked.

When neither of them answered, he chuckled and beckoned they follow him out of the barn.

"My wife is in the house preparing our evening meal. I will take you inside to meet her and while ye eat, I'll finish the milking and ready yer horse. I do not believe there is a moment to lose."

Jay trotted ahead, sniffing the air. They followed Ben through his system of corrals in the deepening shades of evening and up to the door of his house. He opened it, and warmth and light flooded over Charles with a welcome glow.

"I myself have heard rumblings of war among the townsfolk," Ben continued as they preceded him inside. He paused in the doorway to address them with a worried frown as he stroked his grizzled chin. "I know for a fact there be a group of Respiele's men that have taken up residence in Braklyn. They be trouble. They strive to gather those always looking fer mischief. But now...Respiele promises folks wealth and power in exchange for their allegiance and their swords. You had best get there and find help as soon as possible. I fear much blood will be shed afore it be settled."

After introducing them to his wife, Clara, Ben disappeared outside with Jay. Charles and Alainea seated themselves at the table. The space was small but homey. A wood stove radiated heat from the far side of the room and Charles lifted his hands to enjoy the warmth. The lady peered at them with curiosity.

Clara was plump and rosy-cheeked in her long, simple dress of dusky rose. Her glossy brown hair shone in the light of lamps placed around the room. She wasn't an old woman. Charles judged her to be her thirties, like Ben.

"Now then," Clara said with a smile, "may I fetch you

something to eat?" She clasped her hands together and looked eagerly at each of them in turn.

"Yes please," Alainea replied. "We would appreciate that."

Clara bustled about with dishes of food. "Ye look half famished." She peered at them as she set plates on the table with a thump. "And, if you pardon me saying, as though you have been through a war."

Charles looked down at his clothes, realizing they were dirty, torn and covered with bits of sheep's wool and straw.

"You're right," he said. "It's been a hard day."

"Well, no matter," Clara beamed at them again. "Ye are most welcome at our table." She laid a heavy looking spoon and knife before each of them.

Their reception was filled with kindness and attention so much that Charles was overwhelmed. After the ordeal he'd been through thus far, he looked upon these generous people with a kind of awe.

Clara brought them cold meat, a creamy homemade cheese, a bowl of purple, oblong fruit, bread with a rich yellow butter smeared on top, and hot mugs of fragrant tea. Wiping her hands on her apron, she hurried away to fill bowls from a pot bubbling on the stove. Charles caught the good lady's hand as she set a bowl of steaming soup in front of him and squeezed it tight.

"Thank you," he said, looking into her concerned eyes. "This is delicious."

Clara beamed with pleasure before she sat down at the table with them.

"I am glad to help," she said. "It would seem as though ye needed to rest a while and take on some nourishment. Do ye have food for the journey ahead?"

"Enough to see us one or two days." Alainea's response

was garbled as she took another bite of the thick brown bread.

"Do ye mind if I add to it?" Clara bobbed her head encouragingly.

Alainea swallowed noisily. "Thank you, Clara, that would be most appreciated. Please, is there meat in this stew?"

Clara looked surprised. "No, dear. It be only vegetables from my own garden."

"Ah, thank you. It smells wonderful." Alainea smiled at the woman, picked up her spoon, and dug in.

Charles pondered the question as he chewed. *She must be a vegetarian.*

The reason popped into his mind. Alainea was one of the ancient people she'd told him about back at Respiele's fortress—the Garde. These people were close to animals. As close as family. They conversed with them, even knowing one another's thoughts. It stood to reason that she could never eat the flesh of any animal. Things such as butter or eggs might be different. Finding himself also eyeing the sliced meat with distaste, he dug into the soup with renewed energy and left the meat alone.

The door was flung open. Ben stepped into the room with Jay at his heels. His face was creased with worry and he lurched toward the table. "My best mare is ready to go. Ye need to leave *now*. Just this minute I heard a dragon land in the back pasture."

Chapter Eight

Charles dropped his spoon and scrambled up from the table. His body surged with adrenalin.

"Here." Clara rushed to him, pressing a cloth-wrapped package into his hands. She handed one to Alainea as the girl grabbed her bow from the back of her chair and yanked it over her head.

"Thank you both so very much," Charles' voice quavered, and he cleared his throat. He pushed the food into the satchel he carried and rushed around the table to join Ben. "You're wonderful people."

Alainea hugged Clara close. "Yes, thank you. Bolt the door when we are gone and do not open it." She caught Charles' eye. "I shall sit behind you. I have not ridden a horse before."

He nodded with understanding. She'd spent her life locked away in a mountain prison.

Alainea stuffed the parcel into the bag at her waist and followed Ben outside. Charles was right behind them as they melted into the inky darkness. No lamp was used this time.

He could only make out the silhouettes of his friends by the light of a crescent moon that rose far in the east.

The night was still. Not a sound alerted them to the presence of the enemy, but Charles knew they were out there somewhere. Silently, he and Alainea followed the farmer to where he had tied a horse to the railings at the front of the house.

"There is no time to tell ye where to look for help in town now, but Jay will go along. He knows." Ben reached for Charles' hand and gripped it in a final gesture of friendship. Charles felt strengthened.

He reached for the reins, untied them, and drew them over the horse's head before swinging onto its broad back. There was no saddle as it would have made the journey unpleasant for the passenger seated behind it. Charles was well-used to riding horses and shifted forward, speaking to the animal in low tones and running a hand down its neck.

Alainea slid on behind him, wrapping her arms around his waist. A rush of gladness washed over him, despite the seriousness of the moment. Finally there was something he could do to help.

Without further words, Charles urged the mare into a trot, and they made their way along the entrance to the farmyard. Given the worry of being detected, he didn't want the horse's hooves to beat a loud tattoo on the road, which he assumed would be a dirt track, but they needed to cover ground fast. Though he had forgotten that Alainea was able to speak with both the horse and Jay the dog.

"They will take us across country," she whispered into his ear. "You need not guide Pearl, the horse. She will follow Jay who knows the way, even in the black of the night."

Charles patted the clasped hands that clung tightly to his waist.

They rounded a corner and in the gloom, he could just make out the uneven edges of a stone fence that separated the farmland from the road. With a louder *clip-clop*, they crossed the road and trotted up a low hill on the other side. There, Pearl's hooves sank into the grass and the dense growth deadened the sound of her hooves. Despite not being able to see, she broke into a gallop and soon they were flying across the field. In flashes of moonlight, Charles could make out the stealthy form of Jay barreling along in front of them, leading the way.

His legs gripped the horse. It wasn't a happy sensation to not know where he was going. He couldn't see if there was a barrier coming up that might slow them, or whether he should prepare himself for a jump.

He wound his hands into Pearl's mane, allowing the reins to go slack. The horse knew far more than he did about the terrain underfoot. Charles wondered if he was equal to the task. Could he hold both himself and Alainea on the horse's slippery back as it galloped across the countryside?

The horse veered sharply to the left and bolted into a stand of trees. A branch swept both Charles and Alainea to the ground where they landed with a thump in some prickly shrubs. Somehow, Charles stifled his reaction and managed to keep from making a sound as he rolled to a stop and came up on his hands and knees. The horse and Jay came to a standstill, breathing heavily within the shelter of the bluff.

A great *whooshing* sound overhead caused him to duck despite already being almost flat on the ground. A dragon passed over them, its dark shape obliterating the moon. Its rider must be scouring the area for them.

The wind generated by its passing blew the hair on

Charles' head straight up and sent the trees around them into turmoil. The rider was most certainly watching for any sign of movement in the dim light of the moon, but the animals had sensed it before it could be heard by the human ear and had kept them safe.

As the sound of wings died away, Charles and Alainea got to their feet and stood within the shelter of the bush, not speaking or moving a muscle. At length, Alainea plucked at his arm and led him out into the clearing. Jay whined low in his throat and their horse plowed her way from the bushes behind them. Silently, Charles leaped aboard and leaned down to offer assistance to Alainea. She sprang up behind him and they were off once more.

It wasn't safe to even whisper, not that they'd spoken before. Charles listened for sounds that the spy was returning. According to Alainea, the three rider-less dragons would have been sent out with new warriors on their backs. Plus there was another to make an even four that would be out searching for them. Even though chances that one would pass directly over them again were remote, they couldn't take that gamble.

Their horse galloped tirelessly on into the night, occasionally slowing to a walk so as not to frighten a herd of sheep, or in order to bypass a farmyard.

Lights twinkled from a valley below them as they crested a rise and Pearl came to a halt. Her sides heaved with exertion, and no wonder. She had kept up a steady pace for the last three hours, if Ben's calculations were correct.

Alainea shifted her seat and peered around Charles.

"That is odd. It is late, yet most residents of this town appear to be awake." She leaned back and her arms dropped away from him. "Jay says he can find the house where Ben meant us to go. It will be safer to look for it now, staying in the shadows, rather than searching in the morning. We should go."

Charles leaned forward to rub Pearl's sweaty neck. "That's fine with me."

The horse threw her head up and down in acknowledgement. Their pace slowed and each step was carefully placed as the group moved down the hill. The crisp evening breeze grew colder as their elevation lowered and with it Charles' anxiety heightened. He was aware of every noise they made. It was a larger town than he had expected and, so far, most of the inhabitants still had lights in their windows.

Pearl followed the dog as he skirted around the north side of the town and entered a narrow, cobblestone lane that appeared dilapidated and disused. She clopped across the stones and Charles scanned the tiny houses on either side of the street, expecting any moment that someone would rush outside and ask them difficult questions.

He wondered which house Respiele's cohorts had taken over. Perhaps Jay knew. He glanced down at the dog who flitted between patches of soft light from the houses, trotting faithfully onward, his nose up, ears pricked, leading them to the place of sanctuary.

Without warning, Jay stopped and then darted down a side street. Pearl followed, her hooves skittering and slipping on the smooth cobblestones in her haste. Alainea slid down the side of the horse, clinging to Charles as he struggled to pull them both upright again.

"Who is there?" shouted a rough voice behind them.

The sound of boots striking cobblestones floated through the chilly night air. A short, piercing whistle was given, followed by the unmistakable clanking of swords sliding from their sheaths.

This wasn't good at all.

Charles wasn't about to answer such an imperious request and it seemed that Alainea wasn't either. She said nothing and gripped him tighter. Pearl trotted down the street in an attempt to avoid their pursuers.

But whoever was back there wasn't about to give up. The noise of running footsteps continued and then lamps appeared ahead of them on the road. People had been alerted to the presence of strangers thanks to the whistle.

His spirits sank. He and Alainea would be caught, questioned, and returned to the mountain prison to face Respiele—and death, he was sure of it.

Charles looked frantically for another lane to turn down. Neat little houses lined the street, each with a postage-stamp-sized front yard surrounded by low stone walls. But there wasn't a break in between the buildings, and no avenue of escape.

Men's voices shouted back and forth, and the flickering lights of their torches brought out the jutting angles of the houses. Lights became visible behind, as well as in front of Charles and Alainea as their captors hurried to hem them in.

The shadowy figures loomed up from the darkness, holding torches in one hand and swords in the other. The faces of the men that confronted them were made grotesque and menacing in the light cast by the flames. Pearl pulled up short with a snort and both Charles and Alainea nearly pitched over her withers.

"Get down from that horse and present yourselves!" a deep voice bellowed.

They were trapped. Jay growled low in his throat, but then leaped over the fence of the yard nearest them and disappeared into the night.

Could he really have abandoned them?

Alainea slithered from the horse and landed lightly in the street. She stepped forward to meet their captors. Charles dismounted as well. He swivelled to face them, his eyes jumping from one angry face to another, his heart awash with hopelessness. The man who had yelled at them, stepped forward with a limping gait and brandished a sword.

"We apologize for entering your town so late," Alainea began in a pleasant tone. "We are weary travelers from the village of Nell who seek lodging before continuing on toward the shores of Rin Lake, tomorrow. We have family there. Do you know of a place we could stay this night?"

Charles was impressed. She sounded quite normal and was pleased to think that they appeared to be exactly as she had said, simple travellers.

Unfortunately, the man hobbled closer and lifted his torch to study her face.

"I know you! You belong to Respiele." He rounded on his companions. "Bind their hands and bring them to the barracks."

As two men stepped forward, Alainea jumped back, her right hand reaching for her sword to draw it forth. With a clang of metal, one of the men lunged at her and she met his blow with one of her own.

The other man rushed at Charles; sword pointed straight at him. Unarmed, Charles knew there was no way he could win against someone so prepared. He spun and leaped to the right, hoping to somehow evade the man's clutches. He swung at another who lunged at him and knocked him to the cobblestones, but more took his place, surrounding Charles. With one on either side, they grabbed him, their hands biting into the flesh of his upper arms as they spun him around. A third man delivered a rapid fire of punches to Charles' stomach. Then, all three dragged him, wheezing, back to their leader.

Alainea had been overpowered by others in the contingent as well. Over twenty men had assembled by now. Their numbers were too great for either her or Charles to disable. She stood struggling between two burly combatants, panting from her efforts.

"I do not *belong* to anyone!" she spat at the leader. "Least of all Respiele."

The man stooped to pick up her sword and chuckled. "Oh, but you do. And you shall be returned to him. You have his tenacity, but I fear you lack vision. Word arrived this very night that you were missing, and that you had stolen something most valuable."

The man snaked out a long arm and grasped Alainea's throat. He squeezed until her eyes, bright in the wavering light, bulged, and she gurgled helplessly, struggling for air. She sagged between the men who pinned her arms behind her back.

"Leave her alone!" Charles hollered. "We don't have it."

He struggled against his captors, flipping his body, and lashing out with his feet. He caught one squarely between the legs. The man groaned as he dropped to the ground, but before Charles could break free, another arrived and Charles was shoved to the ground and kicked.

As Charles' shoulder ground into the stones, his entire body was jarred. His breeches ripped right through to his jeans and the contents of that pocket spilled onto the road. There were three washers, from a combine he'd been repairing back on the ranch, a few coins, and some of the colourful rocks he'd picked up in Respiele's fortress.

No one but him paid the items any attention at all, but

as he was hauled to his feet he noticed that the pebbles glowed with an odd incandescence he hadn't perceived when he'd picked them up. They were faintly green.

Charles was shoved toward Alainea. He slammed into her as the leader of the group gave orders they were to be tied up and taken away.

"I shall interrogate them myself," he said, before turning on his heel and limping away. As he left the scene, the man tripped and pitched forward into the darkness, his torch flying from his hand and skittering across the flat stones to rest at the edge of the roadway.

The group stopped to stare. A movement at Charles' feet caught his eye and he looked down. The tiny glowing pebbles were gone, but in their place were luminous, lime green vines. They slithered across the cobblestones, multiplying and weaving among the company that stood unaware. Tentacle-like arms wound about the feet of Respiele's men and curled half-way up their legs before they noticed anything was wrong.

They drew their swords, hacking and jabbing at the vines amid cries of fear and protest. Yet even the vines that were slashed in half took on a life of their own. Despite the frenzied attempts of the guards to free themselves, the vines slipped around the men's feet, trussing them top to bottom like turkeys awaiting the oven. Even their mouths were silenced. The leader, some distance away, scrambled up and tried to run, only to be toppled like a tree. He fell with a *whump* and was dragged back, kicking and chopping with his sword. Yet, no matter how he fought, he was rolled atop his companions in a great heap and held there by the writhing mass of greenery.

The only ones standing were Alainea, Charles, and the horse, Pearl. Alainea sprinted to where a torch still burned brightly on the cobbles and hurried back to Charles. She held it up to examine what the vines had done. The men's eyes glinted at them from among the rustling leaves of the plants that held them immobile.

"How did you do that?" Alainea hissed from the side of her mouth.

Charles met her golden eyes glowing with the flame from her hand. He shrugged. He didn't want to say anything about the pebbles while these men might hear him. Instead, he beckoned to her, grabbed the reins of their horse, and struck off in the direction they'd been going before the fracas began. He didn't know how long the unusual vines would hold the men and wanted to be far from there when they were freed. Alainea extinguished the torch and tossed it aside.

They ran as fast as possible. Alainea on one side of Pearl's head and Charles on the other. Charles knew Alainea must be wondering the same thing as he was—how to find the house they'd been looking for and avoid more of Respiele's troops.

They turned at the first opportunity, ran, and turned again in an effort to muddle their trail. Where was Jay? They had no idea which direction to go. All they knew was that they must put distance between themselves and Respiele's warriors.

Alainea paused at the next intersection and looked down each branch of the street. Charles was just about to tell her they should get back on the horse and ride out of town altogether. It appeared hopeless to try to find the house that Jay had been leading them to and they had no idea who else could be trusted.

A tiny sound drew his attention and he saw the eyes of

an animal gleaming from behind a row of thick shrubs ahead.

Pearl almost stepped on Charles' foot as she pulled sharply on the bridle, changed direction, and trotted toward the eyes. Charles was dragged along until he caught his footing and ran with the horse, hoping it was Jay. As they drew closer, the glowing orbs disappeared. They stopped at the edge of a thicket, then paced along the perimeter, searching for a gap. Alainea joined them.

"It *is* Jay," Alainea said at Charles' elbow. "He says we must follow him." Her tone was anxious and she glanced back the way they'd come with a frown. "Pearl is going to return to the farm. The sound of her hoof beats may help to lead our attackers away."

She lay her hand against Pearl's shoulder as Charles flung the reins back over the horse's head and tied them securely.

"Thank you," he said to the horse in an undertone. He also rested a hand on Pearl's neck and received a low nicker in response before the animal lurched away from them and galloped loudly down the street.

Charles turned to examine the hedge in the moonlight. Alainea headed toward a spot where the brush was less dense and pushed through. Charles followed close behind her.

They emerged on the other side of the bushes where a long, winding path, bordered on either side by the same thick hedge, vanished down a hill. The rooftops of houses could be glimpsed beyond the shrubbery on either side, but the path appeared private and overgrown with long grass. Could this be right?

The eyes reappeared, glowing some distance ahead despite the lack of torchlight, and Charles felt the first hope he'd allowed himself all day. It must be the way. Alainea increased her pace to a jog, but as they continued down the path, it narrowed until the spiny branches of the shrubs dragged against their sides, slowing them down to a crawl. They pushed and shoved their way through the clinging claw-like twigs that grasped at their clothes.

Then, the way ended entirely.

Charles squinted around him in the pale light of the moon. They faced a dense wall of leaves.

Jay was nowhere to be seen. Had seeing the dog been a figment of his imagination? Charles' throat constricted painfully.

No, Alainea had communicated with Jay. Then where was he? And where was the promised sanctuary in this accursed town?

The cries of Respiele's men floated to them on the night breeze. Somehow, the warriors had been released from the vines. Their shouting sounded close.

Charles looked at Alainea's shadowy silhouette beside him. Beside them, the shrubberies rustled ominously as the narrow pathway behind them was quickly overgrown by the same strange vines they had witnessed at work before. The two of them were ensnared in a trap they had willingly entered.

There was no way out and Respiele's men came nearer with every passing moment.

Now what?

Chapter Nine

With alarm, Charles felt something slide past his feet. He shuddered as a horrible vision passed before his eyes. He imagined the long seeking vines, their tentacles curling and wrapping around his legs before dropping him to the ground and dragging him off to some unknown torment, but that couldn't happen. The vines had targeted his enemies, not him or Alainea.

The second time the thing brushed around his legs, he bent in the constricted space to feel for whatever was there. A sigh of relief washed over him as his hand met with Jay's rough coat.

The shrubs swished with movement again. Alainea reached back to tug at the sleeve of his tunic, pulling him with her through a gap in the hedge.

Clouds scudded across the moon. Blinded by absolute darkness, Charles stumbled through the opening and along an unseen path, the twigs and leaves beside him almost seeming to guide his feet. They pushed and propelled his body, urging him to move faster as though they were the fingers of some strange gigantic entity. Once, he tripped, but the shrubberies swept under him like caring hands to set him on his feet and usher him forward once more.

After he was hustled along the corridor, the bushes went still. Each arm-like branch retreated into the hedge as Charles and Alainea stumbled to a stop. A sliver of pale green glimmered before them. It was a door, about four feet tall, and it swung open to brighten the darkness with an iridescence from within.

A short, squat woman appeared in the light, signaling with rapid motions of her upraised hand that they should follow her. Jay slipped inside immediately. Alainea and Charles, after a moment's hesitation, ducked low and entered as well. The door swung shut behind them, as though on springs, sealing with a clang. A distinct crackling sound issued from outside. Without seeing it to know for sure, Charles sensed that the bushes had secured the entrance. Once the door was safeguarded, lights flicked on.

The little lady, barely reaching Charles' waist in height, bobbed and smiled before them. Her face was lined, but she didn't appear to be old. Her cheeks were creased with good humour. Her sharp, quick movements reminded Charles of a robin. Shiny gold, triangular glasses perched at the end of her nose, magnifying amber-coloured eyes that looked upon them with gladness.

"Welcome, welcome," she said. "My name is Magda Roudel."

She laughed delightedly and clapped her hands.

She was dressed in a sky-blue dress that ballooned over her toes and was trimmed at the neck, wrists, and hem with white flowers on long stems. Charles squinted at them. They were daisies, he thought, and oddly enough they seemed to be moving all on their own.

More flowers sprang from iron-grey hair twisted into a fat bun on top of Magda's head. These daisies bent low over Magda's forehead in what appeared to be a strange sort of greeting. Although the vision this made was extraordinary, Charles found he was at perfect ease. This was who they had been meant to find. They were safe, at least for the time-being.

"I have been expecting you since Jay came to warn me what was happening on the streets." Magda's face clouded with concern and the flowers on her head visibly wilted.

Charles looked in alarm at the bedraggled posies drooping over Magda's face.

"Nonetheless, you are here now and all will be well for the night. Tomorrow will take care of itself." The little lady beamed at them once more and the daisies sprang to life.

"Thank you, Magda. I am Alainea and this is my friend Charles." Alainea bent to take the hand that Magda proffered, and Charles bowed. He'd never bowed to anyone in his life, but it seemed the only appropriate thing to do when confronted with a woman such as Magda Roudel.

"I am pleased to meet you both." Magda nodded. Every flower stood straight and tall on its stem. "Please, follow me. We must speak."

She bustled into a hallway leading from the entrance. Charles grinned at Alainea. After their wild ride into town and the myriad of trials since his capture, he felt buoyant with relief. Alainea smiled back and he waved for her to go ahead of him.

He followed behind the two women, peering up at the ceiling. There was no visible means of lighting and it intrigued him. No lamps, candles, or electric bulbs, not that he expected there would be electricity in this place. The friendly greenish glow that lit Magda's home appeared to emanate from the very walls themselves, top to bottom.

Charles looked at the wall closely as he passed, trying to figure it out. He trailed a fingertip along one and recoiled with distaste. It was wet—and sticky. What sort of building was this? The material reminded him of the green goo from inside an aloe vera plant. The same stuff his mother had used to treat his cuts and burns when he was little. The walls seemed to pulsate with life, as though he was inside some sort of plant. He was careful not to touch anything again.

They passed through an archway and into Magda's kitchen. It was small but bright, and filled with such a cheery radiance that it seemed to Charles as though they'd just walked inside a lemon.

Magda waved an arm toward a tiny round table at the center of the room and began to assemble cups and saucers at a counter on the other side. Alainea and Charles seated themselves as Magda prepared a drink.

Jay trotted to where two cats dozed in baskets on the hearth. A fire roared beside them. The cats regarded him solemnly, as though the dog were an old friend, and he clambered into a third basket beside them to rest.

Hanging over the flames was a large black kettle. Magda snatched a thick cloth off her counter, grasped the handle with both hands, and lifted it off of an ornate hook. When she had poured the contents of it into three cups, she carried a tray over to the table and thumped it down in front of them. Her eyes crinkled at the corners and she smiled as she handed them each a steaming beverage.

Charles watched her closely and wondered at her tawny eyes, which were almost the same colour as Alainea's.

Magda's appeared to be flecked with green and a shimmering gold.

"We could all use a good hot cup of my tea, I be thinking," Magda said. "It should help to settle our thoughts as you tell me your next move."

She pulled up a chair and hopped aboard to sip her own drink. They fell into a comfortable silence.

Oddly enough, Charles relaxed after his first swallow of the fragrant liquid. He looked into the odd, swirling green depths and breathed in the scent, wondering what it was. The drink was like nothing he'd ever tasted before. The constant state of fear and stress he'd been in since the abduction rolled away from him like a wave. His mind felt clearer already.

He held the tiny porcelain cup between his fingers and regarded the two extraordinary women before him. How fortunate he was to be in such company. It was quite a magical place, this Erinbourne. And the people that lived here seemed to be equally as awesome on one hand as they were frightening on the other.

Charles sighed and settled back in his chair to gaze about him.

Then he sat forward again, his mouth dropping open. Magda's kitchen was amazing! The walls were embedded with the same multi-coloured pebbles he'd found in Respiele's fortress. Some were huge, bigger than his fist, and others were as tiny as the tip of his finger. Yet every size fit together like the pieces of a puzzle to completely cover the space, across the ceiling and down to the floor.

He was sure that every colour known to man was represented, and he kinked his neck in order to take in the remarkable sights above and around him. At first he thought the stones flashed with light due to the flames of the fire, but soon realized he was wrong. Each stone flared from a kernel of flickering light within itself. There were dark shades of ebony, cobalt blue, and gleaming purple all the way to the bright iridescent hues of lemon yellow and pale icy pink.

There were no windows to the outside world, but Charles could see there was no need of them. The room was filled with the light of the smooth, coloured stones.

"The mountain was your home, wasn't it," he mused, thinking out loud. "And I hid in the room where you lived and worked."

He tore his glance away from the mesmerizing stones to Magda's face.

When Alainea raised her eyebrows first at him and then Magda, he added, "Sorry. I mean, did you once live in the mountain where Respiele is now? I recognize these coloured stones."

Magda met his searching gaze over the rim of her teacup, then placed it gently on its saucer. Taking her time, she laced her fingers together and looked over Charles' shoulder, a wistful expression on her face.

"Yes," she answered at length. "I was driven from my home, along with all the other Garde, when Respiele came with enough violence to evict us. We Garde are peaceable folk, unused to war…yet, unsuccessful as we may have been that day, we did not leave without a fight. He killed many brave souls before it was over. The rest of us were forced to flee."

She wrung her hands.

"I entered what must have been your room, to hide from Respiele's men," Charles continued hesitantly, not wishing to cause the woman to recall more unhappy memories. "It was only yesterday I was there, but it feels like a life-time ago."

He drew the remaining few pebbles from his torn pocket and lay them on the rough wooden table. There were three left from the handful he'd taken. Dirty and lusterless, they resembled lumps of clay. "These stones were all over the floor along with broken jars."

Magda reached out, picked one up, and rubbed it along her skirt. Even as she touched the pebble, the life inside that had lain dormant since it had been forsaken, awoke. Shafts of azure light leapt from her palm when she lifted it for them to see.

"It is one of my precious kilodens. Thank you for restoring it to me." She smiled and reached with her other hand to pat Charles' arm. "Many of them were left behind when we were rounded up and ejected from our homes."

She tilted her head and peered at him. "They helped you tonight, in the streets. Yes?"

Charles acknowledged with a nod of gratitude.

"Then I am well-pleased. Yet, the kilodens would not have responded unless they were in the presence of a Garde." She looked at Alainea with a quizzical expression.

"I am half Garde, and have heard stories of you, Magda," Alainea leaned forward, inclining her head in a gesture of respect. "My mother remembers you well. I am honoured to be in your presence."

Magda blushed a fiery red and giggled. "Why, thank you, young miss, and who might your mother be? I am always anxious to hear news of my kin."

Alainea looked up. "My mother is Elspeth Ilstyne of the Araleesh Mountains."

Magda gasped and reached for the hem of her skirt to fan her face as Alainea continued.

"Respiele captured her when you and all of the other Garde were banished. She was beautiful then, I am told. He forced her to cook, clean, and..." Alainea said, her voice hardening, "and become his unwilling wife. I am the product of that union."

She shrugged in a gesture of defeat and managed a watery smile.

"Oh, child," Magda said. "We thought she had been killed. I am sorry Elspeth met with this fate, but glad to know she is alive."

Magda hopped from her chair and enveloped Alainea in her arms. Tears glistened on her lashes. The flowers trimming her dress and poking from her hair fell forward and withered.

Magda dropped her arms away from Alainea and took a step back. She straightened, her back stiffening, and the daisies stood erect. A faraway look glazed her eyes as she cupped Alainea's cheeks in her small hands.

"It was meant to be," Magda said in an uneven voice. "However...unpleasant as that ordeal must have been for your mother, there was a greater purpose in that course of events more than we can know at this point. This purpose will reveal itself in the years to come. Through you, I believe the curse upon this land shall be lifted."

Alainea paled, but nodded as though believing every word. Magda lifted a hand to smooth Alainea's hair before seating herself again and picking up her tea.

"And you, Charles, what part do *you* play? I wonder." Magda turned her lively yellow eyes toward him as she took a sip.

Charles shifted uncomfortably on the hard wooden chair that was far too small for someone of his size.

"I was abducted from another land. I don't really have

anything to do with all this." He shrugged as if to remove himself from the discussion. He felt a bit foolish under this tiny woman's penetrating scrutiny.

What *was* he doing here? It was an excellent question. He wished he wasn't.

"You are wrong." Magda waved her free hand dismissively. "Your destiny lies in Erinbourne."

Magda's cryptic remark startled him and his mind raced. Destiny? This lady had it all wrong.

He laughed, but it sounded hollow even to his own ears. The last two days had turned his world upside-down. He had to admit anything was possible in Erinbourne. Almost to convince himself as much as her, Charles continued to protest.

"No, you don't understand. I'm not even from your *world*. I have no destiny here. My arrival in Erinbourne was accidental."

"There are no accidents." Magda hopped down from her chair.

Before he could object more, she bustled back to her cupboards where she filled a dish with some biscuits. Popping one in her mouth, she hurried back and thudded the dish onto the table, indicating they should help themselves.

"I have a feeling about it," Magda said. "And my feelings are never to be trifled with, young man."

She wagged a tiny finger at him, and the daisies rocked back and forth to match.

Charles' head spun. Was this woman saying she could predict the future of Erinbourne—and that he was in it? Impossible!

"Magda's premonitions are not taken lightly." Alainea turned to look at him as though seeing him for the first time.

A frown creased her brow. "She is a keeper of vivacity and life for both flora and fauna, as well as a healer."

"Hey, no offense meant. I can tell she's a special lady. I just have trouble believing there's actually a reason I'm here." He ran a hand through his hair. "And what, if you don't mind me asking, is a keeper of viva-whatsit and life?"

The room seemed to be getting awfully warm.

Alainea opened her mouth to reply, but Magda cut in.

"I am sure this must all seem strange to you, young Charles." She smiled and with fluttering fingers, soothed the flowers on her dress that had risen with indignation at his words. "In short, I communicate with both animals and plant life. They are part of me as I am of them. The Creator intended it this way and left me this duty to uphold for my people. There is one of us for each Garde clan, but that is more than you need to know. In an indirect way, I am responsible for the vitality and verve of all living things, apart from humans, and certainly of their hue."

"You're in charge of colour?" Charles shook his head as though doing so would help him wake up from this bizarre dream.

"In a roundabout way, yes," Magda said in a soothing voice. "But that is not important at this time."

Charles slumped down in his chair. He couldn't figure it out. Dragons, swords, magic stones, sceptres, and now supposedly his destiny was tied up in this place.

"Tell her," he blurted. His voice sounded high-pitched and fearful. He forced himself to take a breath and master his emotions before continuing. "Tell Magda what happened when I was picked up and dumped off by that dragon. Then she'll know I don't belong here."

Alainea nodded, still directing sideways glances at him. As they ate the sweet treats and finished their drink, she recounted all that had transpired starting from Charles' arrival in Erinbourne and ending with how they had wound up here at Magda's home. When she spoke of Respiele's dragon riders, and how they attacked King Larkender, Magda threw her skirt up over her face with a wail of dismay.

Fortunately, there were several petticoats underneath. They fluttered with this flurry of movement in a dazzling array of colours. Each layer was embroidered with matching flowers. Charles squinted at the scarlet roses revealed on the thin pink material that settled on Magda's lap. These inanimate flowers also appeared to move of their own accord. At the end of the story, Magda sighed in an exaggerated manner and flopped her top skirt back into position before hurrying off to fetch more tea.

"Take a sip. Then, we must discuss the immediate future," Magda said when she returned. She thumped the teapot onto the table. Placing her hands on her hips, she looked at them expectantly. "I shall need to know where you are going and the action to be taken once you arrive?"

As she filled each of their cups, Charles crammed a cookie into his mouth and slumped on his chair waiting to hear what Alainea would say. He had no plan to deliberate over and no idea what would happen from minute to minute in this place.

Alainea slurped a mouthful of the steaming beverage and then, from somewhere inside her voluminous cloak, she pulled a thick piece of paper and smoothed it onto the table. Magda scrambled to her feet in order to see. Charles cradled his hot tea in his hands and stayed where he was. A map of Erinbourne would mean nothing to him. He just wanted to go home.

"I need to find the one remaining dragon egg in Erinbourne," Alainea said. Her face flushed with the intensity and purpose she so clearly felt. "Respiele has hidden it somewhere in the Araleesh Mountain Fortress and holds the egg as leverage over the other dragons. If they do not obey him, he threatens to destroy it. The egg is a male from parents who are long since dead."

She drew a shuddering breath. "It is in stasis at present, but under the right conditions, it will hatch. This egg represents the last male dragon left in Erinbourne. It is the only chance the dragons have to be free and to survive this curse."

There was desperation in her voice. Magda was silent, her head bowed. Of course the situation was grim, but Alainea might as well have announced she wanted to spread her arms, leap from the roof, and fly to New York City for bagels. She wanted to go right back into the hornets' nest and he didn't see how she could succeed. No, how *they* could succeed, he corrected himself. He'd promised to help her.

"How would you accomplish this feat, child?" Magda reached for the remaining two pebbles from where Charles had dropped them and cleaned them on her skirts as she waited for Alainea's response. They flared in answer to the woman's touch.

"Respiele plans to wage war upon Erinbourne, now, while the kingdom is at its most vulnerable. He holds the Amethyst and believes Charles and I have the Golden Sceptre of Power. By now he may suspect the king was rescued, but he cannot be sure. He searches for us day and night knowing if he can secure the sceptre, the kingdom is his. His fury must have been terrible when he found we had taken it."

Alainea shook her head. "Based on what I and my informants could gather, troops will be marching from Respiele's domain tomorrow. This is the route they will take."

She traced along a thin line. Magda pushed her spectacles further up her nose and bent low over the roughly drawn map.

Charles had a sudden vision of her "informants." A pack of rats was more like it. Vermin of any number, had never in his life been considered a good thing until now.

"I hope he has not lied to us about the egg's existence." Alainea twisted her braid with white knuckles. "We must avoid those troops, return to the Araleesh Mountains while it is poorly guarded, and save the unborn dragon...and my mother."

Her voice broke, and a tear trickled down her cheeks as she struggled to regain composure.

Magda patted her shoulder. "Of course, you must. And I might have an idea where to look."

Alainea's head snapped up and she caught one of Magda's hands in her own.

"You do? But how? I have lived there all of my life and have searched everywhere I could think of. Still I have not found it." She gazed at the little woman, her face flooding with hope.

"There was a time when I was familiar with every corner of that mountain," Magda said with a sigh. "I think Respiele would keep the egg close, to retain control of his advantage. I think it will not be far from his private chambers. I have a suggestion where you should look first."

Alainea wiped her cheeks with a sleeve and slid to the edge of her chair.

"Respiele has taken over the tallest spire of the Araleesh Mountain. Yes?"

Alainea nodded.

"In that room is a hidden door. Behind it is a staircase leading to a tiny chamber, used in my time, as a viewpoint. There is a grate built into the floor of this circular chamber that leads directly to the kitchen." Magda leaned toward them.

"Most rooms in the mountain have their own fireplaces, or other means by which to warm the cold, dark spaces." She looked meaningfully at her own walls and the kilodens embedded in them. "Others, that have no such accommodations, are connected to huge fireplaces elsewhere. I believe the very ovens your mother uses to prepare food provide the heat required to warm Respiele's quarters and the secret room."

Magda wiggled in her chair and crossed her arms across her chest with a nod. "Of course, I could be wrong, but…"

Alainea broke in with a wide grin. "No, I think you are correct. I have never found this hidden door and neither has anyone I know. I shall look there as soon as I am able to return.

Can you please direct me how to find this door?"

"Certainly." Magda hopped off her chair and began clattering the tea things onto the tray. "But, if you will allow me, I would be pleased to help you in another way. Yes?"

She slid the tray into her arms and peeped up at Alainea through the tangle of flowers that fell over her brow.

When Alainea inclined her head, Magda said, "Once I show you how to use them, you must take a few of the kilodens with you. Also—since your dragon is not here, I can offer you both the perfect method of transport."

Charles' heart caught in his throat at her final words. He and Alainea followed the direction of their host's gaze as she turned to the fireplace and stared at the three animals lying in baskets on the hearth.

"Felix and Hilda." She bustled to her sink with the dishes. "Nothing can match them for speed. They are able to see in the dark, and their agility is beyond description."

Charles pinched his wrist. Seriously, was he even awake? Out loud he heard himself mumbling a question, shock and alarm thickening his voice.

"You want me to ride on a cat?"

Even as the words left his mouth, he realized how foolish he sounded. He was in Erinbourne. Anything could happen here. He swallowed down his fears and plastered a smile on his face as Alainea turned to him with a laugh.

"Of course." She rubbed her hands together with glee. "I thought I recognized them to be meircats. Is it not marvelous, Charles?"

"Yeah, marvelous." He made an effort to sound enthusiastic, but it was difficult as he took another look at the furry felines. They were quite normal in size. How in heck were he and Alainea supposed to ride those little creatures?

But there was no time for questions. Magda rustled in a cupboard for food to send along for the animals while Alainea pulled the bow and arrows from her back and inspected them. Her sword had been taken from her, but the warriors hadn't thought to strip her of her bow. He wondered what was happening on the streets outside this dwelling now. How would they ever escape when so many eyes were searching for them?

"Here you are, young man. Please carry this for the cats." Magda thrust two packages into his hands. Each was wrapped in a somewhat oily cloth, and Charles didn't ask what they were.

"Thank you," he said. He pulled back his cloak to stuff them into his bag, exposing the long tear in his breeches. A length of ragged material hung almost to his knees, revealing the denim beneath.

"Ooh la, la." Magda hurried to the table for one of the kilodens. Polishing it on her skirts as she returned, she extended it toward him on the palm of her hand.

The stone, smaller than the rest, seemed to melt into a glistening puddle of blue before running like liquid ink across her hand to form a long string. Then, of its own accord, it leapt from her hand and skimmed through the air to Charles' pants before winding itself in and out of the flap of material. Charles looked down at it with amazement. Deftly, the thick blue thread fastened the two sides of the tear together.

"That should do the trick." Magda chuckled with satisfaction and her daisies bent toward one another, nodding in agreement. "May I fill your flask with water?"

"Sure, thanks." Charles answered mechanically, all the while staring at his pant leg. He unslung the flask and passed it to the woman by the strap. He was so bemused, he likely wouldn't have thought of it, and the thing was almost empty.

He wished he could sit down somewhere to let the events of the last two days settle in his mind, so he could make sense of them. But that wasn't going to happen. They were preparing to leave as soon as possible.

It only took about five minutes for him and Alainea to get packed up. Plus, a further five for Magda to explain about the secret door, and how to manage the kilodens she pressed into Alainea's hands. All too soon, Alainea folded her map, shoved it back inside her clothes, and looked at him expectantly.

With a swish of her long dress and its many petticoats, Magda strode to the fireplace and bent low over the baskets.

"Felix," she called in a low, sing-songy voice. "Hilda. Your assistance is required."

One large tabby stood up and stretched luxuriously, with its tail straight and stiff. The other, an orange long-hair, peered at Magda over the rim of its basket and drew its lips back over sharp teeth in a yawn.

"My dears, these young people are in need of transportation. They are on a mission for the Garde of the Araleesh and must return there immediately. It is a great favour I ask of you. Please will you help them?"

Both cats stepped daintily from their beds. They curled around her legs, arching themselves along the bottom of her dress. They were actually a bit bigger than regular cats, and when they began to purr, Charles thought it sounded like someone had started an outboard motor.

Magda looked up from stroking their heads and beamed at him and Alainea. "They have agreed."

As the animals came to a halt, one on either side of her, she swept her hand towards the orange cat.

"Hilda. And Felix." She motioned toward the tabby. "I would like you to meet Charles and Alainea."

Both felines meowed, but while Felix lowered his head in greeting, Hilda sat down and proceeded to lick her paw as though unimpressed with the visitors. Jay remained by the fire, his head resting on his paws.

Alainea inclined her head in a show of respect and Charles, seeing this, did likewise. Both cats appeared pleased with this attention to formality and sauntered forward to circle Charles' and Alainea's legs in turn. Charles got the feeling he was being inspected more than greeted. He didn't dare reach down, as Magda had done, to pet these animals. They seemed far too regal to be touched by a commoner.

"There now, it is all settled." Magda looked relieved, as

though there had been some doubt about it. She stood with hands clasped before her. "We must go. Follow me."

She twinkled past Charles and headed for the only door in the room. Felix and Hilda, side by side, padded close behind. However, instead of turning to the left and out the way they'd come, Magda turned to the right with the cats, Alainea, and Charles on her heels. The walls glowed eerily. The hallway was not as cheery or inviting as the kitchen had been.

Around the corner, plants sprouted from the walls and ceiling in lush profusion. They dangled into Charles' face and trailed along his shoulders. Many of them resembled the vines that had come to their defense earlier. However, these vines were transfigured with blooms. Huge red flowers as big as his head, and heavy with sweet-smelling nectar, dangled in his path. Fuchsia, bell-shaped blossoms sprang from the walls on either side. Petals fluttered in the breeze as they passed through and a few floated to the floor, littering their path with glorious colour. It was beautiful. And all with an intoxicating scent. He breathed deeply as they walked, the perfume making him feel giddy. The hallway made Charles think of pictures he'd seen of springtime in Japan where people walked through cherry blossomed avenues.

Around another corner stood a door of a more regular size. There wasn't much of the door visible behind ferns that hung over it.

"It has been my great pleasure to serve you, young Charles and Alainea," Magda said.

She stopped at the door and turned to face them with formality. Her face was rosy and her eyes glistened as she looked from one to the other. Felix and Hilda seated themselves, one on either side of her like revered Egyptian cats, each staring owlishly forward without expression.

"When you pass through this door you must make no sound. Felix and Hilda know the way well. You have the kilodens? Yes?" Magda smoothed her hair innumerable times, causing the daisies to group together on one side in order to avoid being flattened.

"We are grateful to you, Magda," Alainea said. She stepped forward and went down on one knee to give the tiny lady a hug. "I must ask though, will you please inform all those who would stand with the king that a battle is on the horizon?"

"I will," Magda said.

"Yes, thank you for helping us." Charles' stomach was balling up in knots again. It had been so nice to feel relaxed and safe. Who knew what lay outside these walls? And he still didn't understand how a couple of house cats were supposed to carry them.

"You are most welcome, my children," Magda said. As Alainea stood, Magda reached for Charles' hand, her yellow eyes holding his own. "Trust in what you have been given, in who you are with—and…" she paused to give her next words weight, "in your own ability to make a difference."

He nodded, not knowing how to respond. Magda gave him the briefest of smiles before rotating away to focus on the door.

She grasped the handle with both hands, braced one tiny pink-slippered foot on the wall beside it, and yanked. With a *whoosh* the door opened, Magda swinging along with it, and the cold night air swirled into the hall.

They waited for Magda to lead them, and then passed through, tiptoeing. Charles felt his way down a short set of wooden stairs by the light of the kiloden Magda held in her hand. It was yellow, and its pale rays dimly lit the darkness through which they crept. A fitting colour for her, since Magda herself was like sunshine.

It seemed as though they were leaving by a more orthodox method than they'd arrived. Progressing along a narrow path worn into the grass, the outlines of houses appeared in the gloom ahead. They must be close to a street. Oddly enough, for a front yard belonging to Magda, there wasn't a tree, shrub, or vine in sight.

Without warning, he bumped into Alainea, who had come to an abrupt halt. She was accepting the lit kiloden from Magda. The cats moved around their mistress.

Alainea held the kiloden between her thumb and forefinger, and in its light a strange vehicle appeared. It looked like a mini version of an old-fashioned sleigh made of a thin burnished bronze, with golden runners that curled up at both ends. The thing was just big enough for him and Alainea to fit—if they were lucky. It had high, sculpted, curved sides that might screen them if they hunkered low, and a small bench at the back to sit on.

He didn't know what he'd expected, but it wasn't this.

The sleigh looked like something that might have been used as a prop in a Santa Claus movie. It did *not* look like a way to travel quickly about the countryside.

A protest rose on his lips, but he remembered Magda's warning and clamped his mouth shut. If it was good enough for Alainea, it was good enough for him. He turned his attention to the animals that were supposed to pull it. Attached to the front of the sled with pliable woven cords were the cats. Felix sat in a harness licking a paw and then using it to clean his face, but Hilda was watching Charles. It was a little disconcerting. He shifted from foot to foot as her round dark eyes scrutinized him in the wavering light.

Then, from down the street, a horse neighed, closely followed by the frantic barking of a dog. In the yellow glow, Magda straightened and reached for the kiloden. Alainea handed it back and the light went out. They stood in darkness, silent and still. Charles was almost afraid to breathe. Then he felt Magda's hands guiding him forward and lifting his leg to place it into the sled. He grasped the curved side and pulled himself inside, groping until he found the bench and seated himself.

The horse neighed again and there was a clatter of hooves on the cobblestone street nearby. Alainea wedged herself into the seat beside him. Magda's small hand gripped his arm in farewell. Then, he was flung against the rear of the sleigh as they shot forward into the night. He clutched the side for support, the force of their getaway pinning him to the backboard. Behind them, men yelled in anger, a horn was blown, and the pounding of footsteps caused Charles' heart to miss a beat.

He gulped. Would they be caught after all? How fast could a couple of cats really run? Fear tore at his chest and he willed the cats to sprout wings to get them away from this place. Yet, where they were headed was worse.

Chapter Ten

After the initial jolt of their departure, Charles couldn't feel a thing. He'd braced himself, expecting to be jarred and jerked over Magda's front yard, the bumpy stones lining the street, and then over the rough terrain of the fields beyond the town—but he'd felt nothing but air whistling past his ears and rifling the folds of his cloak. He drew it tighter.

Alainea reached for his hand. Hers was cold and clammy. Charles squeezed it reassuringly, letting his cloak fly where it wanted and reaching for her other hand as well. He chafed them both in his bigger ones in an effort to warm her. She was as worried as he was.

The sounds behind them grew louder. Lamplight flickered off the buildings and voices shouting orders split the air. Would Magda be alright alone? He knew she would. She had allies he couldn't even imagine.

Charles could hear the cats' laboured breathing, and their light galloping footsteps, but it was as though the sleigh was flying. Apart from a few twisting turns, he and Alainea sped into the night, and the sounds of their pursuers faded

so quickly that he wondered if he'd imagined it. The town and Respiele's soldiers, melted away in the speed of their escape.

He could see nothing and, eventually, Charles relaxed. Alainea must have too, because she released her grip on his hand and subsided into sleep, her head dropping to rest on his shoulder. Charles thought he might never be able to sleep again, but eventually he too fell into a restless slumber.

He jerked into wakefulness when they shuddered to a halt.

The shaggy shapes of trees towered overhead and he yawned, wondering how long they'd been travelling. He didn't move for fear of disturbing Alainea who still slumped against him, but craned his neck to see what was happening. The sound of running water penetrated his consciousness, and he realized the cats were bent low at the front of the sleigh, drinking.

The dim outline of a ridge towered overhead. They must be in a ravine, sheltered from prying eyes for the moment, but the sun was coming up. That might make travelling without detection more difficult.

Alainea stirred, pulling herself upright and stretching.

"Where are we?" she whispered.

"The cats are drinking," Charles said. "Why don't you ask them?"

She leaned forward and he supposed she was doing just that. Then she rested back against the backboard.

"We are close to the River Spye and will cross it soon. It originates in the Araleesh Mountains. There is only one bridge this close to Respiele's Fortress, but we must be careful since we cannot risk running into the forces that will be marching forth this morning."

As she spoke in lowered tones, Charles peered at Felix

and Hilda who were coming into focus now that light was emerging in the east. They were much larger than he recalled—huge, in fact. He blinked and leaned forward to examine them again.

They were as big as what he supposed a jaguar would look like. Although he had no frame of reference to judge that by, since he'd never harnessed two jaguars together to pull him across the countryside in a sleigh. He almost chuckled with incredulity at the thought. Yet, here was that very scenario, just a couple metres from his toes.

Yes, these creatures were a heck of a lot bigger than they'd been at the beginning of the night. His view of them was still hazy but he could tell they had flat, broad heads and sleek, muscly bodies, more than half as long as he was tall. Gone were the fluffy house cats with cute faces and pricked ears. No wonder these animals could run so fast.

"…and that has me concerned," Alainea finished. "I do, however, have good news from Dranich. She has arrived at Larkender Castle and the king is recovering well."

Charles was startled to find she'd been talking to him. He'd lost track of the conversation in his astonishment of the meircats.

"Sorry," he whispered, "I missed what you said, but I'm really glad to hear the king and your dragon are alright."

His response felt lame, but he found it hard to tear his eyes away from the enormous creatures in front of him. They'd finished drinking and had seated themselves for a moment of rest, their thick tails curled around their bodies.

She sighed. "I suppose you have never seen or heard of a meircat?"

He shook his head.

"They are like many animals of the Garde in that they have…remarkable abilities. There are very few meircats in all of Erinbourne. Their shape, for the most part, is that of a common housecat. However, when needed, they trans-form." She gestured toward the animals, obviously feeling no other explanation was necessary.

"They're amazing," Charles breathed.

One of the cats, Hilda, stood and a low growl rumbled in her throat. Felix bounded to his feet and both of them stared across the stream into the long dense bushes that brushed the edge of the gurgling water. Hair rose along the spine of each big cat.

Charles and Alainea, followed the cats' gaze. No one moved a muscle.

The snap of a branch broke the spell. The cats whirled around and made for an opening in the trees leading back up the ravine. The sleigh jumped to attention, slamming Charles and Alainea against the side. They grappled for something to hang onto.

A hulking shape lunged across the water behind them, crushing small trees by the stream like kindling, and threw itself across their path, blocking the way. Felix and Hilda, with amazing reflexes, leaped sideways and careened back the way they'd come.

But the beast lunged over their heads and curled itself into a twirling mass that planted itself before them like a wall. It straightened, drawing itself up to full height. Charles thought dazedly it must be eight feet tall. Tentative rays of sunlight illuminated the monster, revealing dangerous-looking spikes down its back, and it held out thick, burly arms to prevent their flight.

The cats turned back on themselves once more, jerking the sleigh in yet another direction. Charles and Alainea tumbled from their seat, clinging to the floor of their vehicle as it went up on one side, slammed down flat, and then flipped over to the other.

What was this horrifying creature?

The monstrous being roared. Charles imagined the very trees shuddered with fear at the rage that erupted from within the creature, but as Charles quaked in horror at what would happen next, he sensed the tension ebb from Alainea's frame. He looked up, struggling to calm his racing heart. The thing must have communicated with Alainea.

She sagged with relief against the side of the sleigh.

"It is Talbot. What a fright." She raised a hand to push back her hair. "In the gloom, he did not know who we were, or that would not have happened."

"Talbot?" Charles repeated the name sharper than he'd meant to. "Who, or what, is a Talbot? And what does he think he's doing scaring us like that?"

Alainea stifled a weak giggle. Talbot seated himself on the mossy earth to converse with Felix and Hilda. Softening her gaze she stared at the enormous being.

"Talbot is a hedgehog of unusual proportion. He is also friend, warrior, and ally of the Garde." She pulled herself up and hopped out of the sleigh to greet the monstrous being that sat erect on the ground nearby. Spines erupting from his back stood like a forest of spears, glinting with menace in the first rays of dawn.

Charles dragged a hand through his rumpled hair and made to get out of the sleigh. He supposed he'd have to meet this Talbot too.

Alainea reached for the folds of Charles' cloak as he drew near and pulled him closer.

"This is Charles," she said, looking up at the creature. "Charles, meet Talbot."

When she glanced at him again, Charles sent her a

silent thank you. He knew she was speaking aloud for his benefit, so he would feel, at least, part of a conversation he couldn't hear. As it was, he could detect only muffled grunts and rumbles from the three animals before him.

The huge hedgehog bowed and Charles wondered if Talbot might be smiling. It was a bit difficult to tell since, when the creature's lips were stretched wide, it looked more like he was baring his teeth into a snarl. Charles took it to be the former, but couldn't help taking a step back.

"Hello," Charles said stiffly. Perhaps he should have been more polite and said he was glad to meet this monster called Talbot, but he was still feeling awed by the ferocity and size of the creature. After the frightening skirmish they'd just experienced, he *wasn't* really all that pleased to make Talbot's acquaintance, so he said nothing.

Thankfully, his thoughts remained private, and he allowed them to wander as Alainea fell into discourse with the three animals. Standing next to the huge animal made Talbot appear even larger, and nothing like a hedgehog at all. Talbot was indeed a fearsome beast and Charles felt gratitude he was on their side.

The woods returned to peaceful solitude. Charles turned his attention away from the conversation he couldn't comprehend and made his way down to the stream. Thin shafts of sunlight wove through the trees and began to awaken small birds. He listened to their cheerful chatter and to the bubbling of the water at his feet. His heartbeats were finally slowing.

He crouched and trailed his fingers through ripples of the ice-cold water. It chilled him to the bone. He dried his hand on the leg of his trousers and stood to stare into the morning sky.

His mind drifted back to home. What would his parents

be doing right now? This was the morning of his third day in Erinbourne and his parents must be frantic with worry over his disappearance. His heart began to speed again with concern for his folks.

There's nothing you can do about that. For now, your course is set in helping this girl.

Glancing back to the sleigh, he was surprised to see that Talbot was gone. Charles manoeuvred through the broken branches of their recent encounter, wondering how such a huge animal could have disappeared so fast.

As he drew closer, Alainea beckoned to him with a smile. The head of a small animal poked out from the pocket of a vest she wore under her cloak. Evidently, Talbot could change form like the meircats, and quickly too.

"Talbot has offered to accompany us. Is that not wonderful?" Her face was flushed, and her eyes sparkled even in the gloom.

Charles felt unaccountably annoyed.

"Yeah, that's great," he said without enthusiasm.

Talbot regarded him from her pocket with round, dark eyes that narrowed as Charles spoke. Charles felt sure not only could the animals understand what he was saying, but could read his mood and tone as well. He told himself that if Alainea was pleased, there must be more to this Talbot than just a huge hulking monster. He'd have to keep an open mind.

Forcing a smile to his lips, he asked, "So, now what?"

"We leave straightaway." Alainea was already stepping into the sleigh and arranging the bow at her side to be more comfortable while sitting. "Talbot has seen Respiele's troops. They met with any folk who crossed the Pontile Bridge to join in this battle against the king, and they march north to skirt around the Maldone Mountains on their way to Larkender Castle. I expect the king to foresee this. Talbot and I agree, King Larkender will meet them where they least expect it, on the Plains of Ileele."

Charles seated himself beside her, pushing aside the rush of gladness from having her next to him, and focusing on his next question. "And so, if they've left, we go back to the fortress?"

"Yes," she said.

Felix and Hilda sprang forward, catching Charles off guard and pinning him back in his seat as the sleigh took off. He looked at the cats now fully revealed in the dappled sunshine that filtered down through the trees. They were magnificent. Muscles rippled beneath their glossy coats and the breeze caused by each stride they took flowed through Hilda's long, glistening fur.

Up through the oddly shaped trees they wound, a branch slapping Charles in the face as he leaned over the side of the sleigh to see if the runners actually touched the ground. He dabbed at his eyes, concluding that somehow they floated above the terrain. It was all quite fascinating. But he didn't think he'd ever be able to tell his family about it, because they'd never believe him.

If he ever got home again, that was.

They paused before breaking away from the treeline and Charles joined Alainea and Talbot in squinting across the hilly ground they faced. The edge of the ravine was quite high and the ground sloped away from them into lush green pastures dotted with brown animals that looked like cattle. Yet, Charles had seen so many strange beasts in this land, he couldn't say with any certainty what they were.

Ahead of them, in the distance, stood a ridge of dark purple mountains. He assumed that was where they were going, and only the occasional bluff of trees seemed to stand in their way. The peaks looked foreboding and he shivered before swivelling away from the sight.

Beyond the huge expanse of meadowland, to the north, snaked a wide blue river that sparkled in the dawn as though the Creator had purposely inlaid an avenue of sapphires to wind among the hills.

Across the river, atop a gentle rolling knoll, stood a village. A thin line of smoke curled into the rosy sky from one of the clusters of tiny houses set down on this side of the hill. A meandering trail led from somewhere ahead of the dwellings along the river and disappeared into their midst.

It was a scene of quiet repose. Charles found it hard to think that war loomed on the horizon for the people of this land. Yet, he had witnessed the violence himself and knew it to be so. He wondered if he and Alainea should be making a detour to warn the residents.

"It is the village of Maldone," Alainea said, as if reading his thoughts. "If possible, I would like to pay a visit to their mayor. They should be informed."

Charles looked expectantly at her. Talbot crawled from her vest pocket and scampered to the front of the sleigh where he climbed up to sit on the ornately curved front. His spines were laid flat and he looked like any other hedgehog might.

Alainea leaned forward and cocked her head to one side. She appeared to be listening intently and Charles supposed Talbot was speaking to her. Feeling strangely left out, he fished around beneath his cloak until he found his water and took a long pull at the flask. He jumped when she spoke into his ear.

"Talbot says we should follow the edge of the ravine as long as possible in case we need to find cover, but the bridge is not far from here." She pointed to a spot where the river curved away and was hidden in thick green woodland. She flipped her long auburn braid over her shoulder and levelled her gaze on him at close range. "Are you alright? You seem tense."

Charles laughed without humour. "Tense! Are you kidding me? Yeah, I'm tense. The most adventure I had… before meeting you, was Thursday night boxing class and a flat tire on my pickup. Now I'm on a mission to save a race of dragons in an alternate universe while riding in a sleigh dragged by a couple of cats. And, suddenly, our fearless leader is a hedgehog. Tense doesn't even begin to describe how I feel." He ended by flinging both hands into the air in a gesture of defeat. "But I have no choice in the matter."

"Yes, I see. And I am sorry for your fate." Alainea looked genuinely remorseful and Charles felt bad for flying off the handle.

This situation wasn't her fault.

"One day, I would like to know what both a tire and a pickup are," she said, pursing her lips. "However, our fearless leader, as you called him, is the only one of us who knows how to get you home, so perhaps you should try to cultivate his friendship."

As she spoke, Talbot jumped down from his perch and the cats lurched off along the fringe of trees lining the gorge. Now that it was daylight, Charles could see the land skim past them at an alarming rate. He grabbed the bronze edge of the sleigh and considered what she had said.

Taking a deep breath, he realized he hadn't gotten off to a great start with the hedgehog. He needed to fix that.

"It's a bit difficult when I can't talk to him," he said, "but if he's helping you then I appreciate him too. Please tell him that."

"You just did." Alainea leaned into the curve, balancing herself as Charles' side of the sled rose into the air. She turned her attention to the scene unfolding before them. "Talbot comes from the south. He lives with the Garde in the Ildune Mountains that form the border to your land where Durgot Flandish is gatekeeper. Durgot watches over the portal between our worlds. That is where you will go in order to get home."

Well, that was interesting news.

Charles clutched the side of the sled, this time using both hands to prevent him from crushing Alainea as they flew around a bluff. Leaving the safety of the ridge and the dark shelter of the trees, they hurtled down the slope toward the grove of pines wherein lay the bridge.

He looked at the little hedgehog who had rolled into a ball to protect himself from the force of their wild ride. Talbot careened back and forth across the sleigh floor, his spines smacking into the sides with a clanging sound at every turn. Reaching forward, Charles snatched Talbot up as he bowled past and lifted him into the safety of his voluminous cloak.

The cats stretched out and ran until their bodies were only a blur. Charles found it difficult to draw breath at the speed with which they descended the rise. There was no room to be able to turn and look behind, but he had an overwhelming urge to do it. They had not been so exposed since dashing for the farmer's barn the day before. His eyes were watering again, this time from the speed.

Straining forward, Alainea lifted one hand to shade her eyes from the sun that was gliding higher in the clear blue sky behind them. Charles followed the trajectory of her gaze. He started so badly that if it weren't for Talbot's quick reflexes, he would have flipped the hedgehog out of the sleigh. Rising into the air from the forest of dark green pines that hid the bridge, was a huge, dark shape.

A dragon.

"It has not caught sight of us yet. But it will." Alainea leaned back rigidly and spoke directly into Charles' ear. Talbot had seen the dreadful sight as well. He dug his needle-like claws into the material of Charles pants and peered into the sky.

Hilda and Felix, if possible, redoubled their pace. The meircats flattened themselves to the ground, their legs moving like pistons, and their breathing laboured and heavy.

"They cannot run like this for long," Alainea said.

It was exactly what he'd had been thinking. What could they do? The sleigh and all who were connected to it were sitting ducks for the dragon who, as Charles well knew, was perfectly capable of lifting them all into the air and carrying them away.

The black lizard wheeled in the sky, rising higher and higher. Surely it must have seen them by now. The dragon moved slowly, its wings catching the mist as it rose off the river as though in no particular hurry. The thought crossed Charles' mind that perhaps the dragon had seen them, but was trying to give them time to cross before its rider spotted them too.

"The rider must be watching the bridge, knowing we will be forced to cross at some point," Charles whispered into Alainea's ear. "We cannot escape his notice for long."

"No, we cannot. But I believe the dragon is trying to help," she said, and then called to Felix and Hilda. "Turn aside!"

Although the wind whipped her words away before they could have reached the cats' ears, they understood her in the telepathic way they communicated and swerved sharply toward the river only a few hundred metres away.

"I must reach the kilodens," Alainea said.

Despite the tight fit she and Charles made in the sleigh, she wiggled herself up until she could force a few fingers into the pocket where she'd put the stones. Charles moved to allow her as much room as possible. Talbot crept beneath Charles' cloak to prevent being swept away in the fierce wind that their speed generated.

"I do not know if this will work, but it seems we have no alternative." She subsided back onto the bench with a groan. With one hand, she hung onto the sled for dear life; with the other, she clenched the brightly coloured stones.

She turned her head to speak directly to him again. "I need only a few."

She pulled back, her yellow eyes searching his in a plea for assurance that they would be alright. With infinite care, she unfolded her fingers and rested the back of her hand on his knee. "Take them all and give me back only the green ones?"

Wordlessly, Charles gave her a quick nod before holding out his free hand. She dropped the stones into his cupped palm.

He braced his feet on the rolling floor of the sled, plucked four sparkling jade-coloured rocks from the small heap in his hand, and slipped them back to her. Alainea's fingers closed over the kilodens, but before she pulled away, Charles squeezed her hand.

"You can do it," he said simply.

Tearing his eyes away from hers, he looked ahead and sucked in a breath. They were a few metres from the rushing waters of a river that was wider than any he'd ever seen. The water flowed deep and fierce between the two banks, whirlpools swirling and waves whipping high from the wind. Despite the danger, the meircats had not slowed their speed and it looked as though they would plow into the churning waters to their doom, if something didn't happen, and fast.

Alainea raised her hand over her head and brought it back as far as she could. At the same time, and despite the flying nature of the sleigh, Charles could feel the bump of a ridge of earth marking the edge of the land before it dropped to the swirling water.

He held his breath. His gaze flickered to where the dragon still hovered over the forest, seemingly unconscious of their presence.

Alainea stared out over the water and muttered words Charles couldn't catch. Then, she flung the kilodens out over the depths of the dark, swirling waves.

Their sleigh plunged over the bank and plummeted toward the river. Charles felt fear rise with bile into his mouth. He opened his mouth to scream, but the sound lodged in his throat. He had a fear of water and couldn't swim a stroke.

Alainea hollered the words she had only muttered before. They were clear to Charles this time, but spoken in a language he couldn't understand. The tiny green stones caught the sunlight and expanded. In a sparkling emerald haze, they bounced like tiny, flat rocks skipping across a still lake. But each time the kilodens bounded off the water, they left a lime-green cord in their wake.

The cords thickened, stretched, and strengthened in an instant. They were multiplying and connecting like vines growing in fast forward, weaving together, twisting to bind and form a shape that was not unlike a rope bridge. It settled over the waves, quieting them with a hush. The sleigh crashed down upon it and it held.

Charles and Alainea were thrown high with the impact, but the tall sides of their sleigh contained them and they tumbled onto the bottom of the sled. Talbot, being so light, was flung wide. Charles sprang from where he'd fallen and caught the little creature before Talbot hurtled like a baseball into the waves.

The meircats didn't falter as the craft slammed onto the surface of the narrow green path. Their long legs propelled them forward, but not without complaint. However, their yowls of displeasure at finding their feet were wet only served to make them go even faster.

Gushing water poured over top of the sleigh, arched overhead, and splashed down on the other side. Alainea and Charles huddled within, not daring to lift their heads and be caught in the flood. The deluge roared around them. Charles could see nothing beyond this wild watery world.

Then, with a bump and a jolt, they were on the sandy shore of the other side. The water fell back, and they were safely across. It was amazing.

As they hurtled up the opposite bank, Charles and Alainea both craned their necks to look for the hovering winged giant.

It was gone.

"Do you think the dragon landed again? To watch over the bridge?" Alainea directed her questions to Talbot.

The hedgehog crawled up the cloak to stand on Charles' shoulder for a look, merely shrugged.

"He says there is nothing to do but carry on," she relayed. "There is no place here we can hide."

And there wasn't. As the meircats breeched the outcropping of land, bare pastureland stretched before them. Yet, although there was no shelter for them, hope rose in Charles' heart. Maybe there was a chance to reach the bluff peeking over the nearest hilltop. If only the dragon stayed on the ground a little longer.

Felix and Hilda did not break stride, but even so, Charles could tell the cats were tiring.

The sleigh powered up the rise beside the river with still no sign of the dragon. Both Charles and Alainea crawled onto the seat again, but they trained their eyes on the forest where they knew the dragon and its rider lay in wait. It was not until they raced across the top of the nearest knoll and dashed beneath the overhanging branches of a thick cluster of the oddly shaped pine trees that Charles exhaled with relief.

The cats slowed to a trot and then stopped altogether. Their heads hung low as they took great panting breaths. Alainea jumped from the sleigh to tiptoe back in the direction they'd come, motioning for Charles to stay where he was.

Uncurling his fingers, he considered the coloured kilodens he still held. They looked like plain, unremarkable rocks. He'd gripped them so hard that deep indentations were left behind in his flesh. He rolled them across his palm, considering the hidden well of magic within each one.

Talbot untangled himself from Charles' cloak and hopped onto the floor of the sleigh before scampering into a corner to pick up a kiloden that had fallen. He tossed it up to Charles, who caught it and added it to the others.

"Put them in your pocket," Talbot said. He stood up on his hind legs, lifted his little black snout into the wind, and sniffed.

Charles stared at him.

"I—I heard you," he said, voice faltering. He fingered

the smooth round stone, its edges still glowing red from being in Talbot's grasp.

Talbot's head swiveled around, and he dropped to all fours. He opened his mouth and squeaked something in reply, but Charles shook his head.

"No, not now. But when you threw me the kiloden I understood what you said." Leaning over, he handed the red rock back. The hedgehog sat up to take it into his two paws, and the kiloden flared to vibrant ruby-coloured life.

"You are one of the Garde," Charles said. "Of course it would work for you, but why does it have an effect on me?"

He waited patiently for Talbot to open his mouth and speak.

Talbot extended the ruby kiloden to Charles, but when Charles went to take it, the hedgehog shook his head. Catching what he meant, Charles simply touched its smooth side with one finger.

"I have not heard of such an instance before," came the surprisingly deep voice of Talbot.

Charles was so shocked that he reared back, then felt the heat of embarrassment as Talbot rolled his eyes and motioned for Charles to rejoin him.

"Sorry," he said. With an apologetic grin, Charles slid off the bench to sit across from Talbot on the bottom of the sleigh. Now that he was able to ask questions, Charles couldn't think of one. "Guess I'm a little rattled."

"Well, get used to it. This could come in quite handy." The rich tones of Talbot's voice rang in Charles' ears. He grinned, wondering how such a small fellow could speak so loudly.

"I understand you wish to return to your own land through the Southern Portal?" Talbot continued as though nothing unusual had happened.

Charles, on the other hand, was having trouble collecting his thoughts. He opened and closed his mouth several times and blinked slowly.

"Are you alright?" Talbot tilted his head to one side, eyeing Charles as one might examine a display of fruit to determine which one was rotten.

Charles gave his head a little shake. He wondered if he could talk to any animal in Erinbourne this way. It was amazing.

"Yes!" he blurted louder than he'd meant to. Then, glancing around with concern, he took a breath. "Yes, I'm fine. And I—I do need to get home if that's possible. You can help me?"

"I can take you to Durgot. He is the gatekeeper and he will get you home." Talbot set the kiloden on the floor, then stepped on it with one paw to maintain the connection. "If Alainea finds nothing amiss, I believe we should rest here until dusk."

He looked to where she had disappeared. "The meircats have been through an ordeal and, although we have been fortunate to evade Respiele thus far, I fear it cannot continue if we push on into the open." He peered at Charles quizzically. "Did you understand my words?"

Charles didn't trust himself to speak. He nodded.

Alainea returned. "The dragon, I believe it was Nurelle, has not flown again. I am sure she was aware of our presence, but hid us from her rider. We have her to thank that we are safe."

Straightening, Charles released his bond with the kiloden and slid back onto the bench. These decisions were not his to make, but his future, as well as theirs, depended on them making wise choices. Speaking with Talbot had brought the reality of his departure home. One day soon he would be leaving this land. It was not as pleasant an idea as it had been even yesterday.

Alainea went straight to Felix and Hilda, asking them how they were and thanking them for carrying them all to safety. Talbot picked up the red pebble and thrust it out to Charles, motioning that they should follow her.

When Charles touched it, Talbot spoke. "Keep it close. Then we may speak if need be."

He hopped over the side of the sleigh to the ground.

Charles released the red pebble into a deep pocket at the front of his tunic, gathered the rest of the kilodens, and moved quietly to Alainea. Dropping the coloured pebbles into her outstretched hand, he searched her face. "Did Talbot tell you about our discussion?"

"Yes." She looked at him in amazement. "I have not heard of a regular person conversing with a creature of the Garde before. However, I suppose few people have even seen a kiloden, nor would they know what it was if they did. Perhaps it has not been attempted until now."

She seated herself cross-legged in front of the cats and waved her hand for Charles to do the same.

Felix and Hilda rested their heads on weary paws to listen to the discussion. Charles was concerned for them. He reached for his flask and the food Magda had sent for them as he lowered himself to the ground.

"Could you pour some water into my hands for the meircats?" he asked Alainea, handing her the drink.

She shot him a look of gratitude and did as he asked. The meircats drank the water greedily, their tongues rough and dry. Charles unwrapped the food and laid it before them on the cloths. Both Felix and Hilda fell asleep before finishing their meal, but Hilda laid an enormous paw on Charles' leg and purred before she closed her eyes.

Charles sensed that Alainea and Talbot had been talking the whole time, but he didn't feel left out any longer. For the first time, he knew he was an important part of this adventure. It was a good feeling.

He shuffled away to allow the meircats more space and angled himself toward Alainea and Talbot. The sun was high in the sky now and light filtered down in dappled patterns past the dense green branches of the trees. There was no wind here.

Charles looked up into the boughs and wondered what sort of trees they were. Each branch was uniform and exactly perpendicular to the trunk.

"Oh no." Alainea's shocked words brought Charles out of his reverie.

He caught Talbot's gaze as she dropped her head into her hands with a groan.

"What is it?" he whispered.

Alainea lifted tear-stained eyes to his.

"When we left the fortress with the sceptre, Respiele sent a decree throughout the land offering a substantial reward for my capture. Talbot just told me." She took a deep, sniffling breath and struggled to pull herself together. "Whoever is with me is also in grave danger. This is far worse than I had supposed."

She took another deep shuddering breath.

"I knew, of course, that he did not like me. I was tolerated, used as his servant and treated as less than those who were paid to do his bidding. But still…" a sob caught in her throat. "I am his daughter."

She buried her face in her hands, and Charles shuffled closer to put a tentative arm around her shoulders. Anger stirred in him. How could any man treat his own child in such a way?

Finally, Alainea wiped her face on the voluminous sleeve of her tunic and looked first at Talbot and then at Charles. Her eyes were red from weeping.

"I shall not be safe in Erinbourne again as long as Respiele lives. Talbot told me the person who brings him my head will receive one hundred pieces of gold." She hiccupped another sob. "But one thousand gold coins will be given to the person who delivers me into Respiele's hands...so he may kill me himself."

Chapter Eleven

They decided to eat and then try to get some sleep. It was smart to set forth again when darkness fell over the land. Their group would be far too vulnerable and easily spotted to continue traveling during the day.

Alainea was worn out, so Charles offered to take the first guard duty. Everyone knew, without saying so, that someone must remain vigilant.

"No, Talbot says he would prefer to take the first shift," she said, her arms clasped around her torso. She sounded tired, but authoritative. "He was not up most of the night like we were. Try to rest."

Wrapping her cloak tightly around her body, she felt the ground for rocks and then settled herself exactly where she had been sitting. She pulled the cloak around her head and closed her eyes. "He says he will wake you when it is your turn."

With reluctance, Charles accepted the wisdom of her statement, but sat staring around him.

The meircats, who were curled around one another for warmth, had fallen asleep in their harnesses and had remained that way throughout the discussion. Although it was only midday, the animals had been running all through the previous night and needed to regenerate before doing it all over again. The air was warm and the breeze balmy, perfect for a nap.

Talbot scurried off along the way they had entered the bluff and disappeared into the shrubberies.

Charles yawned, drew his cloak closer, and lay down on the ground.

Sleep claimed him as quick as his eyes closed—but it was not dreamless. He tossed and turned, reliving portions of the past few days before eventually sinking into a world of his own nightmarish imagination.

Charles stood in a dark, circular cave hewn from solid rock. He wheeled around and around, searching every inch of the space. Perspiration broke out on his brow and his hands grew clammy with sweat as he realized there was no way out. It was a prison of stone, and he awaited his doom. Fear clawed at his heart and squeezed the very breath from his lungs. He was trapped.

Yet, suddenly, he was not alone. Alainea appeared to the right of him. Straight and tall, bathed in a swirling gray mist, she held a gleaming upraised sword in one hand. In the other, an egg of massive proportions balanced on her upturned palm, its shell looking as leaden and cold as the cavern itself. Charles called to her, but the words wouldn't move past his throat.

She did not turn or acknowledge his presence. Her eyes were riveted on an area of the chamber floor that, as he followed her gaze, seemed to sink in upon itself to expose a whirling, ebony whirlpool. A howling wind coiled upward from the space. Charles felt the wind swirl around his body, but it seemed to blow right through him and have no effect.

Alainea, however, began to be drawn toward the gaping mouth of the vortex. Her lips opened in a silent scream and her head rocked back and forth in terrified protest as she was lifted. Her toes dragged across the floor. She appeared frozen in place, her arms outstretched, and weapon in hand, yet unable to use it.

Charles screamed her name. He lunged for her, grabbing at her arm, her leg, the cloth of her cloak. He even tried flinging his arms about her body to halt her progress, but couldn't quite reach. Inexorably she was drawn into the swirling black pit.

Then, to his left, as though a match had been struck, sparks of white flame ignited on the stony wall. Spreading outward horizontally in two directions, the flames sizzled high along the rock face like a trail of lit gunpowder. Reaching the furthest point, at the same moment, both sparks turned downward and Charles began to see the rough outline of a door in their wake. The stone fell away from the interior of the prison and a bright light from outside streamed in.

What was beyond? Charles turned pleading eyes back to Alainea. If only he could reach her they could flee through the opening. Escape was so close. He could feel it.

"No!" Alainea cried.

Her shrill piercing screech filled Charles with horrified dread and then he felt his legs go out from under him. He slammed to the floor. His body scraped over the uneven rock as the black whirlpool sucked him in as well.

With a muffled yelp, Charles bolted upright, panting as though he'd just run a race. He gathered himself. That was some nightmare. It had seemed so real.

He decided there was no way he could try to sleep now. Rising, he took a deep calming breath before tiptoeing to the edge of the tree line where he found Talbot hunkered behind a patch of thick shrubs.

Talbot turned to him with surprise.

"I can't sleep." Charles waved aside Talbot's obvious objections and slid to the ground beside him.

Talbot shook his head in disbelief. Through a few complicated paw movements, he was able to make it known that he would leave to scout out the area beyond the sleigh.

"Got it," Charles said, before Talbot disappeared into the foliage. Still feeling shaky, Charles sank behind a patch of shrubs and considered the dream.

He couldn't remember having one so vivid. It felt like he was actually there. He shook his head to rid himself of the fear that gripped his mind and looked out upon the day.

A clear blue sky greeted him and all looked peaceful with the world. He would never have guessed that a dragon, carrying an emissary of evil, lurked within the quiet green woods below. The sparkling blue waters of the River Spye cut through the lush green of the rolling hills and wound its way along until it disappeared behind a knoll. Charles knew from being on the other side of the river upon that knoll sat the cute little village.

He settled his back against a stout fir tree and centered his gaze on the forest across the river. An ancient-looking stone bridge spanned the waters. It was empty and the trail leading from it narrow.

He rested his head against the trunk and allowed his eyes to close for a moment. The image of a pretty young woman with a long braid of auburn hair and haunting amber eyes floated into his mind. His heart swelled. Was he falling for her? In the space of two days? Naw, that couldn't be. He knew plenty of girls back home and had gone on several dates, but none of them had captured his attention like Alainea.

He sighed, opened his eyes, and then reared up straight.

Someone was driving a horse and cart over the bridge. Shading his eyes against the blazing sunlight, Charles watched them, listening as faint sounds of the horse's hooves clopping across the stones reached his ears. When they hit the dirt road on the other side, the driver lifted his reins and snapped them smartly on the horse's rump, urging it into a trot. The man's actions suggested he was eager to escape the shadows where the dragon sat. Charles followed the pair as they moved along the road before disappearing from view below the rise.

There was nothing unusual about the incident and Charles yawned, realizing how little sleep he'd had over the last two days. He had no idea where the road led and didn't really care. He didn't expect to see the horse and cart ever again.

He got to his knees and poked his head above the bushes to have a clear view of the rolling hills they had to cross on their way to the Araleesh Mountains. His thoughts were so focused on the journey ahead, that when the horse's head, and then the man appeared over a ridge not ten paces from where he was hidden, Charles was shocked. Sliding down, he flattened himself as low to the ground as possible, watching between gaps in the shrubbery as the cart came into view.

Had the guy seen him? He prayed not.

The fellow was mumbling angrily, that much was certain, and Charles strained to hear what he was saying. The wheels of the cart rumbled and rattled over the uneven ground making it impossible to pick out any clear words. Charles stopped trying and concentrated on lying very still until the fellow passed by. But that didn't seem to be happening, because the rattling sounds of the cart ceased, followed by the creak of the wagon and a heavy thump as the man jumped to the ground.

Charles dug his hands into the springy grass beside his head and prayed the man would get back in his cart and go home, or anywhere other than here. The thump of footsteps grew closer. Charles held his breath as the man's heavy boots came into view. He stopped at the bushes that barely concealed Charles and began to examine the broken branches that marked the sleigh's earlier entrance into the grove of trees.

What would the man make of all the snapped branches and mowed down shrubs? Maybe they should have kept going. This examination was too close for comfort.

"I know you be here." The man's voice was soft and warm with friendship. "And I mean you no harm. Tis on the side of the king that I be, and I wonder if there be anything I could do to help."

Charles didn't move a muscle. Without Alainea's unerring judgement in these matters, he had no idea whether to trust this person or not.

The man's boots inched closer and a hand reached out to swipe at the bushes over Charles' head. "Ye might as well come out, lad. I know ye're there. Where be the others?"

With a release of breath, Charles got to his knees and stood, still staying behind the shrubs.

The man grinned. He was shorter and stockier than Charles. He twisted a flat, pancake of a cloth cap in his hands and wore rough brown clothes like the ones Ben had worn. His face was ruddy, as though he had spent many hours under a hot sun toiling in his fields.

Charles decided to talk a little, to feel things out.

"I was just traveling this way—alone—on my way to…" He paused, trying to remember the village.

"Maldone?" the man supplied. He narrowed his eyes at Charles.

161

"Yes! Maldone. Anyway, when I saw you crossing the bridge, I didn't want any trouble so I hid."

"And why would you be expecting trouble?" As he spoke, the man smiled and stepped away from the bush, beckoning that Charles do the same.

After a moment's hesitation, Charles followed. After all, it was one man, and Charles felt capable of using his fists if necessary.

"Not trouble exactly." He ran a nervous hand through his hair. "I just like keeping to myself."

"The name is Drim. And you are…?" The fellow stuck out a calloused hand.

As Charles reached to shake it, he had an overwhelming sense of foreboding. This was all wrong. He shouldn't be standing in the open, conversing with a complete stranger. Yet, it was too late to withdraw. He would shake they guy's hand, send him on his way, and retreat into the trees again.

Drim grasped Charles' hand in an iron-clad grip. He dropped the cap, and his face contorted with anger. Taking a step forward, he grabbed Charles with both hands, and wrenched him off-balance. In a flash, the man pinned Charles to the ground with one arm bent behind him. He pounded his knee into the small of Charles' back.

Charles writhed and fought, but he was immobilized well and proper. His face pressed into the earth as his hands and feet were tied. He blew dirt from his mouth and thought frantically of how he could escape without alerting the man to the presence of the others. This was the worst thing that could happen. Then, when the rushing sound of leathery wings and the thump of a dragon landing nearby reverberated in his head, he ceased to struggle. He was caught. His only hope was that they didn't find Alainea and the others.

The toe of a boot prodded him over onto his back. Two faces peered down at him. Another man, with an angry face and large nose, glared at him, a sharp black sword clutched in his hand. The dragon rider must have seen them after all and had sent the farmer to draw them out. Without a word, the pair of men dragged Charles over to the dragon and, between them, hauled him up the side of the beast and flung him over top, face down.

"You shall be rewarded for your assistance," the second man said to the farmer. "Tell the others to gather and begin the march in one hour. I will return and lead them into battle."

The creaking of the wagon and the plodding hoof beats of the horse told Charles the farmer had left.

The dragon rider swung on board and kicked the dragon viciously. It spread its wings and rose awkwardly into the air. Unable to hang on, Charles slid sideways and would have toppled to the ground if the rider had not snaked out a hand and grabbed a fistful of the cloak Charles wore. Hauling him back, the man wrapped the material around a leather binding several times to secure Charles to the lizard's back before kicking it again.

"You know what to do," the man said with a growl.

The dragon rose just as high as the nearby trees and then skimmed across the tops as it swooped. Charles groaned. They were searching for Alainea. Charles heard the smack of something like a whip, or maybe it was the ends of reins applied to the broad neck of the dragon.

"Do you see? Down there. Now!" the rider barked.

Flapping her wings in slow, steady beats, the dragon lowered herself straight down like a helicopter. Without seeing, Charles knew what was happening below.

The dragon was extending her clawed feet beneath her,

reaching out for the sleeping form of Alainea and rolling the girl into its talons.

Then, with measured strokes, the dragon spread her wings and rose into the sky. The two of them would be returned to Respiele's lair. And there, Charles and Alainea would face execution.

Chapter Twelve

Alainea screamed, and a tremor went through the scaly body of the dragon. It didn't take much imagination to figure out that the dragon wasn't happy with what it had been forced to do.

Charles screwed his eyes shut as they slowly flapped back toward the Araleesh Mountains. He didn't want to see the familiar peaks looming on horizon. He wondered if Talbot had been taken as well. And what had happened to the meircats? Not only that, but what would happen to Alainea's poor mother—and the egg? Charles forced his eyes open to concentrate on the countryside flashing by. Thinking about those he'd let down with his foolish mistake was painful.

He struggled to keep his fear from mounting. He would need every ounce of ingenuity he possessed to fight his way out of this situation, if there was any hope at all.

The wind cut a bitter trail through his clothes as the dragon sliced through the sky. He shivered from both the cold and dread, but knew the ride to the fortress would be quick and there was little time to think. Soon, they were circling the landing platform that Charles remembered all too well.

A dull thud from beneath them caused Charles to wince in remembrance of the painful fall from the dragon's talons when he'd first arrived. He knew Alainea had just experienced it. Then with a slight bump and a skid, the dragon folded its wings behind her and came to a stop. She crouched to allow them off, her head held high and proud despite the tasks she was ordered to perform.

The rider didn't bother to unwind Charles' cloak from the harness. Instead, he unsheathed his sword and sliced it free. Charles slid over the scaly side of the dragon. He skittered off the beast's shoulder and landed in a heap on the rocky ground below.

With his hands tied, it took a moment for him to untangle himself and get to his feet. In that time, the dragon lifted off.

Running footsteps approached, closely followed by shouting and the clash of steel on steel. Respiele's warriors were coming to gloat in the arrest of Respiele's daughter and the fool whose fault it was they'd been captured. Charles imagined he and Alainea would be dragged off to await their death in that lifeless chamber he remembered so well. And it would all be thanks to him.

But when he finally straightened, and looked at what was happening, he almost fell over backward with surprise. Yes, there were plenty of Respiele's men there to greet them, but at least five of them already lay inert on the rocky shelf and the rest were battling a creature of gigantic proportion.

Talbot? Charles had only seen him in the shadowy light of early morning and couldn't be sure.

The creature was huge, although it was hard to tell who or what it was as the creature was upright for only a second before it curled into an enormous ball and rolled like a deadly sphere through the ranks of warriors that raced to defeat it. The beast was covered in long, lethal spines that projected like bristling spears from its body. Respiele's warriors, regardless of their efforts to combat the beast, appeared helpless in the face of its superior ability. It whirled through their midst, slashing and stabbing mercilessly at whoever was foolhardy enough to defy it.

The dragon rider who had brought them leapt forward and plucked Alainea from the ground. She had been injured on the rocks after being dropped and was only just picking herself up.

"Halt! Halt, you accursed beast!" the rider shouted. He held a knife to Alainea's throat, stretching her neck high with the blade while the other held her arm painfully behind her back. A thin line of dark red blood trickled down to disappear beneath the collar of her shirt. Alainea moaned.

Talbot stopped amid the broken bodies. He assumed the wide stance of one who has not finished what he came to do with arms akimbo, dark face menacing, and eyes glittering deadly intent. Every spine on his back was erect.

It was an impressive sight. The rider stared at Talbot, mesmerized.

Charles, adrenalin pulsing in his veins, stooped to pick up a rock. He lunged at the rider from behind and brought the rock down on the man's skull. The man slumped to the hard surface beneath him and Alainea dropped to her knees.

The fight was over only moments after their arrival. Charles rushed to assist Alainea.

"Are you alright?" He helped her to stand, searching her face for reassurance.

"Ah!" Her face contorted with pain as she tried to put weight on her right foot. "Something is wrong."

She leaned on him, her foot dangling.

Charles slid a steadying arm around her. "I'm so sorry."

"It will be fine," she said. Her eyes held his as she attempted a smile. "Thanks to Talbot, and you."

"Are you kidding?" Charles said bitterly. "It's my fault we were caught."

"And look where it got us," she said, gripping his arm. "All the way to Respiele's fortress in record time with twenty of his best guards knocked out of commission."

"But your ankle…" Charles' voice trailed off.

"Nonsense," Alainea said. She looked beyond him to where Talbot was gathering the men who were able to walk and pushing them across the landing area. No one raised any objection to him now. Enough of their comrades lay before them either injured, unconscious, or dead. It was impossible to deny the latent power of the huge creature. They disappeared into a chamber underneath the lookout post. Talbot rolled a boulder in front of the door, then strode to where Alainea stood on one foot supported by Charles.

"Somehow, Talbot knew what was happening and hid himself in one of my pockets before Nurelle snatched me from the ground."

"That's amazing."

"Take out the kiloden," Alainea said in a voice edged with pain. "You need to hear what Talbot says to us."

Charles was still worried Alainea's foot was broken.

"First, let me get you to that rock." He pointed to a boulder to one side. "Then I'll listen."

"There isn't time to fuss with me," she said, but allowed herself to be supported over to the stone. She subsided on it, exhaling in pain.

Only then did Charles reach into his pocket for the red kiloden. With a glance at Talbot to ensure the hedgehog was aware of what he was doing, he set it on the ledge at their feet. Then, he pushed his knee against it as he knelt to probe Alainea's ankle inside the soft material of her long boot. Talbot, in turn, came close enough to rest a toe on the kiloden.

She compressed her lips to keep from crying out. With light fingertips, Charles examined her ankle. She compressed her lips to keep from crying out. Charles tore away a strip of what was left of his tattered cloak and looked for something to use as a splint.

"Only a few of those guards," Talbot said, jerking his head toward the warriors lying nearby, "are dead. The rest are merely stunned by the poison contained in my spines. I shall drag them into that same chamber and bar the door. Is her ankle broken?"

"I don't think so, although there could be a fracture that I can't feel," Charles said.

He found a few green sticks scattered on the rock, presumably coming from when the dragon had reached down to steal Alainea from her sleep in the woods. He chose two and used them to gently stabilize the injury.

"Do you think you could find the egg without her?" Talbot towered over them, the deep rumble of his voice reassuring.

"No one is going anywhere without me," Alainea said. "My mother is in there too. I will drag my foot behind me if necessary, but I will be there."

Her face was drained of all colour, but her eyes burned with fierce determination.

"I can carry her if need be." Charles looked at first Alainea and then Talbot. "We'll manage."

"Good," Talbot said. "Then you and she will continue into the fortress. Be assured these will not be the only soldiers Respiele has left behind to guard his insurance. Keep your wits about you at all times. I will join you as soon as I am able."

Charles tied the loose ends of the makeshift bandage together and took Alainea's hand to help her stand and test it out.

"I will be alright," she said. Her face was wan and pale, but her resolve was unshakable. She reached for her bow and pulled the broken remains of it from her back. Leaning heavily on Charles, she drew what was left over her head and tossed it to the rocks with a clatter. "That will help me no more. I wish I had my sword, but at least I know where to find another."

She nodded to the pile of warriors. She attempted a weak smile, and Charles knew it was as much to cheer him as it was to bolster her own fears.

"Take your pick." Talbot waved a long bristly arm toward the weaponry lying on the ground where the warriors had fallen. He looked seriously at them both. "Take care. I shall not be long behind you."

He clapped Charles' shoulder with a resounding thump. "You have done well."

He bent, picked up the kiloden, and dropped it into Charles' hand before striding across the platform.

Charles was left feeling a little dazed. He'd been beating himself up for his stupidity in getting them all captured and expected his companions would feel the same. Instead, he'd received praise and congratulations. It was strange, but a good feeling.

"I'll get you a sword," he said to Alainea, watching as Talbot dragged two of the fallen soldiers away, one in each paw.

There was a heap of discarded armaments and Charles picked through them until he found one that resembled what Alainea had lost. With an eye on the fateful doorway they had escaped through only days before, he jogged back to her.

"Here," he said, holding it out. He was uncertain how she would be able to use it, but he'd already learned not to question her.

"Thank you," she said. Standing on one foot, and steadying herself by placing her hand on Charles' arm, she took the sword and tested its weight, slashing it back and forth. "Good choice."

Grasping the handle, she used it as a walking stick and took a few experimental hops.

"Coming?" she called over her shoulder.

With a grim face, Alainea slowly led the way back to the door. As far as Charles could see, there was no visible means of opening it, so he waited while she ran her hand down the right side of the huge wooden door to find the hidden mechanism. Then, she used the extended sword to activate the trigger. The door swung wide.

With a quick backward glance to Charles and then beyond him, to scan the empty courtyard outside, Alainea turned to face the bleak inner chambers and unknown dangers within the fortress. She showed little signs of the pain from her ankle, and as he followed her, his chest swelled with pride thinking of the fearless woman she was.

The door slammed shut behind them, seemingly of its

own accord. Charles jumped. The torches that had lit the corridors on his previous visit were gone. They were left in absolute darkness.

He heard scuffling to the right of him and hoped it wasn't guards coming to seize them. Then, there was a slight hissing sound and a soft light lit up the area beside the door.

Alainea's face flickered in the glow of a candle stuck in a crude metal lantern. She lifted it high and hopped down the main corridor. Yet every time she placed the sword onto the stone floor, it made a clanging sound that echoed along the hall. She looked at him with mute appeal.

"It's okay," he said. Moving in front of her, he crouched. "Sheath the sword and give me the lantern. Then, lay across me, hang on, and I'll piggyback you."

"You will what?"

"It's what we call it in my world. It'll be easier to carry you in this way."

With a sigh of pain and relief she did so, and Charles straightened, shifting her higher up on his shoulders and supporting her knees with his arms.

"Thank you."

"No problem."

They set off. She was surprisingly light, even with the heavy sword. He chose his footing carefully on the uneven passage, not wanting to stumble.

When they came to a fork, she pointed to the hallway leading down rather than up.

She's searching for her mother. I would too.

Once Respiele learned that Alainea had stolen the scep-tre, he must have flown into a rage. Who knew what he might have done to the frail little woman.

As they progressed, the hallway became steadily steeper,

and a warren of tunnels branched off the main one. Alainea pointed over his shoulder each time to show the way. They heard and saw no one, which was a blessing, but Charles was on high alert. As they descended toward the kitchens, Charles sensed that Alainea was becoming increasingly agitated. She tapped a finger on his chest where her hands were clasped.

Before every sharp corner, she motioned that he should stay back and they listened before proceeding around it. Twice they heard the scuffling sounds of what sounded like footsteps, and her breath came in short, sharp puffs beside his ear. But after a few moments of anxiety, the sound ceased and they continued on.

It appeared the place was deserted. Could it be that every last one of the warriors Respiele had left behind to guard the fortress, had dashed outside when they arrived? It seemed difficult to believe, but why was no one to be found?

Despite their cautious pace, they soon reached the door to the kitchen. Charles stopped with his hand on the door. Taking a deep breath, he pushed it open.

Nothing moved.

He ducked inside the room, examining it for any sign of her mother. The ovens were cold. There wasn't even a live ember in the fireplaces. Pots hung over top of charred ashes, half full of rotting stew.

Charles wrinkled his nose at the smell, and of musty, partially peeled and rotting vegetables lying on the counter. Cheese and meat lay on the tables. It was clear Elspeth had been taken away in the midst of her work.

Where was she now?

Alainea laid her head against the back of Charles' neck. Her body shook.

"Do you think he killed her?" Her voice was muffled against his tunic.

Charles squeezed her hands on his chest, wishing he had the answer.

"We'll find your mother," he said. It was the only comfort he could offer, and it wasn't much.

"We must leave this place. I do not believe she will be in her bed chamber. If she were free and able she would be here." Alainea wrung her hands. "I knew Respiele would be furious, but I thought—I mean, he and his followers had to eat—I thought he would leave her alone if she could continue to be of use to him."

Tears dripped onto Charles' exposed neck.

"There's no sense beating yourself up now," he said with conviction. "Maybe Respiele took her with them when they left for war? They have to eat on the road too. Or…"

He hesitated to mention it, but his mind had already considered the possibility that Respiele had left the poor woman alone and imprisoned in the dungeon.

"You are thinking of the dungeon?" Alainea's voice was tight and scared.

Charles nodded. Without another word, he marched out the door and up the corridor. He wouldn't have remembered which direction to take to the dungeon, but he did know it was deeper in the bowels of the mountain. However, Alainea guided the way. Again, they met with no one.

Finally, she had him stop outside a closed door.

"I would like to stand please," she said.

Charles straightened, holding her so she dropped to the ground on her good foot. She unsheathed her sword before motioning that he should try the door. He reached for the handle, turned it one way, and then the other.

"Locked," he said breathlessly.

"He put her in there to die. I feel it." Alainea's words caught in a sob. She clutched the sword until her knuckles showed white, even in the dim light provided by the lantern.

"Deep breaths," Charles told her. "Remember that Maurice is still here. He would have helped your mother. Just think. How can we get inside? Is there a hidden lock somewhere, or a key?"

He ran his fingers along the edge where the door fitted flush with the surrounding stone.

Nothing.

"No." Alainea slid down the rough oak. Her sword dropped with a clatter, and she buried her face in her arms.

Then, from inside came a faint noise, almost like a squeak.

"Did you hear that?" Charles leaped forward and banged on the wood.

"Shhh!" Alainea hissed. "Do you want them to find us?"

"Who is them? Who's going to come? We haven't seen a soul. If your mother is in there…" He jerked a thumb toward the prison. "Well, then we have to do whatever it takes to get her out."

He raised a fist and was about to pound on the door again, but then had a better idea.

Wheeling on Alainea, he lowered his voice to a terse whisper. "Use the kilodens."

"I do not know how they could help with this," she said, yet her face registered hope.

Charles helped her to stand, and she felt the spot where they rested in her pocket.

"I don't either. Just have faith," Charles said. He didn't know Magda from a hole in the ground, really, but he believed in that little woman and her strange ways with all his being. "Get the pebbles out and hold them. An idea might come to you. At the very least, put them beside the door. Maybe those vines will go to work and open it for us. Something will happen."

Moving like an automaton, Alainea shoved a hand into her tunic pocket and withdrew the shining stones. In the flickering light of the lantern, they flashed like brilliant stars, their light nearly blinding Charles as they came to life. He watched expectantly.

Alainea closed her fingers over the smooth kilodens, rubbing then rhythmically with a thumb. Rather than setting them down at the door, as Charles had suggested, she stepped back, swung her arm behind her, and pitched them against the solid wood with all her might.

Wherever the pebbles smacked against the wood, they stuck, burrowing themselves into the sturdy oak with a sizzling sound, as though burning clear through.

Charles and Alainea took a step back, amazed. From each kiloden, a crackling bolt of coloured lightning traced a wild pattern across the wood, and in the wake of that colour, the wood cracked wide open with a *snap*. The door split into a thousand tiny splinters that crumbled to the floor.

Alainea and Charles stood stiff with shock, their mouths agape. Then, an unseen creature squealed from within the prison chamber. There was a scrabbling sound and a tiny black nose peeked over the top of the debris.

"Maurice!" they cried in unison.

It truly was the rat. He rose onto his hind legs and beckoned urgently to them before scampering out of the way. Charles scooped Alainea into his arms and strode across the fragments of wood to set her down on the opposite side. The gloom of the place was overwhelming, yet hope rose in Charles' heart that Elspeth would be found alive. Anything else was unthinkable.

Lifting the lantern above his head, Charles followed Alainea as she hopped behind Maurice.

"Mother?" she called with fearful urgency.

The sound of weeping rent the air. Alainea cried out and rushed ahead. Charles caught sight of a shrouded form propped against the wall. Alainea flung herself beside it and fell forward. The weeping grew louder.

Charles drew closer. In the dim light, Alainea huddled with her mother on the stony floor. He could have cried with happiness himself.

He sank to his knees beside Maurice, allowing mother and daughter time to themselves. Maurice looked up at him, looking as glad as was possible for the face of a rat to look.

Alainea's mother was not shackled to the wall as Charles had feared. Although it was likely Maurice and his handy key had made sure of that. Once Alainea was certain her mother was alright, she insisted that Charles use the ruby-coloured kiloden to hear what Maurice had to say. Alainea would not leave her mother's side. She helped Elspeth to drink some water and seated herself next to the woman, their arms linked together. Tears of happiness carved trails down their faces.

"Tith glad I am to thpeak with you, young feller," Maurice squeaked.

Even though Charles expected it, he was still surprised to hear the rat speak, and with a slight lisp too. Maurice was careful to keep a tiny paw in contact with the red kiloden, but even so, Charles had to bend close to catch what the rat said.

"After you took the sceptre and escaped, thith place was

in an uproar," Maurice went on. "Everyone was running around and dreadful afraid of what the mather would do."

"The mather?" Charles repeated under his breath. *Oh— master. Yes, Respiele would have been beside himself with fury once he awoke and found what Alainea had done.*

"He rushed into that there kitchen and dragged Elspeth —well, you tell them." The rat looked pointedly at the lady, crossed his paws over his chest, and fell silent, waiting for her to speak.

"I could not have been so brave if it were not for Maurice," Elspeth said. "He brought me scraps of food and once even dragged a pouch of water up through the grate. A greater friend I could never have."

She tried to smile, but now that Charles was closer, he could see, even in the faint light, that she had been beaten. Her lips were swollen and cut, and purple bruises covered most of her face. Gray hair hung in strings around her head and her dress was ripped all down one side. She fingered it, endlessly struggling to pull the two sides together.

"There is not much more to tell." Elspeth ducked her head.

Charles sensed she didn't want to say too much about the punishment she'd received from Respiele for fear of further upsetting her daughter.

"I was locked in here, but it is thankful I am that Maurice found me and unlocked the chains. Of course, I was trapped though, since neither of us could open a locked door." Elspeth looked puzzled. "How did you do it? Respiele himself took the only key."

Alainea pulled her mother close. "Do you remember Magda Roudel?"

"No one could forget Magda," Maurice interjected, clapping his paws with glee.

Elspeth nodded and her eyes brightened.

"Charles and I met Magda. With her help, we were able to arrive here and break down the barrier to this room. We were also able to save King Larkender. Dranich carried him back to his castle." Alainea pushed the hair from her mother's face and leaned down to look at her closely.

"Respiele does not know the king is alive, or that he is aware of Respiele's plans to wage war on Erinbourne. Respiele and his troops are gone for the time being. But mother, can you walk?"

Shuffling onto her knees, Alainea took both of Elspeth's hands in her own. "We need to get you out of here to somewhere you may rest and stay out of sight. I do not believe we are the only ones left in this fortress."

With difficulty, Elspeth rose to her feet and watched as Alainea stood.

"You are hurt, child," she said with concern.

"I fell. It is nothing, Mother," Alainea reassured her. "I will be fine. Now, we must leave this place."

Elspeth shambled in front of Charles as he carried Alainea to the door. Maurice scampered ahead of them to ensure the way was clear. Then, they made their way down the hallway.

"If we can get you to my rooms, I believe you will be safe for the time being," Alainea whispered to both her mother and Charles. "There is something I must do before we leave for good."

Her mother looked at her sharply. "The egg?"

"Yes."

Elspeth winced as she stumbled over some rough footing. "You have searched for it since you were only a girl. What makes you think it even exists, or that you will find it now? Is it not more important that we flee this horrible situation?"

"It is my duty," Alainea answered. "Magda told me of one last place to look. I must try to save the dragons. Their future rests on this hope and I shall not give up yet."

Charles added to Alainea's explanation in an attempt to reassure her mother, "I will be with Alainea every step of the way. And I would give my life to see she does not come to any harm."

Alainea's head snapped up and her eyes locked with his.

"I see," Elspeth said. Although it sounded as though she saw far more than had been put into actual words.

It took considerable time to reach the door to Alainea's chambers since Elspeth was stiff and sore, but eventually, they arrived. Elspeth lifted the heavy latch.

"Depart, with my blessing," she said, turning to address them. "I shall be waiting for you both here. And for dear Maurice," she added with a wan smile before shuffling into the room and closing the door.

Alainea took a shuddering breath and leaned her head against Charles' back.

"I think I would like to try walking now," she said. "No further time must be lost in the effort to find the egg. If I can secure it, and then pass that message on to Dranich, she will tell the other dragons they are released from Respiele. That would make a significant difference in the outcome of the war."

Gingerly, Charles set her down and she lowered her foot to the floor. She fixed a grateful smile on him before moving with a decided limp along the corridor once more.

Staying close to her, in case she stumbled, Charles noticed that the rat had disappeared. He lifted his hands in a silent question.

"I do not know where Maurice went," she said. "Perhaps he is gathering more of his family to attend us in the event of a skirmish. I can only hope he is."

Her voice trailed away with her final words. Charles knew she was worried. It did seem odd that the only contingent of warriors left in the castle had all been outside when they arrived.

Nonetheless, no one showed up to prevent them from making their way up the narrow winding stairs to Respiele's private quarters. Alainea shifted the sword to navigate the final steep climb. Finally, the staircase opened onto the landing beside Respiele's room. Breathing heavily, Alainea subsided on the top step. It was clear the pain was wearing her down, but she would not allow him to carry her.

With utmost care, they tiptoed to the broad oak door, so like the one they'd just opened to free Elspeth. It was open a crack. Charles was grateful since they had no way to open it if it had been locked, as the kilodens were gone. He supposed he might remember which room it was that he'd found them in before, if there was time. Yet time was not something they could count on.

Alainea aimed a questioning look over her shoulder and Charles gave her an encouraging nod. Reaching out, she pushed the door wide and, without a sound, limped inside. Charles crept in behind her, hardly daring to draw breath.

The room looked the same, except of course, Respiele was gone. Light streamed from the two long slits that served as windows and Charles set the lantern down on an elaborately carved chair. Alainea hobbled to the full-length tapestry that hung on the wall from ceiling to floor and fingered the rich brocade.

"It has been here always," she whispered. "I did not consider there might be anything behind it."

With a sweeping motion, Alainea grabbed the rough edge where the coloured threads had frayed and pulled it back.

There, chiseled into the rock, was a small door of gray hammered metal, half the size of any other in the fortress and rounded at the top. It was so small, in fact, that he and Alainea would be forced to bend over double to fit through. Charles found himself wondering how a man as large as Respiele had managed to navigate the contracted space.

Without a word, they dropped to their knees to study the door closer. How did it open?

Alainea pulled the wall-hanging back further which revealed a small silver knob and tiny keyhole, but it was locked. After some concentrated wiggling of the handle, just in case, Alainea sat back on her haunches to ease her ankle and twirled the end of her long auburn braid in thought.

A slight sound caught Charles' attention. He glanced behind them to the open door. The noses and whiskers of three rats poked around the corner. One of the rodents sidled in and scampered across the room to Alainea. The other two waited for him. As the one drew closer, Charles could tell it was Maurice, although Charles had no idea how he knew it. Before today, all rats had looked the same to him.

Maurice tapped Alainea on her leg, startling her from her reverie. After a quick bow, he reached into the tiny pack that always seemed to be strapped to his middle. From it he withdrew the same tiny key he'd used to unlock the chains in the dungeon. Alainea took it from his outstretched paw, ducking her head with thanks to the little animal. Then, she turned and slipped the key into the lock. With the tiniest of clicks, the metal door popped open.

Grinning in triumph, Alainea caught the thin metal in

her fingertips, pushed it back against the wall, and lowered her head to creep inside. The sword she carried made an echoing clang inside the stone chamber. Her cramped posture had caused it to come undone from her leg and fly wide. She backed out to unbuckle the sword and hold it with both hands along her side. She couldn't fit any other way. When her heels vanished into the cavity, Charles bent to take his turn at the door. His back scraped along the top of the entry, but he made it.

A smooth, curved tunnel led inside the rock. There were steps, but Charles had to duck his head and hunch his shoulders to climb them. They were narrower than the ones leading to Respiele's room, just wide enough for him to pass. Someone had taken the time to whitewash the space, and the walls reflected a hazy light from somewhere above causing Charles to feel better about forgetting the lantern back in Respiele's bedroom. The tunnel wasn't very long, yet it was steep, with notches cut into the rock on either side as handholds if they were needed.

Charles emerged into a small circular space behind Alainea and straightened his spine with gratitude. There was nothing in the room apart from an ancient, disused looking cot, covered with dirty looking furs, and a chair that had been set before a series of long, wide windows cut into the rock. There were a lot of the open-air windows, cut in a semi-circle and offering an expansive view of the surrounding mountains and countryside below.

The person who perched up here, like sitting in an eagle's eyrie watching for intruders, would have had a cold and lonely job. No wonder there was a vent in the room that attached to the fires below. Any warmth would be appreciated in a drafty place like this. Especially if Erinbourne had a winter that was anything like the winters he knew on the prairies.

Alainea, with one glance around the room, laid down her sword and zeroed in on the round opening recessed into the wall, at the junction where the solid rock of the wall met the floor opposite the windows. She went down on her hands and knees, struggling to pull away the grate that covered the hole. The vent was large, but Charles didn't think it was quite big enough to physically crawl down, even for Alainea. She looked at him meaningfully and he hurried to help.

The grate had been constructed using strips of thick metal, forged together into what looked like prison bars. The thing seemed welded into place. Huffing with exertion, both of them wound their fingers through the grill and yanked in unison, counting to three and then hauling on it again and again as they struggled to remove the grate from the floor. The task seemed impossible, yet this was where Magda had directed them to look.

Eventually, after taking a moment to collect their breath and applying themselves to the task again, they managed to move the grating. Just slightly, but enough to encourage them. They threw themselves into fighting to wrestle it free. Then, with a rush it came away in their hands. They fell backwards across the floor, the grate clattering onto the stone.

Charles leapt after it and snatched the blasted thing up. He listened for any sign the sound had been heard and traced from below.

Nothing. Clutching the grate to his chest, he looked at Alainea who was already prostrate on the floor with her head and one shoulder shoved inside the recess.

"It's no use," she whispered in a raspy voice, pulling

herself back out. Her voice sounded on the edge of hysterics and Charles set the grate down quietly to kneel beside her. "I cannot see or feel anything. Have we done all this for nothing?"

She rested her forehead on the floor and her whole body sagged.

"Let me try," Charles said gently. "My arms are longer."

She backed up to allow him room, a flush of renewed hope on her face. Charles flattened himself and edged as far as possible along the crevice before extending his arm into the gap. It was cold, and the rock slightly damp. He felt nothing.

Bracing his feet, he pushed himself further into the hole. He stretched his fingers as far as possible and then, noticed something smooth. It wobbled at his probing touch, almost rolling away from him. Panic rose in his chest. At the point where he could comfortably reach to, he noticed the tunnel angled downward. Holding his breath, he curled his fingers into his palm, trying to limber them, and then, with infinite care, he stretched them out again. He knew where the thing was now. Could he dare hope it was the egg? However, he said nothing of it to Alainea, and reached tentatively for the unknown item once more.

He closed his eyes and concentrated. The tips of his fingers felt for the smoothness of it. Whatever the thing was, it was still there! Working his way along its side, he rolled, what he thought was the egg, toward him. It was heavy and big, yet he imagined how fragile it might be. The ground beneath the object was uneven and it bumped over two or three little potholes. His breath caught with fear. If it really was the egg, it could crack due to rough treatment. He forced himself to move slower. It wouldn't do to rush and have it break after all they'd done to save it.

Alainea lay beside him, saying nothing, which he was grateful for. Finally, after what felt like ages, he edged himself out of the tunnel and readied his other hand to catch what he prayed was the egg. It swayed over the bumpy rock and came into view as it dropped into his waiting hand. He caught it, just barely, since its weight surprised him. Alainea's sharp intake of breath thrilled him to his core.

It was the precious egg.

"You found it!" Unable to tear her eyes away from the egg, she rose to a crouched position and, with deliberation, cupped her hands together to take it from where the egg wobbled on his hand.

Faintly green in some places and slate gray in others, the treasured egg was mottled in colour. Its texture was smooth, like the chicken eggs Charles was familiar with at home, but it was easily the size of a watermelon, maybe larger.

They had done it. They had secured the prize at the end of the rainbow. But now, how in the heck would they get the thing to safety?

Alainea got to her feet. Charles was about to draw his other arm from deep within the cavity when, on impulse, he strained his fingers for another feel.

Alainea leaped to her feet with a gasp. "Someone is coming!"

Chapter Thirteen

"Did you honestly think no one would be watching over that accursed egg?" Laveza's grating voice floated up the stairwell.

Charles yanked his arm from the hole and leaped to his feet, his eyes on the doorway. Alainea stepped toward him, nudging his arm. He looked at her, realizing what she wanted him to do.

Charles shook his head. "You're hurt. You can't."

"This is *my* battle," Alainea whispered fiercely.

He thrust out his arms and she rolled the egg into his before she stepped away, without a trace of a limp. That move must be costing her dearly. She lifted the sword, and rested her weight on her good foot. Her shoulders were set and Charles knew she would give her life to save the egg. He prayed strength into her arms for he knew what a formidable foe Laveza was. Together, they had bested the woman once, but he couldn't help Alainea now. He backed up, clasping their trophy to his chest until his elbows touched the wall behind him.

His eyes flickered from the doorway to the cold gray ovum in his arms. The last of the dragons, unaware of the battle over its fate.

Would he and Alainea be able to protect it?

Laveza took her time. They were trapped and she knew it. With a sneer, she stepped beneath the arch and sauntered into the room, holding her sword loosely in one hand.

"You could save yourselves a lot of trouble if you just put that egg back where you found it," she said. "Not that I would spare your lives, of course. But at least you would save the egg you care so much about, since it will be smashed when I kill you."

Alainea said nothing. Laveza narrowed her dark eyes and a thin smile played on her lips. "I have never been in agreement with keeping the dragon spawn. Respiele should have destroyed the fool thing long ago."

Laveza stepped toward the windows, calm and conversational as though paying Alainea and Charles a social call.

"The sun has disappeared behind the mountain," she said thoughtfully. "Respiele and his army should almost be nearing the castle by now. The only regret I have is that you will not be alive to see your cherished kingdom destroyed."

She addressed this last statement to Alainea and slowly lifted her sword.

"Neither I, nor Erinbourne's king, will be vanquished." Alainea spoke in a gentle voice that matched Laveza's in her silky smooth hatred of the other woman. She swiveled on her toes and lunged.

Her sword clanged as Laveza parried with her own raised weapon. The two women battled each other back and forth across the room. Charles' eyes were riveted on Alainea. Her braid slashed across her back as her arm rose and fell. No one would ever have known she had twisted her ankle earlier that day, for she ducked, leaped, and drove her opponent back toward the windows with every blow.

Then Laveza leapt onto the only chair in the room and came down with force from above. Alainea ducked and whirled out of the way, but Charles heard her ankle snap before her sharp scream of pain rent the air. She crumpled onto the floor, writhing.

Laveza gave a cry of triumph and pounced, driving her sword forward to pierce Alainea's heart. Yet, at the last moment, she swung around and charged at Charles and the egg. Twisting away, Charles strove to evade her. Behind Laveza, despite her anguish, Alainea struggled to rise and fight.

He lifted the egg over his head and ducked as he had so often done while boxing. But the roughly hewn floor was uneven, and his movements were hindered by the awkwardness of the burden he carried.

Laveza was easily upon him. She sank her sword deep into the egg with a sickening crunch and a high-pitched cackle of delight.

Fluid poured from the opening as she withdrew her sword. Red mingled with clear liquid as it splattered on the floor at Charles' feet, soaking his boots. He hollered at the woman with rage. Yet he still could not drop the egg they'd come so far to save.

Alainea screamed in agony. Using her sword as a crutch, she leaped onto her one good foot and launched herself at Laveza, lifting her blade in the air as she flew. Laveza spun to face her, but she was no match for the pain and anger that drove Alainea now. Laveza's body reeled back as Alainea's sword pierced her through. The shining end appeared between Laveza's shoulders, and she dropped like a stone.

Gasping, her body convulsing with shock, Alainea hopped to where Charles stood rigidly against the wall, still cradling the egg. She collapsed against him. Her hands moved involuntarily to caress the fractured shell as she sobbed.

He slid down the wall to thump onto the floor with Alainea clinging to his arm. Resting the broken egg on his knees, he slipped one arm around her and pulled her close. Her grief was acute. He wished there was something he could say to ease her suffering, but nothing could comfort her.

There was no use in telling Alainea what he had learned on his second attempt to reach into the cavern. It would be too much hurt for her to bear. For now, it was enough to grieve with this woman who had become so important to him, and to do what he could to save her from the wrath of a father who wanted her dead.

The other three eggs that his groping hand had felt, had rolled away down the chute when Laveza's arrival had startled him. They had likely smashed into the stone cold ovens below.

Chapter Fourteen

After a time, when Alainea's sobs had quieted, Charles set the broken shell aside. He helped her down the narrow stairs and, picking her up, laid her on Respiele's bed in the lower chamber. He wanted to get her away from the grisly scene of death.

She flopped backward, staring at the ceiling with reddened, sightless eyes. Charles went in search of something he could use to secure her ankle. It was well and truly broken this time and he was concerned, if not set properly and held still enough to heal, that she would be crippled for life. Finding what must have been the handles of several old knives in a drawer by the bed, he did his best to set her bones. Then, he held them firm with another length of material from his tunic. Alainea gripped the bedpost beside her as he did so and gritted her teeth so hard he could hear it, but he knew it must be done.

Afterward, he flung himself down on the bed beside her and waited until she was ready to talk. Shadows were lengthening and soon it would be dark.

His stomach growled and he realized they hadn't eaten anything since the night before. He sat up and rummaged in the pouch he still carried at his waist. The food was crushed, but even crumbs were welcome now.

"Alainea, you should eat something," he said, offering her some of the bread and cheese that the farmer's wife had given them.

"I cannot."

"I understand how you could feel that way," he said, "but you can't allow your body to weaken. Your ankle has to heal and we're still not out of this mess."

"What is the use?" Alainea turned her head away. "I have communicated with Dranich. She is devastated. I have failed the entire race of dragons and plunged Erinbourne into peril."

Charles had to lean close to catch her forlorn words.

"You did everything humanly possible," he said. He bit into the food he'd tried to give Alainea with a vengeance. "No one could have done more. It's not your fault you had a sprained ankle and that deranged hag appeared. I know what happened was terrible, but we can't change history. You did your best. Now we have to get you out of here before someone else shows up to kill us."

Alainea sighed and rolled her head back to stare at him without expression. "It would be better if you left me here. There is no place in Erinbourne I can hide that Respiele will not find me."

Tears rolled down her cheeks and soaked the thick braid of hair that lay beneath her.

"What will Dranich do?" Charles asked. He thought perhaps a change of subject might help. "I mean, it's horrible that the last egg is gone, but at least this frees up the dragons, right? Once Dranich tells them the news, they'll fight for the king."

"Yes," she said listlessly, "they will fight. But without hope."

"Well, we can't just lie here waiting to die. We have to save your mother." Charles stood up and brushed the crumbs from his front. "Come on. I'll carry you if I have to, but we're getting out of here."

Alainea lifted her weary arms to him in submission. Charles caught them to pull her upright. When their faces came close, and seized with the rashness of youth, he brought one of her hands to his mouth. His heart flooded with emotion for her. It wasn't sadness for her loss. Although he was experiencing plenty of that. It was something else he didn't want to figure out just yet. Their eyes met in the dim light of dusk and Charles lingered there, his lips against the back of her fingertips, his heart flooding with feeling for this brave woman. He leaned closer and might have kissed her tear-stained face if not for a squeaking sound at the door.

"It is Maurice," Alainea said, breaking eye contact. "He comes to tell me Dranich is here and wishes to speak with us."

Charles felt his face flush. Alainea allowed herself to be gathered into his arms.

As he carried her to collect the lantern, she said, "I see Respiele's old bow and arrow hanging over there. Can you please help me to get them off the hook?"

Without a word, Charles returned to the bed and gently set her down. Then he strode across the room and plucked the weapons off the wall. If Alainea wanted them, she should have them. Her abilities as a warrior were impressive. Alainea fastened them around herself, picked up the lantern, and gave him a nod.

"Thank you."

Picking her back up, he carried Alainea down the flight of stairs to the broad hallway below. Alainea insisted she be put down at that point, but it was evident after a few hops that she couldn't continue and he carried her on his back again.

After his show of emotion, Charles felt embarrassed and kept his eyes trained on the path ahead, saying nothing. But as they walked along in the flickering light, Alainea lifted her hand from around his neck and rested it on his cheek. Surprised, Charles faltered.

"Thank you, Charles Bramley," she said. "You have saved my life more than once, and I am grateful for you and your friendship. I could not have done this without you."

Charles almost tripped over his own feet and despite the grim situation they faced, gladness rushed into his heart.

Her directions and his long strides soon brought them back to Alainea's chamber. He pushed the door open and Alainea called for her mother. There was a flurry within and Elspeth's worried face appeared.

"Be you well?" She bustled out to reach for her daughter, her already weakened voice cracking under the strain of concern. She smoothed stray hairs and rested a tender hand on Alainea's head. "What happened?"

"Yes, Mother, I am well." Alainea smiled through tears that threatened to spill over again. "But the dragon egg was not so fortunate."

Elspeth blinked rapidly.

"It is gone? Did Respiele…" She left her words hanging and wrapped her arms around Alainea. "Why is she shaking?"

Elspeth directed the question to Charles.

"Her ankle is broken," he answered. "And she fought with Laveza."

"We will explain everything in time," Alainea said. "But for now we must get away from this place. Dranich awaits us outside."

Maurice ran ahead of them the whole way, peering anxiously over his shoulder every now and then to urge them on.

When they reached the last big door, the rat stopped and sat up on his hind legs with paws raised. Charles stopped, unsure what Maurice wanted.

"This is where we must say goodbye," Alainea said. "Please, will you set me down for a moment?"

Without a word, Charles carefully lowered Alainea onto her one good foot. While she and her mother said their farewells to the rat, Charles opened the door and scanned the outside platform area. He expected to see Respiele's forces rushing down the rocks toward him, but he was met with only silence.

Charles took a lungful of fresh air and turned back to add his own thanks and goodbyes. He bowed to the little gray rat. Maurice fixed Charles with a beady gaze and inclined his head in response.

The massive door swung shut behind them as Charles carried Alainea into the courtyard, closely followed by Elspeth. He looked for Talbot and the dragon in the gathering gloom, but there was no sign of either.

Elspeth stood at his elbow, peering into the north. He followed her gaze.

"The war has begun," she said.

A strange glow was reflected in the heavy clouds that

hung there. It wasn't a colour Charles would ever have associated with war. It was a violent purple.

"Dranich is nearby," Alainea said in low tones. "She tells me Talbot left when we were inside. He went to fight when he sensed the battle worsening for King Ludwig. He is able to cover great distances quickly as his larger self. Please, set me down."

Charles did so.

Alainea's shook her head in silent regret. "Dranich is overwhelmed with grief. She would also be fighting in the war, alongside her comrades, but cannot go when she feels a duty and concern for me."

All at once, Dranich was there, looming over the edge of the mountain fortress. Her huge flapping wings stirred up a breeze that caused Elspeth to take a step backward from its force. The dragon's bulk blocked out the evidence of battle that rose into the sky. She landed with a *thump* on the stony shelf where they waited for her. Great puffs of black smoke issued from her nostrils with each breath and as she folded back her wings, her head bowed. Knowing Alainea needed to grieve with Dranich, Charles helped her to cover the few steps it took to reach her dragon's side.

Alainea stretched both arms out to the dragon's angular features, pulling herself as close as she could and sobbing anew. Dranich leaned into the girl. Huge tears rolled down her craggy face, dripping from her chin and splashing onto the rocks like upturned buckets of water. Alainea allowed herself only a minute this way, however. Soon she pulled away, sniffing noisily. Dranich hunkered low and even Charles knew what she was telling Alainea to do.

"If you can help me, Elspeth," he said, "I think we can get Alainea onto Dranich without injuring her ankle more."

Elspeth nodded and moved to support her daughter.

Between them, they managed to seat Alainea and fasten the harness safely around her. Charles looked at Elspeth.

"You're next," he said with false cheerfulness.

It was only when they were all aboard that Alainea, in a voice edged with pain, revealed the spot that Dranich meant to take them.

"Durgot Flandish expects us to arrive this night. His realm of the Southern Garde is a sensible choice since it is vital my mother reaches a safe haven. It is also where you, Charles, must be taken in order to journey back to your world through the portal." Alainea heaved a sigh.

"Afterward, Dranich plans to return to the battlefield. I have asked her to take me along." When both her mother and Charles opened their mouths to protest, she raised a hand to quiet them. "I know what you want to say. It is true, I cannot walk, but I can ride Dranich, and I do have use of my arms."

She fingered the bow slung across her back, but Charles and Elspeth protested in chorus.

"No, my child!"

"That's crazy!"

"Yes, that is what Dranich says too." She winced as she tried to move her foot into a more comfortable position, then continued with a trembling chin. "If I am with the Southern Garde, however…I place my mother, Durgot, and those who live with him in the mountain, in grave danger. Respiele's blood runs in my veins and he can sense my presence. My betrayal is unforgivable. He will not rest until I am dead and I fear he would take the lives of those around me too. It would be better if you let me go."

Elspeth wrapped her arms around Alainea, holding her tight and kissing her forehead. As though a child again, Alainea rested her head against her mother's breast.

Dranich unfurled her powerful wings and with one down-ward swipe, she sent them plummeting over the cliff and soaring over the mountain edge into the south.

The rush of wind as Dranich streaked across the sky would have been exhilarating at any other time. Now, however, it was only a howling whine in Charles' ears. It would be his last journey on a dragon, but worst of all, it marked his final hours with Alainea too. His insides ached at the thought.

They skimmed just over the treetops to avoid detection against a cloudless night. Behind them, the northwestern sky continued to glow with unnatural shades of purple. No one spoke, mostly because it was too noisy, but also—there was nothing to say.

Charles knew the thoughts of his companions rested on what was happening in the battle. It was their world; the people and creatures that inhabited it were their own. He could feel they had lost all hope.

He wanted to do something to aid them too, but what? Punching people was a poor way to win a war when your opponents were armed with weapons of destruction and death. It wasn't his war anyway—was it?

He dragged his thoughts back to the present. A cow bawled from somewhere below and he thought of his parents and the shocking last moments he'd spent in Canada, thrashing about in the claws of a dragon. A lot had happened to him since then. Strangely enough, this place meant something to him now. He cared about what happened to these people.

He bent down close to Alainea's ear.

"Okay, listen," he said, a makeshift plan formulating in his head. "Dranich is *going* to fight, you *desire* to fight, and...I *want* to fight for your people."

Alainea flinched and slowly turned to face him.

"I can't leave Erinbourne now. What if we drop your mom off with Durgot and the three of us left right away? I don't know how to shoot an arrow, but I can help *you* to shoot one. Maybe we'll think of something else we could do on the way."

Alainea clutched at his hand in the darkness and finding it, held on tight.

"Yes," she breathed.

It took time for Alainea's mother to locate the secret entry, but eventually, with Alainea's help, Elspeth opened the great door of the mountain herself and entered alone. Alainea put on a brave face as she hugged her mother, assuring the woman she would return, and soon. They clung together, prolonging the moment they would part. Charles did not meet Durgot, the man he had heard so much about. Yet, he knew from all Alainea had told him that Durgot kept a close watch on the borders of the Southern Portal, and would have doubtlessly known when they arrived.

Once Elspeth was inside, and protected within the Ildune Mountains of the Southern Garde, they prepared to leave. It was the middle of the night before he and Alainea were astride Dranich once more and winging their way toward the conflict.

Charles' stomach was in knots. He couldn't see Alainea, but he knew she was feeling an even greater tension than him.

"Do you see it?" Alainea's voice floated across to him despite the wailing wind of their travels through the midnight sky.

He looked ahead. Yes, he saw what she referred to as the weird, mauve clouds suspended overtop the fighting. They appeared to have grown since he'd seen them last.

"What is that? Why is there a colour over the fighting?"

"Respiele may have lost the sceptre, but he still carries the Amethyst, and wields its power to his advantage. It is that power we see reflected in the atmosphere. I am worried." She shifted uncomfortably. "It lies heavier on the land than when we left the fortress. It is my guess that King Ludwig was still too weak from loss of blood to have accompanied his troops. Without the sceptre they are vulnerable. Or perhaps he is sick at heart and unable to fight."

"Why would he be sick at heart?

"King Ludwig loves his brother," she said simply. "Dranich told me he was on a mission to meet with Respiele, and make him see reason. That was just before the skirmish in the meadow in which Ludwig was left for dead and you were carried into Erinbourne. The other dragons told Dranich about it. The king misjudged his ability to influence the brother he once knew. He was not even given the chance. The Respiele who exists now, cannot be reached with sentiment and reason. His mind has been warped by greed and the sickness that comes upon weak-willed individuals when they are in contact with the Gemstones of Power."

"These gemstones are pretty potent?" Charles watched as the cloud of luminescent colour ballooned higher into the air. It seemed to be lit from within.

"They are," she said. "The gems bestow an ability to rule Erinbourne. That is what makes them so dangerous in the hands of a fool."

The rise and fall of Dranich's huge wings carried them closer to combat with each stroke and Charles started to wonder what they would do when they arrived at the scene of battle.

"Can I help? Could I steady you as you shoot, or hand you the arrows…?" he finally asked.

"Dranich will take over," she said. "She and I are in constant communication. Of course, she has her own methods of attack."

There was a hint of grim sarcasm in Alainea's words and Charles guessed he knew what that meant—fire. This whole visit would make a great story. He decided then and there that if he made it out of this alive, he'd write it all out one day. Mainly so his ancestors could read about it. He couldn't imagine too many people could honestly claim they'd ridden a fire-breathing dragon into a war zone. But who would believe it if he told them?

He knew, without being able to see her in the darkness, that Alainea was readying her bow and fitting an arrow into place. He heard her sharp intake of breath as they drew close enough to see the battle.

"Two of the dragons have been killed," she said flatly. "Dranich just told me. Respiele shot them with his bronze arrows."

She added nothing more. Charles assumed this meant something worse for a dragon than a regular arrow. His heart sank. He wished he could ease her pain, but there was nothing he could say to comfort her.

Fires raged across the land and laid waste to trees that lined the area. Whether they'd been lit by the two remaining dragons circling overhead, or whether they'd been lighted by the people scurrying about in dizzy circles below, Charles couldn't tell. The battlefield glowed with an eerie light, illuminating the struggles of men and women as they engaged in hand-to-hand combat. Swords clanged together, arrows flew, and combatants grappled with one another using whatever weapons they had. There were hundreds of them, but many more lay crumpled on the earth amid the abnormal purple mist.

Talbot was there. He barreled in concentric circles as he took on a whole squadron of Respiele's army, but he was outnumbered. Charles wondered how long Talbot could hold on. Something had to be done.

War was horrific. What was wrong with this man, Respiele, that he would do such a thing in an attempt to kill his own brother and dominate a land that wasn't his to rule? Charles' stomach rolled. He felt faint with revulsion and disgust.

Dranich joined the last two dragons and roared out a greeting. There were answering calls and then the three of them dove to attack Respiele's army. The dragons banked against the north wind and formed a line, swooping down in formation to breath fire on the ranks of men and women who had wronged them for so long.

As they opened their gaping mouths to spurt the first flame, the violet cloud descended on them. It was a choking mist that gagged the great beasts and sent them into a blind tailspin across the sky. Their wings thrashed and tails whipped. Screams of fear and anger mingled together as they fought the sickening scum created by the Amethyst.

Charles gripped the ropes that held him on Dranich. He hollered in fury at the injustice of it all.

One dragon spiralled to the ground, and then the other fell close behind.

Alainea shrieked as the massive creatures dove headfirst into the earth, rolling up great furrows of soil and deci-mating entire ranks of the king's armies where they held their ground against the foe. The majestic creatures ground to a halt and lay still, two splendid dragons crushed by Respiele's army and the wrongful use of magic.

Dranich screeched in agony at their deaths. Charles clung to her as she careened toward the ground. She couldn't see. He leapt to his feet on her broad back and hauled up on the ropes that bound him to her. At the last moment, she nosed upward, a river of useless fire streaming from her mouth.

She wheeled around, propelling herself back along the edge of the battle. Charles dropped back in place. It would be stupid to fall off. Alainea took aim, let her arrow fly, and had another nocked in its place in the blink of an eye. Below, two men fell, but it did nothing to turn the tide of evil. The undulating clouds of mauve seemed to weave around everything in their wake, even weapons belonging to the king.

Alainea made a strangled sound. Charles turned to see her clutch her throat. Then he felt the very oxygen torn from his nostrils.

Dranich pulled up with a scream and flew almost perpendicular to the ground in an attempt to escape the thick, syrupy mist. The stuff was thicker here and Charles traced its genesis to one spot at the middle of the action. The purple mist billowed up into the air in great mush-room-shaped vapors from that point.

"It is Respiele!" Alainea croaked. "The consuming mist emanates from him. He must be stopped."

How? Charles became frantic. People were dying all around him. Soon this madman would take the woman he loved as well. He knew it was so. His heart almost burst from his chest, and he took a sobbing breath before his mind cleared and the answer came to him.

The one last kiloden. The red one. Deep in his pocket it

called to him. He sprang to his knees, praying it would work, and plunged his hand into his pocket to search for the powerful pebble. It seemed small, but Charles knew what kilodens could do. His fingertips touched its smoothness. He pulled it free and yanked one of Alainea's arrows from her sheath. From his tunic he tore a thin strip of material and feverishly bound the kiloden to the tip of her arrow.

He thrust it into her hand.

"Use it!" he shouted. "Take out the Amethyst."

The moment the kiloden was in Alainea's grasp it came to blinding life. Her face flashed red with the blazing light of it. Swift and sure, Alainea fitted the arrow into the notch and drew it back. Her eyes flashed like stars as she looked at Charles. She didn't ask why and only did exactly what he had said.

She took careful aim and released the string.

The arrow whistled through the deadly purple night, cutting a red flame of fire in its wake. Straight and true it flew, slicing through the cloying, unearthly mass that rose from Respiele and the gemstone. It turned aside the thick waves of magic like they were but a meaningless barrier trying to hold back all that was good in this world.

Respiele didn't see it coming. Like a missile, the arrow hurtled on a trajectory toward him. Yet he stood on a pinnacle of earth at the center of the melee, a gloating, foolish man in his supposed victory. He held the raging Amethyst in his upraised hand.

His head was thrown back in a howl of conquest when the arrow and the kiloden caught the Amethyst and sent it spinning into the air above his head. Insidious purple met with the blistering heat of red. The two stones of power matched each other, spinning and sizzling like explosives about to detonate, streams of sparklers raining to the ground about the man below.

Respiele shrieked.

He leaped for the Amethyst, clawing for the precious stone that had won him short-lived dominion. Only the gem whirled up into the air over his head before Respiele had even gathered the presence of mind to reach for it.

The glittering kiloden and the Amethyst trailing waves of nauseating purple strove together higher and higher, and with their climb they drew all the profane purple power with them. The mauve mists that had so clouded the king's armies were whisked into the heavens in a twirling vortex of colour.

Both gems winked out of sight. The curtain of dense purple fog dissipated and was blown away in a breeze that rose in the west.

The king's warriors shook themselves as though ridding their brains of a foul stench. The numbing effects of the Amethyst had disappeared. They picked up their weapons, and began to drive Respiele and his legions back. Respiele flung himself onto a horse and charged through the ranks of men who still strove to valiantly serve him, knocking them aside in his haste to flee the wrath of his brother. Seeing this, his army turned tail and also fled. Some were successful in their escape; others were not.

As Dranich circled slowly overhead, many of the disillusioned people who had joined Respiele in his bid to take over Erinbourne were rounded up and marched away by Talbot and the king's army.

For the first time in days, Charles laughed. Moving sideways in the straps that held him safe on Dranich's back, he reached for Alainea and hugged her. She flung her arms around him and hugged him back.

Charles released Alainea at the sound of a piercing screech and looked toward it. Revealed in the light of the burning fires was Respiele. He had galloped his horse atop a high hill and had lifted a thick bow to his shoulder. Before Charles could holler a warning, Respiele's arrow spun through the air toward them. Charles grabbed Alainea and tried to flatten her against the dragon.

The arrow flew with such force, Charles could hear it coming, but he wasn't fast enough. He screamed a warning to Dranich who veered sharply away, but the arrow aimed at Alainea seemed to be guided by a homing device. Charles felt the wind as it passed him and knew she had been hit when a muffled shriek flew from her lips.

Respiele's arrow had found his daughter. Charles prayed Alainea had not been mortally wounded.

"Alainea! Are you alright?" he cried, but there was only silence.

Again an arrow whistled through the air. Dranich spun and zigzagged, tracing a wild pattern through the night as she sought to evade the killer arrows shot from below. She angled on a trajectory further from the madman on the hilltop. And then one last missile zinged through the night sky, Charles felt the thud as the arrow found its mark, somewhere beneath him.

The dragon lurched sideways. She flailed her great wings, dropping abruptly and plunging them across the sky.

Charles rolled toward Alainea, one hand gripping the thongs that held him atop the great dragon and the other feeling for Alainea's face. His fingers reached her cheek and came away wet.

Was it blood?

"Alainea?" he shouted. His voice sounded foreign and frantic. "He hit you! Are you alive?"

"Yes. I wish he *had* killed me." Her body spasmed, waves of sobs wracking her body. "Dranich was impaled with Respiele's bronze arrowhead."

She subsided into paroxysms of pain that tore at her body. Charles knew she could say no more. He ripped another strip of cloth away from his garment, leaving his stomach bare, and felt for her wounded arm.

"I have to bind the wound or you will lose too much blood," he yelled.

Her arm was limp. She lay across Dranich, uncaring whether she lived or died, but Charles cared. He found the wound and dressed it as best he could.

Had Dranich really been impaled with an arrow? Her body was rigid beneath them as she pulled herself into the air. With all of her former strength, the dragon swept them through the starry sky. But he knew, when Alainea continued to cry, that it must be true.

Dranich, the greatest dragon of them all, was doomed.

Chapter Fifteen

Into the night they plowed, clinging to Dranich. Charles stroked Alainea's hair with one hand, and with the other he bunched the folds of her garments as she lay prostrate across Dranich's back. He didn't need to read her thoughts to know her heart was breaking in two. She curled herself into a tight ball of misery and cried, unheeding of the straps that bound her to the dragon's back. Charles was worried she might tumble off and be lost in the landscape below. He wound the cloth of her cloak and tunic around his hand, ensuring he could save her if she fell, but also to try, in some small way, to impart strength in time of her grief.

Dranich was dying.

With every lift and stroke of her wings, Charles sensed the dragon's body weakening. Occasionally, she dropped so low that passing trees would brush her underbelly and then, with a groan, she would strain to lift herself higher.

Alainea pleaded in vain with the dragon to turn back to the scene of battle. She begged Dranich to save her strength, to turn around and to find King Ludwig and his Golden Sceptre of Power that could heal her wounds. But Dranich would not go. Sobbing with every word, Alainea told Charles that Dranich explained how her priority was to see Alainea safe. She was determined to carry her back the Ildune Mountains, to Durgot, and to be reunited with Elspeth. Dranich would not risk their lives in trying to save her own.

Charles was awed by such love. He remained silent throughout the journey. There was nothing he could say that would help and felt very much the outsider in these last moments shared between the girl and her dragon.

Despite the grievous injury, Dranich managed to have them back at the entrance to Durgot's domain by sunrise. A shard of golden light broke over the eastern horizon to Charles' left, and he lifted his head to look out upon the Ildune Mountains.

He dropped his gaze. Everything ended now. Alainea would say goodbye to Dranich for the last time and he would have to say goodbye to Erinbourne—and to Alainea.

Even if he wanted to see her again—he didn't think that was possible—it would be the ultimate long-distance relationship. And that was if she even liked him, and he very much doubted she did. No, Alainea was consumed with a pain he couldn't begin to understand. His departure would be the least of her worries, and that was only right. He'd only been here for what? Four, maybe five days? It was ridiculous to think he'd formed such bonds with the people of Erinbourne, and with the land itself.

He ignored the threads of luminosity that turned the cobalt blue of a moonless sky into the pale pastels of morning. His mood was black and heavy. He didn't want to see the sun or think about this world carrying on without him.

His eyes rested on Alainea who was quiet now. Her sobs had subsided and she sprawled in an exhausted heap beside him, face down, arms outstretched and her hands curled around Dranich's knobby scales.

Charles recognized the patch of grass ahead of them where Dranich had landed last evening, and prepared himself for a bumpy landing. He was astonished at Dranich's force of will and strength. Yet, the dragon's breath was hoarse and rasping in the still morning air and her body quivered with the enormous strain she had put on herself.

She was an amazing creature.

Charles put a protective arm over Alainea as they slumped lower and lower in the air. He loosened the straps around her body as well as his own, knowing she couldn't think beyond her grief. Alainea didn't look up or make a sound, but her shoulders began to heave. She knew what lay ahead. Charles only hoped he could somehow help her to get through it.

And then, they were only a few metres from the ground. Dranich angled her wings, creating drag, holding herself rigid, till her body shuddered and failed her. Her huge wings trembled, unable to sustain the effort required to bring them down for a secure landing. One at a time, her wings crumpled and slammed to her side. While her head had always before been above her body, now it disappeared beneath. The massive creature tumbled headfirst over and over across the grass. Charles and Alainea were flung high and to one side where they toppled end over end before coming to a halt. Had they still been strapped to Dranich, they would have been crushed.

The dragon slammed into the jagged boulders at the base of the mountain and came to rest in a mangled heap.

Alainea rose onto her one good foot. She fell weeping, and then hauled herself upright again to hop painfully to the side of her cherished Dranich.

The dragon sprawled on her stomach, her head curved back from where her neck had smashed against the rocky verge and her long, barbed tail stretched across the torn grass behind. Alaina collapsed at Dranich's head. She wrapped her arms around the dragon's face and stared into her huge, half-opened eyes. The waves of pain radiating from the pair were palpable.

Charles picked himself up and stood a respectful distance away with his hands clasped, but Alainea beckoned to him. With uncertainty, he walked toward her.

"Dranich wishes me to thank you for all you have done to help us." Alainea turned her head to look up at him, her eyes red and hollow in her pale face. "She and I both know you risked your life to help us last night, and because of what we were able to do, together, Respiele was defeated. That outcome is the only part of what happened that makes her death worthwhile."

Alainea gazed back at Dranich. "And also, that she was able to bear us to Durgot."

She whispered the last few words.

Charles struggled to swallow before he could get out the simple words he wanted to say. "I'm glad I could help you. I wanted to be there because…well, because I care about you all, and your world."

He'd meant to make his caring a little less encompassing than the whole of Erinbourne. He wanted to make it personal. Sure, in the beginning, he hadn't been given a choice about whether he wanted to be there, but his feelings had changed. He'd helped Erinbourne, because of Dranich, Magda, Elspeth, the rat Maurice, Talbot, the farming folk they'd met, and the meircats. But mostly, he had helped this world, because of Alainea. Yet, there was no time to say any of that.

Instead, Charles laid his hand on Dranich's face. The dragon swiveled an eye to focus on him, then held his gaze for several long, unmistakable moments, before it drifted closed. Her thoughts flooded through Charles, leaving a prickly sensation head to toe, and he knew, without speaking her language, having a magical kiloden, or asking Alainea to interpret for him, what Dranich was asking him to do.

She wanted him to look after Alainea when she was gone.

Although he wasn't sure how he could fulfill that request, seeing how they were from two different worlds, he knew what his heart urged him to say. He would keep the oath as best he could. He wasn't sure where a dragon's ears might be, but Charles leaned close to her face, knowing she would hear and understand when he whispered.

"I will."

He climbed onto a boulder, in order to allow Alainea and Dranich their final moments together, and dropped down to sit and stare at the mountain. The hidden doorway was up there somewhere, but it was undetectable now. He squinted at the rock face. Walking through that door marked the final step toward exiting this world and entering his own.

He did not see Dranich draw her final breath. Yet, he knew when it happened since Alainea's shuddering wail echoed about the mountains.

His heart reached out to her in this tragic moment. He placed a steadying hand on the rock beside him and revolved on the rocky perch to stand.

Alainea had pushed herself away from the dragon, her

arms lifted to the heavens with tears streaming down her face. She made not another sound, but raised her face to watch with reverence as Dranich slowly transformed.

It was as though the quiet breeze that had ruffled Charles' hair since they landed, began to gust from all four corners of the land, converging above the body of the great dragon, Dranich. As the winds met, they formed a vortex that grew in strength and intensity until it began to sweep every loose branch and blade of grass unto itself.

As Charles watched, the body of the legendary dragon began to fragment, returning to the dust from which all beings, plant or animal, are formed. The tiny pieces twinkled on the breeze like brightly coloured stars. They continued swirling, particle by particle, up to meet with the whirlwind overhead until it was a churning mass of light that billowed up to a dizzying height too high for the human eye to see. Then, the winds died. The particles drifted lower in the sky, and were carried away on the wind to each of the far ends of Erinbourne.

Alainea sat for a long while with her head bowed. Charles waited for her with chin in hands and eyes downcast, feeling as though what he had witnessed was the most beautiful ceremony he'd ever seen. Finally, she turned to look at him.

Jumping from boulder to boulder, Charles landed beside Alainea and helped her to stand before pulling her into his arms. She leaned against him, laying her head on his chest. Her tired arms hung at her sides. Alainea's tears were spent, and so was her strength. She sagged and would have collapsed if Charles had not steadied her.

"Dranich and I have been together, secretly, since I was five," she said. "But she is with the Creator now. So much loss. So many loved ones dead for such a foolish purpose."

The sound of rock grating on rock interrupted them and Charles looked up. One of the huge rocks above them on a ledge was slowly rolling aside. The small figure of a brightly clothed man peered around the edge. He wore a floppy blue hat with wide brim, and a long trailing suit of the same colour fluttered about his ankles. In his hand was a long gray staff.

"Durgot," Alainea breathed. A sob caught in her throat. She pulled back a little, to acknowledge the tiny personage. Charles, scooping Alainea up, picked his way toward the gap. There were a few stumbles over rocks, but he took his time and chose each step carefully.

The little man, silhouetted at the opening, waited for them. This must be the gatekeeper.

When they stood before Durgot, Charles set Alainea down and, being a tall woman, she bent nearly double to hug the little man. When she straightened, holding Charles' arm for support, he awaited his introduction.

"Greetings," Durgot said, bowing so low his beard scuffed the rock at his feet. "We meet in the midst of a most melancholy circumstance, young man, but I am gratified to make your acquaintance nonetheless."

He doffed his hat in a sweeping gesture of welcome.

Charles found himself doing the same. He'd never experienced so much formality in his life as he had in Erinbourne, nor heard so many long words in one sentence. It was old-fashioned and a bit difficult to follow, but he knew he had an instant liking for this fellow.

"Hello," he replied. "I'm very glad to meet you, Mr. Flandish."

Durgot used the floppy brim of his hat to wipe away a few tears that had worked their way into his lengthy gray beard. He gave Charles a tremulous smile. It was a meeting made difficult by the awful circumstances of their arrival. And they still didn't know for sure what had happened in their wake. Had Respiele been defeated? Or had he located the Amethyst, despite their efforts, and rallied his troops to destroy the king? Was Talbot alright? And King Ludwig?

Sadly, he knew the answer to one of his questions. Every last dragon in Erinbourne had been killed.

"The name is Durgot," the man said, replacing the hat on his head. "I do not hold with formality between comrades, and you, young sir, are henceforth, unequivocally, a comrade."

Charles' head was spinning.

"Durgot, I wonder if you might just take us inside," Alainea said, her voice tired and raw from crying. "Your vocabulary is too much for us common folk to tackle after a hard night. Please, I need to lie down and Charles has carried me far too long already."

"Apologies, my dear!" Durgot leaped aside and ushered them inside the narrow opening. "Follow me."

Charles picked up Alainea and stepped into the chamber. Durgot paused to trigger a mechanism that closed the door with a resounding crash. Then, holding his staff before him, he hurried ahead, calling back to them over his shoulder. The staff seemed to be more of a strange lantern than a walking stick since the tip of it radiated light into the dark stone chamber,

"I shall endeavor to speak in simpler terms," he said in a remorseful voice. "You must follow me closely and mind the uneven floor. It is not far to the Enchanted River and then Alainea may lie down in the boat."

He swung toward them and added, "Under no circumstance must you allow even a drop of the Enchanted River to touch your skin. It has disastrous results."

Although Charles eyed the water suspiciously after this dire warning, he didn't question it.

True to his word, the river he'd spoken of was not far, and a small, flat-bottomed craft lay on the rocky bank beside the rushing black water. Charles gently deposited Alainea inside of it and waited while Durgot arranged a light blanket over her legs. She closed her eyes.

"Broken, is it?" he asked, pointing at Alainea's bandaged foot. "And her arm?"

"The ankle is broken, yes," Charles said. He lowered his voice to a whisper. "And her arm was grazed by an arrow last night."

Durgot gave him a reassuring nod. "All will be well once we reach the house and reunite her with Elspeth. She awaits her daughter's arrival most anxiously. We have been worried about all of you."

Durgot held the boat and motioned that Charles should wedge himself inside. Then, Durgot slid into the prow and released his grip on the rocky bank.

The waters lapped at the sides of their craft and gurgled noisily as they were borne swift and sure to the middle of the stream and sped into the gloomy underbelly of the mountain. The yellowish light from Durgot's staff cast eerie shadows on the rough walls of the cave. Soon, their small boat approached a low shelf of rock with little distance to spare for the boat, let alone its passengers. Durgot instructed Charles to lie as flat as possible. After they passed beneath the shelf, they bobbed along for some time without saying a word. Charles would have liked to ask a multitude of questions, but Durgot raised a finger to his lips and pointed to Alainea who had fallen asleep with the rocking motion of the waves.

They shot out from under another stone shelf and into a

wide open space that reared into the darkness over Charles' head. Durgot produced his long staff and slid it into the murky water to send them scudding over to bump against the inside bank. He grabbed a short rope that was secured to the rock with a spike and held them steady.

Without a word, Charles clambered out and then got down on his knees to lift the still slumbering Alainea into his arms. He warily shuffled away from the water before standing. Durgot fished the boat out of the stream, being careful to avoid any drips, and laid it along the bank to dry.

Navigating the complicated staircase to the upper level was tricky, but together he and Durgot hoisted her up each step.

All three of them stood at the massive doorway to Durgot's domain. From a belt around his waist, Durgot withdrew a large, intricate key and fitted it into an ancient-looking lock. With a snap and a click, it sprang open and Durgot pulled the door wide to reveal the homeland of the Southern Garde.

Chapter Sixteen

Elspeth stood on the other side of the great door, hopping from one foot to the other in anticipation of their arrival. Alainea had awoken and Charles gently set her down to greet her mother. The two women embraced, but as they pulled away, Elspeth held her daughter at arms-length and studied her face.

"She needs medical attention," Elspeth said. A frown of concern furrowed her brow. "We must get her inside at once."

Once inside, Alainea collapsed onto a chair at Durgot's kitchen table. Her face was drawn with pain as first the wound on her shoulder was cleaned and a bright orange salve applied, and then her ankle was inspected and re-bandaged by her mother's tender, loving hands.

As Alainea's injuries were attended to, Charles and Durgot sat down with them. Charles filled the others in on all that had happened the night before. Elspeth looked at him with glowing eyes when he came to the part where

Alainea had shot the kiloden to destroy Respiele's chances of winning the battle, but caught her breath in a gasp when he spoke of how their foe had turned his wrath upon his own kin.

"That vile man!" Elspeth, who stood at Alainea's side reached up to caress her daughter's cheek.

Charles couldn't have agreed more, but further discussion was halted when Alainea begged to retreat to one of Durgot's bedrooms for a rest. Charles stood to assist her, but she waved his help away. Instead she hopped the length of Durgot's hallway to lie down while leaning on Elspeth's arm.

Charles looked after her, concern furrowing his brow as she disappeared around a corner.

"She will mend," Durgot said quietly, following Charles' gaze.

Durgot took off his hat and hung it by the door along with his coat, and Charles looked around the kitchen for the first time. It was painted cherry red and filled with plants, but his gaze was drawn to a huge triangular set of clocks on Durgot's wall. One of them chimed, making a loud tinkling sound unlike any clock Charles had ever heard. He stared at them, wondering what they were for as Durgot walked to his cupboard and withdrew a covered tin box, two glasses, and a pitcher containing a dark brown liquid. He beckoned Charles to follow him and set off along another short passage.

Charles ducked under an archway where long trailing ferns hung low and into a sitting room. Durgot motioned to a seat and placed the tin with the other items on a low table between them. Then, he sat himself in a plush, green armchair by one of several long windows that ran from ceiling to floor of his spindly red house. Wooden shutters had been flung aside and sunlight shone through the opening, causing Durgot's graying hair to shine like silver. A fat bumble bee droned in one window, took a turn about the room, and zoomed out another.

Durgot sighed and poured each of them a drink before prying the lid off the tin box. Inside were a selection of brightly coloured, iced cakes.

"Thank you," Charles said, picking up a glass and lifting it to his mouth. The drink was creamy and chocolaty like what he might have had at home.

Durgot popped a cake into his mouth and reclined comfortably with his legs stuck straight out in front of him. Charles found himself wondering why the man had such large chairs when he himself was so small.

"Her recovery will take time of course," Durgot said, brushing crumbs from his blue waistcoat. "Thankfully, there is plenty of that here."

He reached for a pink cupcake and took a bite. It was almond flavored and delicious. He swallowed and looked at Durgot.

"Respiele wants her dead," Charles said in a flat voice. He hadn't meant to disclose that information. He had thought perhaps it wasn't his to reveal, but he was worried that Alainea never would, or that she had some crazy idea of how she could remove herself from everyone she cared about in order to keep them from harm.

"Ah," was all that Durgot said. He bit into his cake and chewed. Then, without meeting Charles' eyes, he asked, "Was it his arrow that scored her arm?"

"Yes. Is that worse than any other?" Charles felt his face go hot as fear pulsated within his chest.

"It…well, it is not good news, but I am sure she will

be fine." Durgot drummed the arms of his chair in anxious rhythm, sounding as though he was trying to convince himself as much as Charles. "I expected Respiele would wish to make an example of Alainea, but still, I had hoped he would not sink that far. She *is* his daughter."

Durgot gripped the chair with sudden anger. "The young Respiele I once knew no longer exists."

There was profound sadness in Durgot's tone, and he looked as though it were an effort not to say more. He shook his head and stared out the window.

Charles pushed himself further back into his matching chair and looked around the room as he waited for Durgot to explain further. It was an interesting place. The whole house was, for that matter. Much the same as Magda's home, it was filled with plants. Although Durgot leaned more towards ones with huge red and purple flowers, and trailing ferns, than vines. Also, these plants didn't crawl up every available inch of space inside the rooms. A few were hanging from the ceiling, but most lived on the floor in pots filled with soil, like normal vegetation.

Durgot's walls were lined with shelves of books. Charles twisted his head to read a few of the titles. Only they didn't seem to be written in English, so he gave up and reached for another cake.

"Respiele and Ludwig were as close as two brothers ever could be, once." Durgot leaned forward with a smile on his face. "Unfortunately, they quarreled. As I have reflected on it over the years, I believe the gemstones were having a negative effect upon the younger Larkender brother even then."

Durgot fixed Charles with piercing amber eyes. "Erinbourne's Gemstones of Power have the capability to do so, you see. Only a person of purest heart and intention may carry them. Any other would be corrupted."

He took another sip of tea.

"In any case, Respiele left Larkender Castle an embittered man and vowed to overthrow his brother, King Ludwig, and wrest the throne from him by force."

"He had some sort of purple rock." Charles leaned forward too, understanding flooding his mind. "Respiele took it from the king, right? It was the Amethyst, from the sceptre that was dropped into my world."

"Respiele stole that gem from Ludwig the day he left the castle. I am not sure why he did not take the sceptre itself. Perhaps he felt it would be noticed sooner and his escape foiled. In any case, that one gemstone has been his undoing. He was not fit to carry the Amethyst and the enchantment of it has perverted his mind." Durgot sighed deeply. "However, he is able to use a warped form of its magic to empower him, which makes the man all the more dangerous."

"But somehow, a few days ago, Respiele found out that King Ludwig was coming, and sent his dragon riders to fight with him near here, right? That's when they thought they'd killed him and they took the sceptre."

"Yes. There was a great battle just the other side of my Ildune Mountains. Ludwig had journeyed, after all these years, to see his brother in hopes of reconciliation. It was a vain hope, and imprudent of him to bring the sceptre on such a fool's errand. He had no idea of the depths to which Respiele had sunk."

Durgot grimaced. "It all took place high in the air over the mountains. There was a deadly clash between the dragons. Two of Respiele's coerced dragons and their riders, against the king. During the conflict, the rider who had snatched the sceptre collided with the barrier between our worlds and crashed through. Nothing has ever happened like that before, and hopefully never will again."

Charles could imagine it all now since he'd been in Erinbourne for a while. His thoughts went back to his present concern. "But Alainea will not stay here, Durgot. She believes Respiele will hunt her down wherever she is, and kill those whom she loves as well as herself. I'm afraid she will try to go off somewhere alone...to a place where she has no one to stand with her, in order to sacrifice herself."

Durgot scrubbed at his beard. Crumbs trickled to the floor from the silvery curls where they had been imprisoned.

"Yes, I see. Well," he said, hopping to the floor, "you will know best how to help her, I am sure."

With that cryptic statement, Durgot grabbed Charles' empty cup from where he'd set it on the table and went to fetch more tea.

Charles sighed. How was *he* supposed to figure this out? He had to get back home. He had no knowledge of how things worked in Erinbourne, or how to keep Alainea from harm. She was the warrior, not him. All he knew was that he was concerned for her. He ran a hand through his hair that already stood on end and leaned back in his chair with a yawn. It had been a long night. Actually a long few *days*, truth be told.

He wanted to ask a few of the questions that had been floating in his brain. Of course, there were some subjects either too painful or too grand to ask about now, such as where Dranich had gone, who the Creator was, how Erinbourne had come to be in the first place, and what would happen now that the dragons were all dead. However, he was too tired to voice them. His head drooped and his eyes closed despite efforts to keep them open.

Charles opened his eyes and stared at a stark white ceiling. Where was he? He rolled his head on the pillow to follow the sunlight that streamed through several circular windows to his right. A breeze fluttered the foliage of the large ferns hanging over his head. He jumped back in alarm as a few of the long tendrils brushed across his face. That must have been what had woken him.

Reality rushed over him in a flood. He was in Durgot's house, but how had he gotten into a comfortable bed? He didn't remember anything after sitting in the chair. Had Durgot carried him upstairs? That little guy?

Charles shook his head in disbelief and climbed out from under the blankets to stretch. Cracking his head on the sloping ceiling woke him up further and he rubbed his head before he bent. He got down on his hands and knees and crept closer to one of the windows to peer outside. Like the windows in the main part of the house, there was no glass, and he poked his head right out the hole to gaze at his surroundings.

It was an amazing sight. He hadn't really noticed everything yesterday when they'd arrived. He'd been too consumed with grief and concern over Alainea to look at things. Now, as he took in the space that surrounded Durgot's home, he realized it was an open area carved at the very center of the mountain. At the far edge of lush, planted fields, the outer rock of the Ildune Mountain reared up to meet overhead.

It looked like a market garden coupled with the finest

orchard Charles had ever seen. Row upon row of fruit trees led away from Durgot's door below, and in another area, patches of vegetables grew high. A stream splashed along the face of the mountain far into the distance. Although they appeared to be hemmed in on every side with rock, the sun shone bright. It was amazing and Charles promptly added another question to his list.

How was this lush area of life possible inside a mountain?

"Charles!" Durgot shouted from the other side of the door, and Charles looked up sharply, cracking his head again. "Your presence is required in the sitting room. Immediately!"

Now what was the matter? He scrambled away from the window, grabbed the boots he'd been wearing before someone had kindly removed them and set them by his bed, and hurried down the long flight of stairs outside his bedroom door.

He knew something was wrong with Alainea as soon as he entered the room. Neither she nor Elspeth were anywhere to be seen, but Durgot rushed to him.

"She is fevered and delirious," Durgot said, wringing his hands. "It is sorry I am to tell you, young sir, but I believe Respiele's bronze arrows harbor a venom that is deadly even in small doses. If it had done more than graze her arm, she would have passed from us already. As it is, we may still be too late."

Durgot's amber eyes filled with tears.

Charles felt the blood drain from his face.

"I need to see her," he said, turning blindly to look for the hallway where Alainea had disappeared the day before.

"Wait." Durgot trotted beside him and tugged at his sleeve. "You need to know during the night I sent for the only cure that can save her now. Hold faith in your heart that Talbot may be found and the remedy be brought in time."

"Talbot?" Charles stopped despite his urgency, but Durgot trotted past him, leading the way to Alainea's room.

Charles hung back, partly from fear at what he might see, and partly to plead fervently with the Creator of this world, asking that Alainea be spared.

In those few short moments, he accepted that he loved her.

It hadn't taken months of dating, like friends of his had done when they went out to movies, shared dinners, or did any of the other host of things couples did to learn whether they were compatible. No, it had taken less than one week to develop these feelings in his heart. One glorious week in which he had learned so much about this loyal, fearless woman who was willing to give up her life for those she loved. He was in awe of her. Charles prayed he would have the opportunity to tell her.

He entered her room. His eyes flew to the bed where she tossed. A colourful patchwork comforter covered her and shook with the force of her shivering.

Elspeth sat on a plain wooden chair at her head, wringing a cloth into a basin of water and placing it on Alainea's forehead. The woman looked up as Charles entered. She had been weeping. She reached out a hand to him, and Charles strode forward to grip it.

Alainea's countenance was gray in colour, and Charles clamped his teeth together to keep from exclaiming in shock. Her lips were parted, her breath ragged and sporadic, and even though her eyes were closed, she moaned as if seeing sights that terrified her. She flung her arms to and fro with the restless rolling of her head.

Charles dragged another chair over to sit beside Elspeth. Alainea's injured arm had swollen to twice its normal size. The flesh was engorged and red with thick cords of purple veins running angrily up and down it.

On a table at the other side of the room, Durgot was preparing a fresh bowl of the orange concoction he'd applied to her wound the day before. Then, after filling another basin with steaming water from a pitcher he'd brought from the kitchen and laying clean bandages on a table beside her, Durgot and Elspeth administered first aid to the gash again. Alainea fought them. Delirious, in a world of her own suffering, she pushed them away, mumbling incoherently. Yet, the deed was done to the best of their ability and Durgot took the soiled linens away.

"I'll sit with her for a while if you'd like a break," Charles said to Elspeth as she made to take up her vigil again.

"Thank you, lad," she replied, brushing the straggling hair from her tired eyes. "I shall be in the kitchen. One call from you will bring me running."

She managed a tremulous smile for him and tiptoed from the room.

Charles smoothed the bedding near his knee after Elspeth had gone.

"You're going to be okay," he said with a catch in his throat. He pulled out Elspeth's chair and seated himself. He leaned close to Alainea's ear and whispered, "Fight as you've never fought before, Alainea. I—I love you."

His presence beside her, or the words he spoke, made no difference in her anguished moans or in the fever that raged through her body.

Charles, Durgot, and Elspeth sat beside her much of that day with only brief minutes spared for themselves to stretch or get a drink. Durgot had his duties as gatekeeper to attend to, so he was gone longest.

That evening, Charles sat alone with her, staring sightlessly at the floor, head in hands, and reliving moments of the past week.

Alainea cried out and sat straight up. Her good arm thrashed at the air as though holding her trusty sword. The other arm swung lifelessly at her side. Charles looked at it closely, noticing with horror that the swelling and angry redness had spread. It had seeped up her neck, puffing her skin as it went, and appearing to place a stranglehold on her throat. Her veins popped out a livid purple in her face and her back arched with a sudden stiffening as her spine contracted.

Charles leaped to his feet, calling out for Elspeth as he did, and caught Alainea in his arms as she crumpled and lay still. He laid her back on the pillow, fear scratching at his heart. From the worried looks Durgot and Elspeth had shared, he knew Alainea's situation was worsening. He only had to look at her to see it now. Her mouth was open as she gasped for air and the livid purple threads moved like living beings across her face. She was losing the struggle for her life.

"Hang on," Charles said, gently pushing the hair from her brow as Elspeth rushed into the room followed by Durgot.

Charles tore himself away from the one person he cared about most in this world and rushed blindly from the room. He couldn't stay and watch. The feelings of helplessness were too much to bear. Dashing into Durgot's kitchen, he flung himself from one end of the room to the other, pacing back and forth, his mind lost in the agony of thought. He couldn't go on without her.

A bell clanged, the noise issuing from one of the clocks and running footsteps came from the hallway.

Durgot dashed into the room, his face as white as the beard on his chin. He skidded to a stop to stare at the time-piece that took up the whole of one wall. Charles had watched Durgot consulting the set of clocks every time he'd been in the kitchen and figured they must have something to do with his work as gatekeeper. Now, the dials on one of them spun crazily

"He has come!" Without another word, Durgot turned and flew down the hallway leading to his front door.

Charles was left standing there, a kernel of hope growing in his chest. He raced after Durgot and pulled the already open door a little wider to peer out. The man's feet had barely touched the long flight of stairs leading up to the entrance of his home and now he was running toward the southern gate, a ring of keys jangling in his hand.

Someone was here. Was it Talbot?

Charles left the door as it was and ran back to Alainea's room. Elspeth turned as he entered; her eyes huge as she stood near her daughter's writhing form. Alainea's head rolled to and fro as she struggled to fight a losing battle for oxygen. The poison was sealing off her larynx.

Charles reeled back in horror. Alainea had kicked off the covers. Her legs were the colour of rust and had swollen to twice their normal size. Her back arched with each strain to draw breath. But the breaths were coming few and far between now.

"Durgot has gone to meet someone at the front gate," he said, meeting Elspeth's gaze. "Do you think it's…?"

Alainea made a gurgling sound and fell back. Charles rushed to her side. Her eyes were wide and staring in her grossly misshapen face. They flickered toward him in a second of lucidity, but then closed as the choking sound ceased. Her body went slack.

Elspeth wailed and fell to her knees at Alainea's bedside.

"No, please no," Elspeth cried. She clasped Alainea's engorged face between her hands and wept.

The door to the room slammed back on its hinges. A massive, bristling figure swept into the room, its face as black as thunder.

Talbot.

Something green and sparkling flashed in his paw. Talbot rushed to Alainea's side and placed it on her chest, over her heart. Then he stepped back, and everyone watched as the Emerald, one of the Gemstones of Power went to work.

A humming sound filled the room as the shining gemstone vibrated with such intensity that it rose a few centimetres in the air over Alainea. The emerald began to revolve. It whirled at a speed so great that it became a green blur sending sparks of energy shooting across the room like tiny, fizzling firecrackers.

Durgot had entered the room behind Talbot, and all four of them stood around her bed, rooted to the spot.

Had the Emerald arrived too late? Charles held his breath.

Then, Alainea moved. This time, however, it was not the frantic actions of a person fighting a foe that attacked from within. No, it was the restless movement of one who has slept for far too long and wakes, knowing it was time to arise and greet a new day.

Alainea opened her eyes halfway and her eyes focused. The livid purple streaks of poison were already receding and the redness had faded, but most of the swelling remained.

Elspeth sobbed over her daughter anew, but this time for joy. Durgot turned to hug Talbot, but then veered away at the last moment, eyeing the enormous hedgehog's long spines, and grasped Charles around his middle instead. Charles laughed and hugged him back.

Alainea would live. Then realization hit him like a sucker punch to the stomach—and he would have to go home.

Chapter Seventeen

Charles stayed three more days, until he was sure Alainea was fully mended, before he even spoke of returning to Canada. It was with gratitude he learned afterward that the Emerald had not only saved Alainea's life, but it had healed her broken ankle too.

The two of them spent idyllic afternoons wandering in the gardens within Durgot's domain, and sitting to talk beside a waterfall that spilled into a crystal pool near the orchard. Alainea, of course, was a more subdued woman than she had been prior to losing Dranich, but she bore her grief well and spoke of her beloved dragon often.

After all they had been through together, they now held hands as they walked, but for all that Charles was unsure whether she felt as strongly about him as he did for her. It was a subject they didn't discuss. Nor did they talk about his leaving, or if they'd ever see one another again. This left him dreading the moment he'd have to say goodbye. He knew he should be getting back home to his parents, but how could he leave her?

Charles had met many more of the Garde people who lived in the Ildune Mountain too. They were all small folk who appeared quietly and without fanfare to work in the fields every day. Elspeth was acquainted with many of them who had been displaced from the Araleesh when Respiele drove the Garde from their homes.

He and Alainea were meandering along a well-worn trail, gathering a basket of fruit for their dinner and almost to the house, when Talbot beckoned to them from the deck that ran around Durgot's thin, red dwelling.

That was a surprise. Talbot had left soon after rushing in to save Alainea and hadn't been seen since. He must have returned with news of the outside world. The hedgehog disappeared inside.

Charles pulled Alainea to a stop before they reached the stairs. He set the basket of fruit he carried on the path and caught both her hands in his.

"I want to talk to you before we go in," he said.

"Alright." She looked at him with a quizzical smile and plopped down on the bottom step, pulling her hands away to straighten her hair. She drew her knees up to her chest and rested her chin on them before sighing with contentment. "It's so peaceful here. I wish I could stay."

Charles had been about to tell her he had to leave the next morning, among other things, but her words arrested his thoughts.

"What do you mean? You're not still thinking you have to run away, are you?" He sat beside her and bent to look into her eyes. "You can't be! That's suicide."

Alainea lifted her head and set her jaw at a defiant angle.

"I must," she said. "I cannot endanger all of the Garde who live here, knowing that Respiele will not rest until he has finished the job he set out to do. We both know he wants me dead and has been thwarted again."

She reached for the basket of ruby red apples and chose one. "There is nothing more to say."

She crunched into the juicy fruit.

"I have a better idea." Charles braced one foot on the step beside her, bent, and took the apple from her hand with a grin, before biting into it himself.

"Hey!" Alainea jumped to her feet with a laugh and Charles held the apple over his head where she couldn't reach.

A loud, irritated chirping interrupted their banter and they stopped to see Talbot standing on his hind legs above them on the staircase.

"He says he called us for a purpose," Alainea translated.

A chill ran up Charles spine. What was it this time? Without another word, he picked up the basket and the two of them sprinted up the steps to enter Durgot's home.

They burst into the kitchen where Durgot, Elspeth, and Talbot awaited them with grave faces. Alainea pulled out a chair and flung herself into it, breathing heavily. Her close call with death had taken a toll on her body and she was still recovering. Charles edged up to the table, worried about what he was about to hear.

"Sit, lad," Durgot said, gesturing to a tall stool that stood beneath the wall of strange looking clocks.

Charles carried it over and when he was seated, Talbot, who was sitting on the table in his smaller form, began to speak while Durgot translated for Charles.

"You do not know what transpired that night of the battle before you, Alainea and Dranich arrived." Talbot crossed his paws in front of him and closed his eyes as if in remembrance. "We were losing the war, as you saw, and

King Ludwig's army was on the verge of defeat. If not for the quick actions of Dranich and yourselves there would have been no victory. The king is much indebted to you all."

Talbot paused for Durgot to catch up, and he peered around the table, nodding thanks to each one.

"Respiele escaped once the effects of the Amethyst were removed from the equation, but his forces are depleted and he cannot be as cocky as he once was. Unfortunately, the Amethyst was not found and we fear Respiele secured it for himself once again. However, the king has made one request of the young man who travelled from another universe to assist the land of Erinbourne."

Charles leaned forward, almost falling from his perch. The king wanted a favour—from him?

"Of course," Charles said in surprise. "Naturally, I would help him."

Talbot gestured to a blue velvet bag that lay unnoticed on the table beside him. It was about the size of Charles' hand and tied around the top with a golden drawstring.

"King Ludwig wishes you to take the Emerald back to your world for safekeeping until such time as Erinbourne needs it again." Talbot waited for his words to sink in and then continued. "Erinbourne's Gemstones of Power have caused quite enough trouble of late and we feel it would be best to separate them for a time. As they have no effect whatsoever on you, we must ask if you would be willing."

Talbot fixed Charles with a piercing stare.

"I—I would be honoured." Charles slid from the stool as though he were about to be knighted and inclined his head. Then, as relieved smiles appeared around the gathering, he cleared his throat to also speak.

"I have something I wish to say as well," he said. He looked from one face to the other and his heart filled. "I was completely unprepared for what happened to me these last few days, in more ways than one. I was brought here against my will and wanted nothing more than to get home and away from this crazy place."

He glanced around, thinking perhaps he'd offended someone with his description choice, but they appeared fine so he continued. "I was carried through a portal into a world I didn't know existed, hanging from the claws of a dragon. I was chained in a dungeon, shot at, threatened, kicked, and hunted like a criminal."

He turned a beaming smile on them all. "But I also met the best people I've ever known. I've broken out of prison with the help of a beautiful girl and a friendly rat. I rode on a dragon, the most magnificent creature that ever lived. I've talked with animals, experienced magic, and—" He stopped short and felt his face flush red with a mixture of hope and embarrassment. "I've fallen in love."

Elspeth gasped as Charles crossed to where Alainea sat, knelt before her, and took her hands in his own.

"I don't know how this sort of thing is done here, but in my world when a man asks for a lady's hand in marriage, he gets down on one knee."

Alainea's eyes grew large. She sucked in a breath and held it.

"I've never known anyone like you, Alainea Ilstyne. You're strong, courageous, and brave, yet you have the softest heart of anyone I've ever known. I admire and respect you and offer you a lifetime of happiness, with me. We could both go back to my world and be married. You'd be safe there," he added, as though trying to sweeten the offer in any way he could.

"You wanted somewhere to hide from Respiele that wouldn't endanger your family and friends in Erinbourne, right? Well, I'm offering it to you with a heart full of love. Will you marry me?"

Alainea squeezed his hands and brought them up to her cheeks. A tear trickled through his fingers as their eyes met and she nodded.

"Yes, Charles. I will marry you."

***

There was much celebration and congratulations, but Durgot slipped away. When he returned, he brought with him a long, gray staff etched with runes from top to bottom. It was similar to the one he carried himself, but this one bore the initials AI.

"This is a Runestaff," he told Charles and Alainea as they stood in his kitchen. "It is my gift to you, Alainea. A Runestaff will only respond to the people of the Garde. Take it with you and keep it from harm, for it is the only way to open the portal from the other side."

Alainea accepted the staff tentatively at first. With light fingers, she stroked the wood, feeling the runes beneath her hand, then looked at Durgot's face wreathed in smiles. She gripped the staff in both of her hands and lifted it up to examine the beautiful carvings.

"Th-thank you, Durgot," she said. Her voice cracked with emotion. "You have done so much for me and for my dear mother. Yet I must ask you to do one more thing."

She pushed a stray hair from her face.

Durgot stroked his beard and raised his eyebrows as though he knew what she would ask before she uttered the words. Alainea stepped to Elspeth and slid her arm around the older woman's shoulders.

"Will you protect my mother until I return?"

Durgot chuckled, and Elspeth smiled back at him.

"Indeed, I shall," he said. "And not just I. There are a host of Garde here who will be more than pleased to take her in and ensure her safety."

When Charles left for home the next day, Alainea was at his side. Durgot, Talbot, and Elspeth accompanied them through the great door and across the Enchanted River. Together they wound their way along the narrow chiseled pathway leading to the small chamber that marked the portal between their worlds.

Alainea and Charles hugged Durgot and with great ceremony, shook the tiny paw that Talbot extended to each of them in turn. Charles then turned to the woman who would be his mother-in-law and wrapped her in his arms.

"Thank you for trusting Alainea with me," he whispered into her ear. "I promise to cherish her always."

Elspeth took his face in her hands and kissed his cheeks.

"I know you will," she whispered back, her eyes kindling with warmth.

Then it was time for Alainea to part from her mother. They clung together, their mingled tears splashing onto the rock beneath their feet.

"Come back to me one day," Elspeth said. She clung to Alainea's hands until the last moment and then reluctantly let go.

Finally, Durgot raised his Runestaff. Where the image of a sun on the staff had lighted their way along the darkened passage, now the image of a mountain lit up under Durgot's hand. The light blazed a brilliant white and soon every rune on the staff flashed with a silver flame. Durgot lifted the Runestaff over his head and thrust it into a notch in the rock beside him.

There was an answering rumble of sound like thunder

and a sliver of lightning split the rock in two. With a mighty crack, the sides were forced apart and in the blazing breach, Charles could see the fields of home.

"Now!" Durgot hollered.

Alainea reached for Charles and tugged at his hand. Though tears glittered on her eyelashes, she smiled at him. And so, with his heart feeling as though it might burst with happiness, he stepped through the fissure beside the woman he would spend the rest of his life with. They had only a moment to turn and lift a hand of farewell to those they loved in the land of Erinbourne before the portal slammed shut.

It was like the dream he'd had, except the ending was much better.

"Come on," Alainea said.

She vaulted onto a boulder, rapped her Runestaff down onto the rock as though she were claiming uncharted lands, and threw her arms into the air. Flinging back her head, she used her one free hand to shake free the long auburn hair she always kept in a braid. The wind rushed down the Rocky Mountains and lifted it up to stream behind her.

Conscious of the Emerald, and his responsibility to the people who had entrusted it to him, Charles secured the precious velvet bag in his pocket before he leaped up beside her. Then together they looked out upon the world they would conquer together.

It would not always be easy, but it was their own humble beginning.

Chapter Eighteen

Kayden laid the last sheet of paper of his manuscript on the pile in front of him and stared with misty eyes at the dying embers of his fire. He hoped he had done justice to the story of his grandparents and written a true account of the events that took place long before he was born.

His grandfather's memoirs had been detailed, and there'd been a few revelations in them. He knew at least some of the story would come as a shock to his grandmother when she read the book. Mainly the part about the other dragon eggs, even though she knew there had been at least one that had escaped detection.

It was about time Alainea returned to her homeland. After Malahd had been defeated, and he and Rosalyn were married, he'd spent time travelling throughout the land of Erinbourne. It was then that he had met his great-grandmother, Elspeth. No one had told him she was still alive before that. Thanks to the way time moved in this land, she had not aged much, but Alainea had never been back. He would insist that Gran return with him next time he was in

Canada. At least for a visit. She always vowed it would be too painful for her to return, but it had been long enough.

Charles rose, picked up the manuscript, and hurried to his desk. He set the pages inside the drawer to keep them from harm. Then, he walked back to the fire and poked it to liven up the coals before he threw on several logs. He shivered and rubbed his hands together. Hours had gone by since he'd seated himself to read and the room had grown cold.

Raised voices once again caught his attention from outside the thick stone walls of the castle. Evening cast long shadows through the heavy glass of the windows. Kayden wondered what turmoil was taking place outside. He'd better check into it now.

Turning on his heel, he snatched his cloak off a hook by the door and yanked open the door of his study. As he took the wooden stairs two at a time, a woman screamed and children began to cry. He quickened his steps as Alandrial roared. The sound of it echoed off the walls, closely followed by yelling and the noise of huge wings beating the air.

Kayden flung open the huge double doors that were the front entrance to Larkender Castle and rushed outside. The courtyard was chaos. Talbot was there, in his large form, running back and forth in an attempt to calm the people who had gathered outside. Alandrial was perched on one of the tallest turrets of the outer wall of defense, his mouth wide and screaming a warning into the dusky sky.

Rosalyn appeared at the door clutching a sword in her hand. She ran up to Kayden and clutched his arm.

"What is happening?" Her eyes were wide and fearful.

Alandrial screeched again. Pivoting at the same time, Rosalyn and Kayden looked heavenward.

Kayden reeled back a step, his mouth falling open at the sight.

Rosalyn narrowed her eyes to slits as she stepped forward with Kayden to meet this new threat to the peace and tranquility of Erinbourne. How could it be? Kayden blinked, not believing what he saw. Was it a dream? An attack? Or a homecoming?

Rising over the forest into the western sky loomed two massive shapes that blotted out what little sunlight still hung there. Then, as the people shrieked in fear and scattered to make way for the invaders, two enormous dragons settled onto the grass beside the River Glee that ran beside Larkender Castle. The dragons swung their horny heads back and forth as if looking for something or someone. Throwing back their necks, they spewed jets of fire from their craggy jaws. Sparks rained down upon the frightened crowd.

Hissing and spluttering fire along with its words, one dragon spoke.

"Who is in charge of this world?"

More by Helen Row Toews

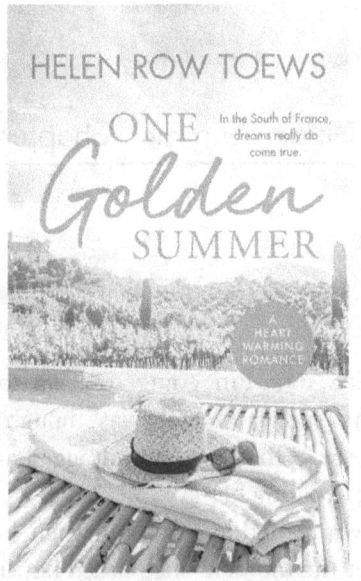

vinci-books.com/onegoldensummer

When fate whispers of second chances, Angelina Fisk finds herself swept away to the sun-drenched hills of France.

After a wrongful dismissal, Angelina finds herself chaperoning her love-struck cousin on a trip to France. As a guest at the chateau of the enigmatic billionaire Julien Belliveau, Angelina is determined to uncover his secrets while fighting her growing attraction.

Turn the page for a free preview…

One Golden Summer: Chapter One

"Sorry Angelina, but I'm going to have to let you go." Glenn Sudbury spoke forcefully, as though expecting an argument. He took off his cap and dragged an arm over his dripping brow, avoiding her eyes.

She'd known something was up when he had hurried out to meet her the moment she parked her truck in the lot. By the time she climbed out and locked it for the night, he was there. Now, they stood together in the gravel. Her, shading her eyes against the setting sun of a long day's work, and he, shifting uncomfortably from one foot to the other.

"Go?" she said. "Go where exactly?" Lifting her pony-tail of long black hair, she flipped it off her neck. It was hot and Angelina was tired. She swung her coat and lunch bag over to the other arm and tried to understand.

Glenn stared over her left shoulder as he replaced his hat and continued in a loud monotone that sounded rehearsed. "You've worked hard for this company over the last six years, and I appreciate it, but management has fielded several complaints about your driving this week," he shrugged and looked away. "You've become a liability I can't afford."

"A liability?" she repeated. It was finally sinking in. "You're firing me?" Her voice rose and she took an unsteady step back, shaking her head. The things she was carrying dropped to her feet, unheeded. "I've done my very best for this company and love my…" she began.

"Not firing—exactly," he interrupted in a strained voice. "But I've received reports that you've taken risks with a loaded truck and shown a disregard for traffic laws. This company has zero tolerance for that sort of thing and a clean accident record. I can't afford to lose it now." He was choosing to ignore her last remark. "Anyway, it's more like laying you off," he added.

Glenn's eyes flicked to meet hers, then slid away. He bent to pick up the items she'd dropped, shoved them into her arms and turned on his heel, signalling the end of their discussion. She stood in a stunned silence.

"You'll get two weeks' severance pay in the mail," he called back over his shoulder. "Clear out your truck and leave the keys on my desk." He crunched across the driveway to where other trucks were parked behind a chain-link fence and disappeared from view.

Angelina couldn't believe it. Shock rooted her to the spot. She'd been fired. Kicked out. Told to get her things and clear off. She shook her head again, trying to make sense of the absurdness of it all. But a voice inside her head told her it made perfect sense. And it had *nothing* to do with her driving.

Kenton. That snivelling little jerk! As she collected

herself and marched back to grab her sunglasses and extra sweater from the truck, she relived the last two weeks of work.

Kenton, the boss' son, had returned from university and lost no time in swaggering around his father's gravel hauling business like he owned the place. He was there each afternoon issuing heavy-handed orders to the office staff, riding along with the drivers to tell them how to do a job most of them had done for thirty years, and making a general nuisance of himself.

He was full of his own importance, looking to take over the family business with zero understanding of how to run it or treat employees with respect. To top it off, he was encouraged by a father who was blind to his son's faults. Angelina suspected it started when Glenn's wife had died, leaving him to raise the boy alone. Even now, the young man could do no wrong.

Still, apart from doing her best to avoid him, she'd thought nothing of it until she noticed him watching her with a predatory look that caused her to cringe. He was trouble. Twice he'd asked her for a date after a safety meeting, which she rebuffed with a smile.

"You're too young for me," she'd joked, sidling for the door. "Are you even twenty yet?" His father had overheard the exchange, she was sure of it. Yet the man had shot Angelina a look of annoyance. Had Glenn really expected her to accept the advances of a kid ten years younger than herself, just because of who he was?

However, her refusals didn't deter Kenton, they seemed to make him even more persistent. Then, one day, things had gotten worse. She grimaced in remembrance.

He'd climbed into the truck beside her, announcing he was coming along to 'assess her skill set.' She'd felt more than a prickle of alarm. But how could she refuse the boss' son when his father was standing behind him, grinning with pride like the Cheshire Cat? After all, her fears were nothing more than suspicions born of women's intuition. She resolved to ignore him and get on with her job.

She was carrying a heavy load of sand bound for a paving company outside of town and needed her wits about her. As she drove past city limits and began to gear up, he made his move.

"Angelina, baby, you have a body that could drive a man wild," Kenton crooned. Unbuckling his seatbelt, he slithered across the bench seat and slipped an arm around her shoulders.

"What do you think you're doing?" she ground out between gritted teeth. "Stay away from me Kenton, I'm not interested!"

"I think you're wrong. I've seen the signs…besides, I'm pretty irresistible. You and I could have a lot of fun together this summer, baby. Just think about it." He leaned in to nuzzle her ear. Angelina's throat constricted as a wave of cheap, nauseating cologne rolled past her nostrils. Keeping her eyes on the road, she used one arm to push him away.

"Kenton! No! I just want to do my job, okay? Get back to your side of the cab like a good boy."

"I say the attraction is mutual, you just don't know it yet." He pulled back for a moment and looked at her hungrily, like an animal eyeing its prey.

Angelina glanced at him with a scowl. His face was flushed and determined, his breathing rapid. He was almost salivating, for heaven's sake!

"I told you I'm *not* interested and I'm warning you to leave me alone."

Kenton didn't listen. His hands grasped for her again,

this time he touched her breast. Angelina's stomach churned with revulsion. She whacked his arm away while keeping her eyes on the road.

Braking suddenly, she felt the load of sand shift forward, and took a deep breath to calm herself lest she cause a problem with the truck. Then, Angelina geared down before cranking the wheel and sending them into a driveway that wasn't part of the route. She stopped and reversed out to head back the way she'd come.

Kenton slammed against his door with these unexpected moves, and then fell against the dash. "Where do ya think you're goin'?" he hollered. "You have a job to finish. And that wasn't safe." The hungry look was replaced with an angry one. He straightened and made a show of dusting himself off.

She remained grim and silent, focused on taking Kenton back to his father. The kid was going to cause an accident and she wouldn't risk it by putting up with his harassment.

"Fine," he yelled. "You take me back to the shop. I got something I need to tell my dad, *the boss*," he sneered. After that he was sullen and silent, sitting with his arms crossed and a foul look on his face.

When Angelina pulled through the gate and up to the office, he didn't even wait till she stopped. Kenton threw open the door and jumped to the ground before slamming it closed.

Good, she'd thought. She was furious with the little creep and only too glad to be rid of him, but that's when the complaints over her driving began. Glenn had called her into his office that night after work and explained that someone had called in to report she'd been involved in a near collision. Angelina knew exactly who had complained.

Though knowing her work ethic, she'd thought his father would have been too sensible to fall for it.

Apparently not.

Angelina came back to the present with a sigh. She stroked a hand along the dashboard of the truck that had been like her second home for the past six years. It felt as though she were leaving an old friend.

Sure, after high school she'd worked the sort of jobs that were what her parents had expected. She'd even spent three long years in business college, taking an office administration course, but it wasn't where her heart was. That year she'd spent working as an executive secretary in a law firm had left her feeling dry as dust. It just wasn't for her.

Angelina loved driving. The feeling of escaping four walls while the wind whistled past her face through an open window was exhilarating. She loved shifting through the gears and the thrill of knowing she could handle the large vehicles that were traditionally considered a man's domain. It was unconventional, but it was her.

Pulling her sunglasses off the dash, she took one last look to make sure she had everything. She slid out, slammed the door, and rushed to throw her things inside her own vehicle before heading into the office to toss the truck keys on Glenn's desk.

Emerging moments later, Angelina paused. A couple of the guys she worked with were striding toward her, concern written on their faces.

"Hey, tell me it's not true?" Garry, the first to reach her, bent down to search her face. "Glenn just told us this is your last day."

She shrugged. "It's true alright."

"It was Kenton, wasn't it? I overheard him talking about

you in an…unpleasant way." Mark, a grizzled man in his sixties, slammed a fist into his palm. "Do you want us to do something about it? We have no problem confronting Glenn and I'd take particular pleasure in chatting with Kenton." His face darkened with anger.

Garry nodded in agreement. "That boy needs a tune-up for sure." He turned to peer through the office door. "Is he in there? I'd like to have a *word* with him myself."

Angelina smiled with wobbly lips, blinking rapidly. "No. You guys are great, and I appreciate the offer, but that would only get you fired too. I couldn't stay here anyway. Not now."

She investigated the faces of these men who'd given her a hard time when she first started working for the company. 'A girl,' they'd said with a certain amount of contempt, 'pretending to drive a truck in a man's world.'

It hadn't been easy in the beginning, but she'd persevered, done her job, and done it well. She'd won their admiration and respect. It meant a lot to her, and she hated to leave this way. However, she didn't want to be around Kenton, and Glenn appeared blind to his son's flaws.

"It's okay, really it is," she said. Acting on impulse, she gave them both a hug. "You take care of yourselves and watch out for Kenton, he's dangerous." She flipped her ponytail behind her, took a deep breath, and forced herself to grin. "I'll be fine. Maybe a break is just what I need."

Angelina collapsed at the kitchen table in her apartment and bent to untie her steel-toed work boots. She kicked them aside. *Won't need those for a while.* A knife twisted in her chest as she wondered who would hire her now. She was worried that the supposed driving incidents she had, coupled with the false complaints, would follow her and mar her driving record whether they were true or not. Would Glenn do that to her? She didn't trust the man any longer.

It had taken a long time to even be hired at that company. She was a woman, had no previous work history, wasn't taken seriously in this world still dominated by men, and knew she didn't look the truck-driver part. Glenn had told her she looked too young and was far too inexperienced. Of course, wearing a red frilly dress and heels to that first interview had been a stupid idea. On top of all the other drawbacks, she'd looked too *pretty*. That wasn't conceit talking, she knew, it was just a fact.

However, she'd always taken pains with her appearance. Once she got the job, there wasn't any reason she should let herself go just because she drove trucks for a living. True, wearing makeup, a nice pair of jeans, blouse, and bright red lipstick every day earned her the mockery of the men she worked with. But in time they'd stopped whistling and teasing, and accepted her as a professional who knew her way around a truck.

Angelina padded across the kitchen and opened the refrigerator. Where was that Moscato? She moved ketchup, a day-old Greek salad, and a large container of yogurt before wrapping her fingers around an almost-full bottle of wine and pulling it forth. Grabbing a glass, she carried both into her tiny living room. It felt good to flop onto the sofa and put her feet up.

She rested her head back among the pillows, lifting the icy glass to take a sip. The soothing liquid trickled down her throat. With a sigh, Angelina closed her eyes and tried to block out the last few hours.

It was not to be. Her cell phone sprang to life, alternating between fits of beeping and vibrating on the table where she'd left her boots. She disregarded it, and a smile crossed her lips as it stopped. As the sound started again, she froze, the buzzing so insistent that the phone toppled from the table and clattered to the floor.

"*Damn!*" Angelina set her glass beside the lamp at her elbow. Jumping up she ran to retrieve the frantic technology. *Who was it? Aah, it figures.* She stared at the number as she swiped a finger across to answer the call.

"Hi Mom."

"Hello honey. What's wrong?" her mother's voice floated into the room as Angelina set the phone on speaker, placed it beside her wine, and dropped into the comfort of her cushions once more.

"You can't possibly think something's wrong from two words." Angelina rolled her eyes. How did the woman know? Sixth sense? Mother's intuition? Dumb luck?

"I can hear it in your voice. Are you alright?"

Her mother's concern almost released the tears that were ready to flow. Before Angelina spoke again, she drew a deep breath and steadied herself. Might as well get it over with sooner than later.

"I was—let go today."

"What! Why?"

Angelina summed it up in as few words as possible, then reached for her wine and thumped her feet onto the coffee table again.

"Oh sweetheart, I'm sorry. That's so unfair." Her mother clucked her tongue, and despite herself, Angelina smiled. She'd seen her mom do it a thousand times.

"I'd like you to come over here for supper." Mom was using her 'no argument' voice. "That's the reason I was calling you. Marcie and Alec are driving out from the city, and they asked specifically that you be present. Your sister has some big announcement to share with us."

Angelina could feel her mother's sympathy like a warm embrace and loved her for it. Except she didn't feel like facing her family tonight and going through the whole miserable tale again. She wanted to lick her wounds in private. Just her, the bottle of wine, and perhaps that hefty bar of chocolate she'd stashed in the cupboard last payday.

"No thanks Mom. Tell them I'm sorry, but I can't do it tonight." She dragged a tattered old blanket from the back of the sofa and picked at the tufts.

"Getting out of your apartment is the best thing," her mother insisted. "Don't argue, Dad will come get you. I'm sending him to the store for parsley anyhow. Be ready in fifteen minutes." She hung up.

Again, Angelina rolled her eyes. Her mom meant well, she knew that, but the woman couldn't leave well enough alone. Reaching for her glass, Angelina downed what was left and poured herself another. If she had to go, she wasn't changing for the event, apart from her shoes, of course. They could take her as she was, a thirty-year-old truck-driver with faded lipstick and a black mark on her reputation.

Dad reached for her hand and squeezed it tight as he pulled into the driveway and turned off the car. Apart from a hug at the door, he hadn't asked her a thing about the trouble she'd had that day. She appreciated it.

"I know you wanted to stay home," he said, looking into her eyes and smiling ruefully. "But maybe it will do you some good to be with people who love you."

With a final squeeze, he let her go, pulled the baseball cap he always wore lower over his thinning hair, and climbed out. Her father, Mark, was a tall, slim man. Since Sharon, Angelina's mother, was plump and petite, it had always been accepted that it was from her father that Angelina had gotten her height of 5'8". However, Dad had a slight stoop now from years of hard work on the family farm. It had been sold when he retired due to ill health.

That was when they'd moved into town and purchased a cozy bungalow with a pretty white veranda. It was smaller than the house they'd had on the farm, but they both enjoyed being closer to friends and having more time to spend with family.

Rounding the hood, Dad beckoned to her and then, as she didn't move, he walked over to open her door. Accepting his outstretched arm, she allowed herself to be helped from the vehicle and led into the garage.

Despite her protests, she'd taken the time to change into clean jeans and a green mossy-coloured silk blouse that matched her eyes. She had released her hair from its elastic, brushed it out, and reapplied lipstick. But she didn't feel any better for it. Her feet dragged as they mounted the steps and prepared to enter the kitchen.

Her mother flung open the door, short, dark curls bouncing as she enveloped her daughter in a long embrace. Her green eyes, the same shade as Angelina's own, reflected the sympathy she felt. Angelina's sister Marcie followed close behind to throw her arms around the pair. They stood together for a long moment before pulling Angelina into the room where the delicious aroma of roast beef filled her senses. She breathed deep. It was home and her family's love was palpable. Maybe she did feel a little better.

Angelina looked around the inviting kitchen, a sense of

comfort flooding over her. She and mom had painted the kitchen a bright, cheery yellow before her parents moved in. Then, her dad had installed new white cupboards along with an updated countertop. Together the three of them had chosen stainless steel appliances to complete the fresh new look.

Over the sink, a south-facing window, hung with pale blue curtains, looked out into the back garden. Since Dad was the official dish washer, he often remarked it did his heart good to look out at the flower beds and vegetable patch as he worked.

A long table sat at the center of the space. Beyond that was the living room where deep, comfy sofas invited guests to stay awhile, and a huge television set graced the wall.

"I'm *so* excited you came!" Marcie burst out. "Mom told me what happened, and I think that stinks, but it couldn't have come at a better time!"

Angelina looked down at her sister's flushed, grinning face and realised something momentous had taken place. Marcie had more of their father's features and sandy-coloured hair and their mother's build. Angelina smiled, and then squealed in surprise as, despite her diminutive stature, Marcie grabbed her around the waist and almost lifted her off her feet as they twirled about the kitchen.

"What is it?" Angelina demanded, laughing. Marcie slowed, let go and bent over to catch her breath. Her husband, Alec, nodded with encouragement, beaming from the hallway. Their parents watching, joined hands in anticipation.

Straightening, Marcie threw her arms in the air. "I'm pregnant!" she screeched. "We found out today."

"Wow." Angelina was dumbfounded. "That's fantastic!"

For the last five years, Marcie and Alec had tried to have

a baby. Recently they'd seen doctors and specialists, but no one had offered any reasons for the problem, or any solutions. Now, this wonderful news—an answered prayer. Angelina grabbed Marcie again, held her close and kissed both her cheeks; the wetness of her sister's tears mingling with her own.

"I'm so happy for you both," she said. Moving to Alec, she hugged him too and then the whole family met in the center of the kitchen to share in the joy.

When they all stepped apart to blow noses and mop faces, Marcie linked arms with her fair-haired husband and spoke again.

"I have more news and it affects you directly, Angel."

That had always been Marcie's pet name for her little sister. Angelina turned, listening for what could possibly add to the happiness the two had already shared.

"There's more?" their mother said in bewilderment. "What? You won the lottery?" She dropped into a chair and fanned her face with a bunched up tea towel.

Marcie nodded with barely suppressed glee. "Sort of. I've got a ticket to France in my purse that I won't be using. I can't take any risks now." She glanced up at her husband and patted her tummy. "I want you to have it, Angel, and take the trip I'd planned. Is your passport current?"

Angelina nodded, the grin fading from her face.

"Great. There are a few other details I'll have to tell you about too, and we'll have to pay a fee to have it transferred to your name, but this is perfect! I was going to beg you to ask for a holiday to go. But thanks to that idiot at your workplace, you now have unlimited time."

Angelina felt dazed. *France?*

"When?" she asked weakly. "Why? And I *don't* have unlimited time. I have bills to pay, same as you."

"Tomorrow!" Marcie whooped, ignoring the latter part of Angelina's statement. "I'll explain everything as I help you pack."

"Pack? I'm *not* leaving for France tomorrow. Are you crazy?" Angelina laughed, but there was a hysterical edge to her voice. She paused, watching, and waiting for her sister to agree, but it didn't happen.

"You can't be serious?" When both Marcie and Alec nodded, affirming it was true, Angelina slumped onto a chair beside her mother. Dad leaned against a counter listening intently, but saying nothing.

"Here," her mother tossed the tea towel to her daughter. "You need this more than I do."

Angelina's hands shook as she lifted the damp cloth and began to beat the air in front of her face.

"We're perfectly serious," Alec said, moving to pull out a chair and sit beside his sister-in-law. He spoke earnestly, leaning forward and searching Angelina's face with concern. "It's a bit of an involved story. Marcie was planning to meet your cousin, Sarah, in Montreal tomorrow morning and fly to Paris in the afternoon. Sarah's been there visiting some family on her father's side, and apparently made friends with a mother and son who are in Canada on holiday from France. They asked Sarah to go back with them and to invite a friend if she wanted."

"Why haven't I heard of this until now?" Mom questioned in a reproachful voice.

Marcie looked sheepish. "I didn't think you'd approve."

"Nonsense. I'd like to go to France myself," Sharon announced, grinning. "What do you say Mark? Maybe *I* should go with Sarah?"

"I couldn't possibly get along here without you," her husband responded, crossing the linoleum to lay a hand on either of Sharon's shoulders. He bent to kiss the top of her head.

She patted his hand. "Of course, I won't go anywhere, but someone needs to keep an eye on that young girl."

Angelina paused in her frantic fluttering and looked at her sister. "So…what's the catch? Why you? No offense, but I can't imagine you'd be Sarah's first choice as a friend to take to France."

Marcie giggled. "I knew you'd be suspicious." She stepped to the table and sat on Angelina's other side with a huff of air. "Honey, could you get me a drink?" she asked her husband. As he rose, she smoothed her blue cotton dress over her knees and took a breath.

"I was going along because I'm worried about Sarah. She's only just turned nineteen and is quite naïve, as you know. I don't know these people, and that concerned both Aunt Esther and me. It sounds like Sarah has fallen for this French fellow and figures he'll ask her to marry him. A similar situation happened last summer. Remember?"

Angelina remembered. The whole family had lived in fear until the girl had been found living in a garden shed somewhere in Montana.

Marcie braided her fingers together and for the first time since she'd arrived, Angelina saw a shadow cross her sister's face.

"I don't believe these people asked Sarah to visit although she raves about their kindness, and they did pay for both plane tickets," Marcie clasped her hands. "I think she foisted herself upon them, but she won't be dissuaded. All that aside, Aunt Esther begged me to go along and keep an eye on her."

Marcie shrugged at Angelina's doubtful expression and explained further. "Sarah liked the idea of me coming since

I'm married and, in her mind, wouldn't be competing for the guy's attention. I'm sure he's wealthy which prompted her grand ideas of marriage. I sincerely doubt he has the slightest inclination of doing so. My fear is that he plans on having a fling with her and then throw her aside. Anyway, I couldn't refuse. It was a two-week holiday to France, and someone must go with Sarah. Who could say no?"

"Me." Angelina spoke with emphasis. "The incongruity of the situation defies understanding. I mean, I'd love to go to France…but contrary to popular belief, this isn't as great a time for me as you seem to think."

"Oh, I know," Marcie caught one of Angelina's hands and pressed it between her own. "It's been a horrible day for you. But look at the bright side—"

"The bright side?" Angelina interrupted with a shout. "There's no bright side to being fired for something you didn't do."

"Okay…well maybe I didn't choose the right words. But you have to admit, suddenly you have no responsibilities and there's no one in your life to keep you here." Marcie spoke encouragingly, clearly not realizing that what she said was having a negative effect on her only sibling.

Angelina stared at the floor. Marcie was right. She had no one in her life and no job to prevent her from going, but hearing it spoken so casually, hurt.

It had been three months since Bryan had left town without warning or even a backward glance her way. After dating for a year, they'd talked about making things perma-nent and settling down. She'd deserved more than to be dumped without so much as a word of explanation. Since then, Angelina had shut herself off, vowing she was finished with men and their treacherous ways for good. Today had only solidified that belief further.

"You know what," she said, standing up and tossing the cloth aside, "I'll do it. Someone has to protect Sarah from this guy...or, knowing Sarah, maybe the guy will need protection from her. Anyway, who better for the job than me."

One Golden Summer: Chapter Two

Angelina stood up with the rest of the passengers on the flight from Edmonton, Alberta, to Montreal, Quebec, and grasped her carry-on luggage before making her way down the aisle and off the plane. She tried in vain to push the wrinkles out of the wide-leg khaki capris and white tee she'd chosen to wear. With a matching jacket, the outfit made an attractive, yet comfortable ensemble for travelling.

Reaching the terminal's restaurant area, she adjusted her backpack into a more comfortable position and stepped to one side, allowing people to hurry past her as she consulted her phone. Sarah was supposed to have texted by now, but the cell phone registered nothing.

Sighing, Angelina started walking, keeping watch for somewhere she could get a good coffee.

"Angelina!" cried an excited voice. "Over here."

Whirling around, Angelina saw Sarah push a suitcase aside and, when it toppled over in front of her, leap over it to rush across the lounge. The people she was with remained seated.

"I'm, like, *so* happy you're here," the girl gushed, as she flung her arms around Angelina's shoulders. Then, lowering her voice, she whispered, "Do you see that hot guy I'm with? He's *so* cute and he has piles of money. I just know we're going to be together. I want you to watch for signs that he loves me, okay?"

Angelina drew back from Sarah with a laugh and held the young woman at arm's length. Marcie's fears were not unfounded.

"I'm glad to see you too, honey," she said. Sarah was even prettier than Angelina remembered. Her curly blonde hair had been trimmed into a stylish bob, a light scattering of freckles dusted her nose, and big blue eyes regarded Angelina with complete seriousness. She wore a fitted, one-piece romper of light blue with a pattern of tiny pink flowers dotting the material and had added a touch of gloss in the same colour to her lips. She was delectable and innocent. Angelina scowled in the direction of the 'hot guy' and mentally armed herself. Her job started now.

"Why don't you introduce me?" Angelina's voice sounded like steel and Sarah glanced at her with a frown forming between her eyes.

"Okay..." With a toss of her curls, Sarah linked their arms and led them across the busy aisle. The man she'd been sitting with, rose to his feet. "Angelina, this is Julien Belliveau. Julien, this is my *older* cousin, Angelina." All of a sudden, she sounded very formal. The girl leaned toward Julien to add. "My mom and her mom are sisters."

The emphasis on *older* wasn't lost on Angelina, but she was fine with that. She *was* older, and hopefully wiser, as this man would soon discover. In watching him stand, she wouldn't have been surprised if he'd clicked his heels together as he stiffly came to attention. He looked very—put together, and she remembered, with a pang, where she'd spilled coffee on her t-shirt that morning.

"I'm pleased to meet you," she said, stepping forward to extend her hand with a forced smile. Unfortunately, her rubber-soled wedges caught in the carpeting. She lost her footing, only saving herself from a fall by involuntarily reaching out with both hands and splaying them against Julien's chest.

"Yikes!" she shrieked as his own hands came forward to steady her. "Please forgive me." She glared down at the floor as though the carpet was at fault.

"*Pas de problème.*" He answered in French and bent down to look in her face. "Are you alright?"

"Y-yes, of course. I'm fine," she stammered. What a foolish thing to do. Mentally she kicked herself for her clumsiness.

Her eyes met gray ones without wavering as she struggled to gather herself. She'd purposely worn her highest wedge heels with this meeting in mind and now it had come to ruin. She already enjoyed an elevated height, but wanted the additional stature that a few more centimetres would provide. Her plan was to look this man in the eye and hold his gaze. Falling into his arms had *not* been a part of her strategy.

He was far taller than her, even in her heels. She thought perhaps 6'3" and not bad looking either. His sandy-coloured hair was cut short on the sides, but was longer on top and brushed straight up to fall over his forehead. A few flecks of silver at the temples told her he was at least in his mid-thirties. He had several-days growth of a moustache and beard on his rugged face. He looked casual, but still well-dressed in jeans and a white button-up. His eyes narrowed as they met hers and he grasped her hand in a powerful grip. Not to be outdone, she gripped him back.

"*Enchante*," he said, inclining his head. If he was surprised at her firm handshake, he made no sign of it. Letting go, he turned to include his mother in the introduction. "And I would like you to meet *ma mere*, Elyse Belleveau."

Angelina swivelled her attention to the mother, who didn't look more than fifty-five. She was petite and slim, an attractive woman with impeccably done makeup. She wore a chic, cream, monochromatic blouse paired with tailored trousers, and had shoulder-length, chestnut-coloured hair.

Planting her feet solidly, and extending her hand once more, Angelina wasn't taking any chances this time. She smiled warmly as they shook and was rewarded with genuine friendliness.

"*Enchante*." Elyse repeated the French word and followed it up with the meaning. "So nice to meet you." The lady paused after each word, and they were delivered in a much thicker accent than that of her son. Angelina got the impression his mother didn't know much English and had only learned the phrase in order to use it at times like this.

"It's lovely to meet you as well." Angelina took a step back and untangled her arms from her backpack, allowing it to swing free as she looked again for a coffee shop. She could feel Julien's hard gray-blue eyes boring into her soul, or so it felt, and hastily moved further away, needing space and time to think. The silence that had fallen between them was already strained.

"Will you sit down?" Julien asked, ducking his head to indicate the seat next to Sarah. You are seated in first class with us." Angelina shook her head as though to clear cobwebs. His accent was quite captivating.

"Oh," she said, feeling colour rush into her face. "You didn't have to do that Mr. B——"

"Julien," he interrupted smoothly.

"Right. Well, you didn't need to do that, Julien," Angelina closed her eyes as she stumbled over his first name. "I could have sat on my own in the economy section without suffering any harm." She forced another smile to soften her words, but secretly was cursing under her breath. It would have been nice to be alone for the voyage.

"Of course, you would not be harmed," he said with irritating cheer. "Yet, I thought you might want to sit with your *plus jeune cousine, n'est pas?*" With an expressive shrug of his broad shoulders, Julien turned the question into more of a statement. There was almost a hint of a smile in his words and Angelina shot him a look. However, he stooped to set Sarah's luggage upright and Angelina was left to think she had only imagined it.

Fortunately, she had studied French in school. While she was by no means fluent, she understood what the man had said. He was pointing out the fact that she was much older than her cousin. Well, he could snicker if he wanted. Ten years wasn't *that* much.

"Thank you," she said, pressing her lips together as he handed her the ticket without another word.

Then, as they stood awkwardly, she went on. "Would you excuse me? I really need a coffee and perhaps the ladies' washroom." Catching Sarah's eye, she lifted her bag slightly. "Mind watching this?

"Sure." Sarah tilted her head to one side as she glanced back and forth between Julien and Angelina. Shrugging, she moved to sit down. "Our flight doesn't leave for another forty minutes anyway."

"Thanks. I'll be back in fifteen." She dropped her bag at Sarah's feet, slid the ticket into her purse, and bustled away, not looking at Julien or his mother again.

Grab your copy...
vinci-books.com/onegoldensummer

www.ingramcontent.com/pod-product-compliance
Lightning Source LLC
Chambersburg PA
CBHW011424010726
47494CB00011B/2497

9781036701604